S0-COP-801

PRAISE FOR JOHN MANTOOTH

"John Mantooth writes with enviable grace, vigour, ease. These stories pulsate with the inevitable pain of familial love, and loss, and the horrors of the human condition while remaining peopled with unforgettable characters who move through their lives toward moments of personal realization and doom that can only come from the Southern experience. Mantooth has here collected a group of stories that exceeds the sum of its parts. You won't regret picking up this collection and will think on these amazing and heartfelt stories long after you've closed the covers. Absolutely brilliant."

—John Hornor Jacobs, author of *Southern Gods*, *This Dark Earth*, and *The Twelve Fingered Boy*

"The stories in John Mantooth's powerful debut collection turn a blazing spotlight on those living at—and beyond—society's margins. In sinuous, elegant prose, Mantooth maps the journeys that have led his characters to dead-ends and disappointments. Mantooth spares his characters nothing, including sufficient self-awareness to understand their roles in their personal catastrophes. These characters grieve their griefs on universal bones, and when they stumble onto hope, it is a small, tough thing that promises no miracles, only the possibility that life tomorrow will be a little better than it was today. This is impressive, assured work, not to be missed."

—John Langan, author of *Technicolor and Other Revelations*

"John Mantooth's short stories crackle with intelligence and violence. He writes about desperate and simple lives gone not-so-simple, and those lives beat with a savvy and familiar broken heart. His down-and-out characters are ugly and beautiful, and most importantly, compelling. John is the real deal, and I think I hate him for it."

—Paul Tremblay, author of *The Little Sleep* and *In the Mean Time*

SHOEBOX TRAIN WRECK

JOHN MANTOOTH

ILLUSTRATIONS BY
DANNY EVARTS

ChiZine Publications

FIRST EDITION

Shoebox Train Wreck © 2012 by John Mantooth
Interior illustrations © 2012 by Danny Evarts
Cover artwork © 2012 by Erik Mohr
Interior design © 2012 by Samantha Beiko
All Rights Reserved.

This book is a work of fiction. Names, characters, places, and incidents are either
a product of the author's imagination or are used fictitiously. Any resemblance to
actual events, locales, or persons, living or dead, is entirely coincidental.

Library and Archives Canada Cataloguing in Publication

Mantooth, John, 1971-
        Shoebox train wreck / John Mantooth.

Short stories.
ISBN 978-1-926851-54-9

        I. Title.

PS3613.A358S56 2012   813'.6   C2011-907676-4

CHIZINE PUBLICATIONS
Toronto, Canada
www.chizinepub.com
info@chizinepub.com

Edited and copyedited by Helen Marshall
Proofread by Samantha Beiko

 Canada Council   Conseil des Arts
        for the Arts   du Canada

We acknowledge the support of the Canada Council for the Arts which last year
invested $20.1 million in writing and publishing throughout Canada.

 **ONTARIO ARTS COUNCIL
CONSEIL DES ARTS DE L'ONTARIO**

Published with the generous assistance of the Ontario Arts Council.

For Bill Mantooth (1945-1997)

SHOEBOX TRAIN WRECK

TABLE OF CONTENTS

A LONG FALL INTO NOTHING

I met Larry Bryant on a cold morning during the spring of 1981. I was a senior and rode the school bus because we couldn't afford a car and my father had to be at work too early to take me. We lived pretty far out, near the Black Warrior River, in an area some people might have called poor—or if they were feeling less kind—rough.

The first time the driver, Mr. Jennings, stopped at Larry's trailer, I thought he must be having engine trouble. There was no way anyone could live in such a place. The trailer had been burned and the whole front side was gone. Someone had strung up shower curtains to keep out the elements, but most of that had been ripped and pieces were scattered about the yard. When I saw the flashing lights and the stop sign extend on the left side of the bus, I sat up, anxious to see who would emerge from the squalor. When no one came out, Jennings blew the horn two short blasts, shrugged, and released the handbrake. Just as he started to pull away, a tall, broad-shouldered kid appeared in the doorway of the trailer and strolled across the trash-strewn yard like it was a Sunday afternoon walk in the park.

I pressed my forehead against the dirty glass, fascinated.

This guy was in no hurry. Normally, Jennings would have gone by now, but I knew he'd let this kid on because he was new and didn't know the rules. But then he'd chew him. Eat him alive like he had done Reggie Calhoun last year. Reggie had been so embarrassed by Jennings vitriolic attack that he'd played hooky for a week.

Except . . . I don't know what it was. This kid was pretty big. Jennings was bigger, though. That wasn't it. It was more the way he carried himself. The way he held his chin out, like he was proud of his greasy hair and ragged clothes. It was the way he looked out past the bus at something only he could see.

I don't know . . . To this day, I still don't know.

Whatever it was, Jennings saw it too. There was a moment of almost unbearable tension, as the new kid climbed onto the bus, when I thought Jennings might tear into him, but it passed with Jennings grumbling something under his breath. Larry took no notice of him. Instead, he scanned the bus, looking for a place to sit. His eyes fell on me, and he worked his way toward the back where I was seated in the very last row.

"So," he said, settling into the seat across from me, "what do you do around here to kill the goddamn time?"

Violence was something I learned about early on. My mother shot herself when I was eight, and although I was spared the sight of her body, I heard the door to her room slam just before she unloaded the 45 into her mouth. I heard that too. Dad, drunk on whiskey, still had enough sense to get me out of the house. It was a firecracker, he'd said. I must have looked at him like he was a fool because he shoved me hard toward the front door and told me to play, okay Jake, just go outside and play. I was still outside playing when they carried her off in the body bag.

Though Dad never offered much in the way of an opinion about why Mom shot herself, I had some ideas of my own. She couldn't take living with her husband anymore. She couldn't take being passive. She couldn't take it anymore. Period. My mother's suicide worked on me. Even when I wasn't thinking about it, I felt it there gnawing at me, whispering. And something else was there too. The adrenaline rush of violence. It was a side of me that only broke to the surface sporadically, like an unwelcomed guest. A fight at school that left the other kid bleeding and sobbing on the bathroom floor, the silk scars on my forearm that felt even better than I had imagined when I carved them with a straight razor. The blind surge of anger that ached to be released when I thought of my mother, and even more so, my dad. Even when I managed to keep the violence down, I could feel it deep inside me, a steady thrum of blood that felt like a birthright.

I suppose it might have all been different if Larry had chosen somewhere else to sit, but all the sleepless nights have taught me the futility of thinking like that. So I accept what happened even if I can't understand it, this puzzle of events that nearly thirty years later, I am still trying to assemble.

Larry was a senior like me, but he could have passed for a man in his twenties. He was long-haired, sullen, and utterly intimidating.

We'd ridden in amicable silence for three days when he leaned across the aisle and said, "What we need to find," he said, "is an easy target."

"Huh?"

"How about her?" he said, gesturing to a girl a few rows in front of us. Mae Duncan. Fat girl, extraordinaire.

"Mae?"

"Yeah. The fat bitch."

I shrugged. I didn't understand where this was going.

"What's your name," he said, his tone changing, becoming friendlier. There was something ingratiating about him then. I wanted to like him. Lord knows why.

"Jake," I said and stuck out my hand.

When he took it, his hand felt cold, lifeless.

"Little help!" Jennings called as he always did when he had to turn the bus around at the stop near Ben Self's driveway. It was a hell of a turn for a bus, and I'd always felt proud he'd entrusted me to help him do it.

The tricky part was where Ben lived, on a bluff facing out over the Black Warrior River. Jennings had to nose into the Selfs' driveway and then put the bus in reverse, while cutting the wheel hard. No problem there, Jennings could handle a bus. The problem was what he had to back into—a sheer forty-foot drop into fast moving water, riddled with jagged rocks. Jennings and the school administrators had been after the county for years to put up a guardrail so at least he'd have something to bump against before the bus plummeted out into nothingness, but the county didn't give two shits for what the principal and a bus driver wanted, and Jennings was left having to rely on students to help him.

Anyway, I was supposed to call out to him when he got near the edge. The first few times he had me do it, I hollered stop too early, and he couldn't make the turn. I learned from trial and error the back of the bus had to be practically hanging out over the bluff in order for him to avoid the pine trees in front.

Because of the danger of this manoeuvre, Jennings demanded absolute silence when he made the turn. Even the little kids who had never been close enough to the back to see what dizzying fates we were tempting, fell strangely silent, and when Jennings made the cut and put the bus in drive at last, there was a palpable sense of relief. It was a like a collective sigh, a hushed whisper that said, we did it, we pushed the limit, but we did not die today.

I opened the back door and leaned out, aware of Larry's eyes on me. He muttered something, but I ignored him, concentrating on the pavement below. It would turn to grass and then to nothingness. The grass came. I waited, leaning forward. The Black Warrior streaked past. A hawk skimmed the surface of the river, its beak grazing the silver current.

"Stop!" I shouted.

Jennings stopped.

He cut the wheel hard. Put the bus in drive. I shut the door. The tension was gone.

I turned to look at Larry, but he was standing, admiring the river through the window.

The bus stopped suddenly. "One more time!" Jennings shouted. I'd been too cautious. He'd have to back up again to make the turn.

He put it in reverse. I reached for door release, but Larry's hand was there first. "I got it," he said.

"But—"

"I got it," he repeated in an eager tone that made me feel like any argument would be silly.

I slid back into my seat. He opened the door, leaning way out. "Keep coming," he said.

Jennings, who I had long suspected was hard of hearing, didn't notice the voice belonged to someone else.

"Got plenty," Larry said. "Come on."

I stood behind Larry to look out. What I saw made me grip the seatback with both hands. The bluff was gone. We were teetering on the brink of disaster.

"A little more."

"No," I said, but my voice wasn't strong enough.

"Good!" Larry called out and smiled at me.

Jennings grunted and put it in drive. The back tires were poised on the very edge of the bluff. Any further and we'd have slid right off into the river.

The bus lurched forward and Jennings had no problem missing the trees.

Larry and I fell into an uneasy rhythm: mornings he spent in the seat beside Mae, chatting her up so well that in a week she was smiling at every word he said. In the afternoons he sat in the back and took over—without really ever asking—my responsibility helping Jennings. He seemed to have an innate sense about just how far to go without sending the bus plummeting into the Black Warrior, and he delighted in nudging us right up against that line. Once or twice, leaning against the side window, watching the lip of the bluff disappear, I was sure we were doomed, but just when I thought Jennings couldn't go further, Larry would call him off with an ecstatic, "Whoa there, Nellie!"

One day he told me he was going to be visiting Mae's house after school. "It's on," he said. "Parents out of town. Fat girl's going down." This little rhyme seemed to please him to no end.

I tried to imagine Mae on her knees, her heavy tits sagging almost to the floor, as she regarded Larry's dick with that stupid, wanton smile she always gave him. Something about this image both sickened me and turned me on.

"Hey," he said. "You should come."

"Nah, sounds like you two will need some privacy."

"Fuck that. I don't care about privacy. You can watch. Hell, you can participate if you want."

"What about Mae?"

"What about her? She's a fat whore. You know what fat whores are good for?"

I shook my head.

"Catching cum."

"What?"

He punched my arm. "You a virgin or something?"

"Hell no."

His eyes darted around my face, never meeting mine. I think, in all the time I knew Larry, I only locked eyes with him once.

"Well, shit. Come with me this afternoon. You'll see how fun a fat girl can be."

Just then Jennings shouted out for "a little help," and Larry popped out of his seat to open the backdoor.

Mae's house was worse than I ever imagined. I'd seen the place where she got off in the afternoon, but that was only her bus stop. I knew she had to walk a long dirt road to reach her home, and I'd assumed it was a dump, but dump didn't quite do it justice.

The windows were broken. All of them. The siding had been ripped clean off the front of the house, and somehow the whole place leaned to the right. Her yard—if you could call it that—was littered with rusted bicycles and kitchen appliances. A stained sheet hung over one broken window, flapping in the wind.

Larry approached the window with the sheet. He caught it in his fist and ripped it down. We peered inside letting our eyes adjust to the darkness. She was on the couch wearing a pair of cut-off jeans and bikini top. When she saw us, she smiled, offering us that same "please pet me" smile I'd seen for weeks on the bus. I wanted to leave.

It wasn't just that I felt sorry for her. I also felt sorry for myself. What was I doing? Why was I letting this new kid, this bully, pull me along in his wake? I didn't have an answer. I still don't, though the perspective of time has given me some ideas.

We went inside. Some things happened. They were all bad.

When we left, Larry was laughing. He put his arm around my shoulders and pulled me to him, giving me one of those best friends forever hugs. I remember smiling, even though I felt sick inside.

I think about what happened next the most. It was a warm day, almost spring, the sky painted a double-coated shade of blue, the bare tree branches reaching out for something that was not there.

Larry sat down in the seat across from me. "I'm bored," he said.

"What about Mae?"

"She's used up. Too easy."

"I thought that's what you wanted."

He shrugged. "It's like there's no goal anymore. She just lays there and lets me do whatever the fuck I want."

The last couple students climbed aboard as Jennings cranked the bus. Mae was one of them, swivelling her hips to keep from getting stuck between the rows of seats. From the look on her face, I saw that Larry had already made his feelings clear to her. Still, she kept coming, until she sat down in the seat directly in front of Larry.

"Something you need?" Larry said.

She shook her head, her eyes flashing with an anger I didn't think she was capable of.

Larry ignored it and scanned the bus. "What about that girl up there?" he said, pointing at one of the younger girls, a sixth or seventh grader. I didn't know her name but she had an eye for the older boys and a body to match.

"She's a little young," I said.

"It must be boring being you," Larry shot back, a challenge in his eyes. Jennings pulled out onto County Road 22, and the tension in the back of the bus was palpable. "I mean, what the fuck do you get out of life?"

18

Before I could answer, he turned and grabbed a handful of Mae's hair in his fist. She let out a low whimper and said, "Don't touch me."

Larry pulled her hair back even farther, so her neck was bent. Her face was flush and her eyes darted to me.

Since the day I joined Larry at her house, she'd ignored me. Even though she was compliant with Larry's every request that day, I could tell she wasn't comfortable with me being there. I thought she hated me, but maybe I was wrong.

"Let her go," I said, and was immediately disappointed in the lack of strength in my voice.

"Did you say something?"

"Let her go, Larry. Do you have to be so mean all the time?"

Larry let go of her hair and placed his palm on the back of her head and shoved hard. "Nah. You're right. I need to be a nicer person. I'm going to be nice to her." He pointed directly at the young girl in the front of the bus. Then he got up and brushed past Mae.

For the next several miles I tried not to think about anything.

"Little help!"

Larry rose and made his way to the rear of the bus. He threw open the emergency door and leaned way out into the opening, using both hands to brace himself on the doorframe. Over time, he'd become even more daring, and sometimes it seemed like he wanted to fall. Larry, I had come to realize, felt constrained by everything. He was always looking for the boundaries not because he wanted to stay behind them, but because he wanted to move past them. Me, on the other hand, I was looking for something absolute, some secret, some reason for why things stayed together and why they fell apart.

"Come on," he said, leaning out the back of the bus now with only one hand positioned on the doorframe to keep him from falling out into the river. The other hand was in the air, waving Jennings on.

"Whoa!" he shouted. "You're good to go."

I felt myself relax; I felt the bus relax, a general sigh of relief because once again we were back on track, certain disaster averted.

But disaster can never be completely averted. Like violence, it always lurks, waiting for the right moment to explode and make you wonder why it doesn't happen more often.

I heard her before I saw her. When she rose from her seat, there was the sound of her blue jeans and her blouse scraping against the torn seats. I turned and saw Mae's eyes locked in on Larry, both arms extended like some of those pictures you see of Frankenstein's monster stumbling forward.

She hit him with all of her weight, and for an instant, I thought she was going to go with him. The momentum of the bus moving forward, combined with Mae's heavy blow literally shot Larry through the opening. For one fascinating moment, I saw him frozen, his body arched like a diver setting up to bend and tuck and turn into a perfect needle nose descent. But none of that happened. Instead, something even more miraculous did.

He flailed his hands and one of them managed to catch the door release—a slender steel bar. Somehow, improbably, he held on. Somebody closer to the front screamed.

Jennings slammed on the brakes.

I leaned out and saw there was nothing between Larry's dangling legs and the rocky rapids below. If his hand slipped, he'd plummet into the teeth of the river. He twisted his body around and reached out to me with his free hand. His other hand was already beginning to slide off the door release. I knew if I didn't reach for him, he'd have to take a chance and lunge for the door opening. He'd probably get his hand back in and be able to climb back onboard. Probably.

"What the hell is going on?" Jennings demanded.

I knew there was a window, however slight, that had opened. An almost imperceptible space in time when I could do something, something big, something important, something right. I reached one hand out for Larry, bracing myself against the door frame with the other. He took it. Even as I felt his rough hand cover mine, I knew Larry couldn't be as evil as he appeared. But at that moment, I didn't care. All I cared about was making sure he couldn't hurt anyone again.

"Come on," I said reaching out my free hand. "Give me your other hand."

He looked at me then, his eyes locking right on mine. I nodded, reassuring him. He looked afraid. Damn if that look doesn't still haunt me. Why is it some of us can feel pity when it is least deserved while there are others of us who cannot even fathom the sentiment?

He must have read the pity in my eyes because he let go of the door release bar and reached for me.

It was easy. Much easier than I thought. Just before I did it, I heard Jennings behind me, telling me to hang on, he'd pull the bus forward and goddamn why had we let him back up so far? I also heard the blast of a 45 and my father again: just go play, okay Jake, just go outside and play.

I let go.

His eyes stayed locked on mine as he fell. I'd like to believe I saw a kind of recognition in them, a flicker of insight that took most people years to obtain. I'd like to believe in the instant before his body broke on the rocks below that he thought about how cruel and pointless his life had been and how his actions had only brought pain to himself and those around him. I'd like to believe a lot of things. But in reality, I don't believe much of anything these days.

Jennings grabbed me from behind and pulled me back

into the bus. It was only then I realized I was halfway to falling out myself.

I was sobbing. I'm not sure for whom.

Jennings heaved me into a seat. "It ain't your fault. You tried, son. You tried."

And I did try. In my own way, I tried to do the right thing, to turn the violence that needed to jump out of me like an ungrounded current into a kind of heroic act. Thirty years later, I'm not sure I succeeded. I'm not sure how to put together the pieces of my life. I turn the events over and sometimes try to force them into something like meaning, but those constructs are only temporary, as enlightening as learning truth isn't absolute and the world is a series of indecipherable paradoxes. In the end, I always come back to that long drop, the look in Larry's eyes as he fell, the rocks waiting beneath. This is absolute, I tell myself. Truth, I tell myself. Greater good. I did the right thing because there is a right thing.

But then I remember my own indiscretions, the fumbling, half-skewered world of my childhood without a mother. And I think maybe when I let go of Larry, I dropped someone else off a cliff as well, somebody who loved him. Somebody who needed him. I don't know.

I do know this: Larry wasn't the only one who fell. I've been falling too. The difference is he found what he was looking for: a hard line at the bottom that could not be crossed. My greatest fear is I'll fall forever and never find the bottom.

THE WATER TOWER

"There's an alien in the water tower."

Heather held the door open and squinted at Jeremy Reddin, her eyes slow to adjust to the bright summer day. He stood at the front of her trailer, dressed in camouflage fatigues, glasses crooked on his sunburned nose. As usual, Heather had to resist the impulse to reach out and straighten them. Above him, the sun passed its zenith and hung lazily in the western sky. His dirty-blonde hair caught the light and filtered it toward her in soft hues.

"Clyde found it yesterday, floating right in the tank. I overheard him talking to Ronnie Pearson about it. You know the rooms in our house are thin as paper. He said it was light blue, the colour of a vein. Tiny, but a big head. Ronnie said that made sense 'cause aliens are smarter than us, but if you ask me, it's pretty dumb to end up dead inside a water tower."

Heather wondered where all this was going. With Jeremy, you never knew. He took the special ed classes in school. It wasn't so much that he wasn't smart or couldn't learn; it was more that he was just Jeremy. He would never fit in anywhere in life. His older brother, Clyde, just let him tag along because

Jeremy would do his dirty work, like stealing whiskey from their father or sneaking up to Jenny Willoughby's window to take pictures of her. Heather was Jeremy's one friend, and even she could only take him in small doses.

"Anyway," he said, after he caught his breath, "I thought you might like to see it."

"So let me get this straight," Heather said. "You want me to walk all the way through the woods, clear out to the train tracks to see something dead in a water tower?"

Jeremy smiled. He had a good one, and when he did it at just the right time, Heather always liked him, always wanted to root for him. "I got a feeling about this," he said. "This could be big. But we've got to beat Ronnie and Clyde out there. Summer school lets out in like an hour. They'll go to Clyde's house to drink for a while." He glanced at the sky. "I'd say we've got until dark." Reaching into the pocket of his shorts, he pulled out a slim, silver camera. "Digital. If this is what I think it is, I'm going to have pictures to prove it."

"And what do you think it is, Jeremy?"

His grin widened. "An alien, of course."

Heather laughed. Not at him exactly. No, his enthusiasm was revved too high for that. She laughed because she wanted to go . . . well, she wanted to get out from under the same roof where she had spent the better part of a long, hot summer trying to avoid her mother and especially the men that came over in the afternoon.

She looked at Jeremy, his big smile still plastered across his face. Someone had given him a bad haircut. Probably Jeremy himself, considering he barely had enough money most of the time to get a roast beef sandwich at Hardee's, and his dad didn't believe in personal grooming. Despite all this, something was right about Jeremy. It was hard to say what, exactly, but it was there. She knew it.

"Okay," she said. "I'll go. But I want my name on any

pictures you take. It would be nice to beat the Barrows to the punch."

"Barrows?"

"Ronnie and Clyde." Jeremy frowned like he sometimes did in class when he didn't understand. "Never mind," she said. "Let's get out of here."

Heather had no sooner said the words when an old blue truck spun its tires out on the road and turned down the worn gravel drive leading to her trailer.

Heather's mother appeared framed behind the kitchen window, a silent face next to the smudged glass. Heather saw her take a drag of her cigarette and watch the truck roll toward the house. She did not look in Heather's direction.

At a certain point, somewhere past the junkyard, out beyond the little pond that, over the years, had been used to dump the things even the junkyard didn't want, the woods changed. Artefacts from a different world slowly began to appear: remnants of a car buried under kudzu vines; a pile of beer bottles so old the labels had faded into obscurity, bled white by the long sun; a pair of trousers, half buried in the mud. A plough had lain too long in the sun and turned a fleshy white so it appeared to Heather like a skeleton, wooden arms stiff and outstretched, grasping for something just out of reach.

"There's a whole world back here," Heather said.

"Yeah, my dad told me about it once. The water tower, these ruins, all of it was once a town. I forget the name."

"What happened?"

Jeremy shrugged. "Don't know. I guess folks went in for trailer parks and electricity. No power out here. But it's got something else." He looked around. "Soul. Yeah. It's got soul."

Heather smiled.

"What? You know what I mean. You've been to places before that suck the soul out of you, right? Like the trailer park where you live. No soul. Soul sucking, but no soul. Except when it rains. Everyplace has got soul then."

Heather grinned. Jeremy was right. This place did have soul. On their left, a creek weaved between the trees. A wooden fence leaned precariously over the water, one of its poles dangling free and occasionally dipping into the slight current. A snapping turtle lay sunning itself on a moss-covered rock, and overhead the tall pines swayed mysteriously, giving Heather a pleasing touch of vertigo each time she looked up.

She saw how this might have been a community. The structures, little more than vine-covered ruins, were sinking deeper into the earth with each passing year. The homes had been burned, the walls black and raw. Inside the least damaged, Heather found bedding and clothes and some dirty magazines.

"This is where David Masters and Jessica McKissick used to come," Jeremy said. "Me and Ronnie used to climb that tree—" He pointed at a tall, leaning oak. "—and watch them. They put on a hell of a show. At least until she got pregnant."

"Jessica McKissick? I didn't know she was pregnant."

"She was. Then she wasn't." Jeremy leaned over close to Heather and whispered, "I think she had an abortion, or maybe just got rid of it."

"Did her parents know?"

Jeremy shrugged. "I doubt it. Ronnie and me and David, of course. We might have been the only ones. I could tell because she started wearing big sweaters and jackets and stuff. Anyway, once that happened, the show stopped."

"It's just hard to believe. How she could get pregnant and hide the whole thing from her parents?" Heather said. She was intrigued, especially by how a girl could get pregnant, have the baby, and her parents never be the wiser. "So, she got rid of it?"

Jeremy shrugged. "She doesn't have a baby anymore. My brother saw her a few weeks ago. He said she definitely wasn't pregnant."

Heather thought of her mother, perpetual drink in one hand, half-smoked cigarette in the other. Thought of her mother's long face, always so blank and uncurious, always ready to speak without thinking, to criticize without understanding who she criticized.

Heather tried to picture herself pregnant. Tried to think of how it would feel to have a life growing inside her, kicking and turning and needing. Would her mom notice? Possibly not. Weeks might go by without interaction between them. If Heather put a little more effort into it, she could go forever without her mother seeing her.

The last time Heather saw her father was two years ago, at the end of sixth grade. Because her mother wouldn't take her, Heather had saved the money for cab fare and travelled down to the VA where her father lived full time. He'd been in the Gulf War and had come back with shrapnel embedded in the back of his neck and spine, but that wasn't why he was off.

According to her mother, it was just his crazy gene kicking in.

"What happened to him," her mother had said shortly after he was committed, "will happen to you one day, too."

Heather, only eleven, wanted to know why.

"DNA."

"Huh?"

"The stuff in your blood that makes you, you. You're a Watson, Heather. You've got the same genes as your father. I should have known when I married him, his elevator would eventually get stuck." She breathed out a long column of smoke, watching it drift lazily across the room. "Just like his father and his father before him."

Heather didn't see her father as crazy. In fact, she considered him—had considered him—the sanest person she knew at the time. Sure there had been moments when he seemed different, at odds with the world, and that was what made him special. They were alike in that way.

When she was nine, he'd taken her to Disney World, just the two of them. He told her she was a princess, just like the real ones.

"Real ones?" she'd said.

"Cinderella, Snow White, Sleeping Beauty. All of them. You're a princess too."

"They're not real, Daddy."

He smiled, surveyed the park, as if to spot one in order to prove his point. At that moment, the park seemed deserted, forlorn almost, in the twilight of the late afternoon. His smile faded, turned to a look of confusion. He touched her shoulder.

"You're going and going until one day you find there's nowhere to go."

She waited, her nine-year-old mind spinning, trying to make connections that were not there.

"You look in the mirror. You realize the person looking back is you. That's when it falls apart."

Heather said nothing. His smile came back. "Hey," he said, "a princess."

Heather followed his gaze, but she saw only the long shadows of the sun falling across the park.

The last time she'd seen him, at the VA, he had said nothing at all. He looked past her, his gaze fixed on the wall behind her, where a dark, mud-coloured stain, possibly blood, had resisted all efforts to clean it. Her father's lips moved soundlessly. He might have been praying. Or cataloguing all the ways such a stain might have ended up on the wall. He might have been reading some secret language in that stain, some otherworldly alphabet only he knew. Maybe Heather would know it too, one day. This was what she liked to think when she thought about her father. He wasn't crazy. Instead, he had uncovered the secrets of the world, lifted the veil over them and found himself stunned to silence by what he had found.

A house appeared, shimmering in the distance, eaves dripping with Spanish moss, front door stripped bare of paint, the colour of flesh. The yard, if you could call it that, was a mess of trash and weeds, tangled together with the undergrowth, which to Heather seemed to creep forth from the trees like fingers searching for something to touch.

The smell was of man, not trees.

"Better steer clear," Heather whispered. She knew there were meth labs out here. And crack houses. And other places that stopped being anything except dead ends. Dying places.

Too late. Jeremy had already seen something that held him mesmerized. Heather followed his gaze to the makeshift porch, where an old rocking chair creaked in the wind.

"That's my dad's hat," he said.

A red hat lay in the seat of the chair.

A shadow moved inside the house past a window and was gone.

"Let's keep going," she said, though her heart wasn't in the words. If she'd been in Jeremy's shoes, she would want to investigate too. There was something about parents, Heather thought: whatever they did, they pulled you along too. Even out here in the woods, in the middle of a place that might as well not exist. You were always part of them, even when they stopped being part of you.

"Is this where he goes?" Jeremy said. "Don't tell me this is where he goes." His voice was angry but weak.

"Maybe it would be better—"

"No. I'm going in."

She followed him.

The door swung open soundlessly, revealing a darkened room. A naked woman lay on a couch, smoking something that did not look like a cigarette. She was old, her body wrinkled and crushed by gravity. She brushed long gray-black bangs from her eyes and exhaled a stream of smoke.

"Who are you?"

"Where's my dad?"

"Your dad?"

"His hat is on the porch."

The woman sat up, making no effort to cover herself. Her breasts, once large, now hung down her chest like empty bags.

"What's your name?"

"Jeremy Reddin."

She nodded. "He never told me."

"That he had kids?"

"That he had any other than the one that died."

Jeremy looked at his feet. "There's me and my older brother."

The woman took another toke. "And little Sam."

"He only lived for an hour."

The woman leaned back on the couch and closed her eyes. Her knees opened, revealing a dark bed of hair between her thighs. Heather looked away.

"Yeah, but I hear it was a good hour," she said, her eyes still shut, a look of complete relaxation on her face.

"Where is he?"

Without opening her eyes, the woman pointed to the back of the house. "Out where the graves are." She took another drag.

Heather followed Jeremy down a short hallway and into a bedroom covered with clothes and trash and a smell Heather recognized as menstrual blood. A door on the other side of the room swayed in a slight breeze.

Passing through the door was like passing into another world, or at least another time. The trees swallowed up the sun back here, forming a perfect canopy of dark green, like pictures Heather had seen of tropical jungles. It made Heather think of hiding under the covers with her father when she'd been a kid.

Jeremy sucked in a deep breath. Stood still. Looked at the clearing where a man lay on the ground, his arms wrapped around something, his broad back turned to them.

"Dad?" Jeremy said.

The man did not move.

Jeremy took a step closer. Heather waited, tense. Unsure how to stand. What to do other than watch.

"Dad?"

There was no response, and for an instant, Heather thought he might be dead.

Jeremy crouched next to the man. Heather heard the woman's voice behind them.

"He's in the mud," she said dreamily.

Jeremy turned and grimaced at the woman before reaching for his father. He grabbed his shoulders and rolled him over on his back. The man moved his head and mumbled something. Jeremy wasn't listening. His attention had turned to what his father had been holding—a rock, a crude marker. He knelt and read the inscription in silence.

The woman stood beside Heather now. She had a needle in her hand. The sharp point dripped with a fluid the colour of honey. Heather watched as the woman plunged it into her own arm, squeezing the syringe, as her face went from serene to ecstatic to unknowing.

Once drained, the syringe fell from her fingers, and she stumbled past Heather. When she fell on top of Jeremy's father, he barely seemed to notice. They lay together like that, still. Everything was still except for the tall pines agitated by the wind.

Jeremy stepped around them, his face wet with tears. He paused on the other side of their bodies, looking at them. The woman said something to him that Heather couldn't make out. Whatever it was made Jeremy break. His shoulders drooped. His face twisted into a mask of agony. His thick glasses slid off his nose and landed in the grass.

He cursed loudly and reached for them, but came up empty. Heather started forward to help him. Before she could get there, in his blindness, he managed to crush them underfoot.

They'd been walking for nearly two hours when the sun disappeared and the rain began. The journey slowed to a crawl, as Heather lost her way several times, and had to backtrack through the muck to regain her bearings. Jeremy was little help without his glasses, and the deeper they travell-ed into the woods, the more Heather lost her grip on the world she knew. The trailer park seemed far away and unimportant, a different world.

As they walked, Heather thought very little about the alien or the water tower. At this point she expected to find neither. Instead, she thought of the snippets of sounds and images from the house they'd visited earlier. She kept seeing Jeremy's father prone on the ground, arms flung around the grave stone, as if he might pull it into himself, and somehow embrace all of his might-have-beens. She saw him turn over, dead-eyed, and not recognize his own son. She heard the woman's cigarette-stained voice.

He's in the mud.

Heather knew mud was a name for heroin. She'd learned that in health last year. And if she had to guess, based on the way the woman and Jeremy's father acted, they were using heroin. The woman's statement seemed to go beyond slang to describe where the man really was, as if he were trying to find his traction, trying to climb out of a pit where solid ground no longer existed, where one slip led to the next, until he was wallowing in it, drowning instead of moving.

This is what she was thinking when the trees parted at last to reveal a dark sky. The rain had turned to a fine mist, and a pale sliver of moon hung above the sunset. The water tower loomed in the distance on the other side of a wet meadow.

Like everything out here, rust held sway. The actual tank was roofless, whether from a storm or the hands of man, Heather could only guess. The corrugated tin had turned to a burnished red beneath all the rust. Four stilts held it off the ground, nudging the lip of the tank in line with some of the nearby treetops. Railroad trestles, eaten by time and weather, formed a half-realized path to the tower before disappearing in the high weeds.

"I see it," Heather said.

Jeremy said nothing and quickened his pace. Heather knew the water tower had become like a totem to him now, a goal he had fixed in his mind. It mattered little what was actually there—most likely a dead bird, stripped of its feathers or a poor raccoon that drowned inside the murky silt.

Underneath the tower, water dripped from the slats overhead and landed on their upturned faces. On the other side, they found a badly mangled ladder. Several steps were broken or missing, but Jeremy felt around for one of the solid ones and began to climb.

Heather followed, pulling herself over the open spaces where the steps were missing, willing herself to the top where she joined Jeremy on the wooden catwalk. She peered over the lip of the tank.

Inside, past endless rivulets of corrugated tin, a shallow pool looked back at her. A foreign smell came up from the tank, causing Heather to hold her breath. She saw no alien. She saw nothing in the dark.

The tank shuddered as Jeremy grabbed the rim and shook. The water, dark and shiny as oil, lapped against the sides. Nothing surfaced.

He gave the tank another shake. "It can't be too deep."

"Maybe the Barrows were just bullshitting," she said.

"No. There's something here." He pulled himself up. "I'm going in."

Before Heather could stop him, a sound came from the logging road. She turned and saw a truck rumbling toward them from the east.

"Hurry," she said. "I think your brother's here."

A thud welled up from inside the tank, followed by a groan of pain. "I'm in," Jeremy said.

As Heather pulled herself over the rim, she looked at the moon. A gleaming silver arc, carrying the stars in the same way a mother carries her children, rocking them to sleep, singing the day shut, opening the night. As she fell, she told herself she would keep the moon in sight, a constant to guide her where all other markers had failed.

She hit the water and then the bottom, first with her feet and then when they couldn't sustain the impact she crumpled to her knees, cracking them hard against the tank. Rolling over in the shallow water, she found the crescent moon, cradling the stars. When the pain in her legs begged for her to scream out, the moon calmed her like any good mother would.

"I think I messed up my ankle," Jeremy said.

"Don't talk," she said. "Look at the moon."

"What?"

"It'll calm you."

Jeremy turned his face up to the moon, its slivered shine opening his face up, glinting in the tiny space of his squinted eyes. Despite the pain, despite the smell, despite the terror she felt at being ridiculed by Ronnie and Clyde, this image of Jeremy was too much. He looked smaller somehow down here, more defined, more in focus. The shadows hid his faults, the moonglow highlighted everything good about him and Heather could see now there was a lot good about Jeremy. Seeing him like this now, in this other world, made her feel like a part of something mysterious and grand and sad. A great, silent secret. She shivered.

Two doors slammed outside the tower. Voices boomed.

"You're buying me a twelve pack if there's nothing here, Clyde."

"How about you buy me a case if there is?" Clyde said. He sounded confident. Heather looked around the tank, but it had grown even darker now and she could barely make out Jeremy, much less an alien.

"If I see an alien, I'm going to extract the bastard and sell him on eBay."

"Well, get ready to extract. Here. Take a flashlight."

Heather heard them struggling up the ladder, cursing as they came to the missing steps. She had no idea what to do. In seconds, flashlights would expose them.

She looked back at the moon, as if an answer might come from there. There was none. In fact, the moon had slipped away, obscured by the clouds. She thought of her father. Maybe that's what happened to him too. Maybe the clouds had simply rolled in.

This thought made Heather angry, even while she found it soothing. If clouds rolled in, they could roll away. It made sense. But why had it happened at all? And why was she here in this water tank waiting to be humiliated? Heather felt the urge to hit something, to strike out.

Backing into the curved wall of the tank, she kicked it twice with her heels as hard as she could.

"Was that you, Ronnie?"

The voices were above them now.

"From down there."

Heather knocked again, this time with her fists.

"Oh shit."

"You didn't tell me the fucker was alive."

"It wasn't."

A series of furious knocking came from the other side of the tank as Jeremy began to hit the walls. Heather joined him and together they made the tower wobble on its wooden legs. Soon she was throwing her body against the walls as the water sloshed around her knees. The sky was completely dark now and the stars seemed to list from side to side as they rocked the tank. At thirteen, Heather had never been drunk, though she imagined this was what it must feel like. The sky appeared to spin above her, to come loose from its fragile place. She had no idea how long this lasted. It seemed like forever.

When they stopped, she was soaked and exhilarated. There was little doubt the Barrows had split. To be sure, she calmed her breathing and listened. Outside, an engine turned over and tires scattered gravel.

"Awesome," she said. Her words echoed in the dark tank, plinking off the tin walls, falling soundless into the water.

Jeremy said nothing. She heard him breathing nearby.

"Jeremy?"

She reached for him in the darkness. He was there, beside her. Taking her shoulders, he turned her gently. At first, she thought he was about to kiss her, but rather than lifting her face up to his, he tilted her head down.

"There's something touching my leg."

The clouds around the moon dissolved. Moonlight played over the water, making the smallest ripples shine like silk. There, bathed in moonshine, near her feet. It had been there all along; she'd probably brushed against it without even knowing, unaware of the deadness touching her legs. She felt a sudden urge to wipe them clean.

Jeremy spoke the question, even as it formed inside her mind. "What is it?"

Heather knelt for a better look. Blue and bloated, almost fishlike in the murky water. Hands splayed apart as if the creature had been pleading. Both knees bent, the creature's feet in the air. Heather counted the toes. Ten. Ten fingers. She lifted her gaze to the head. Proportionally too large for its body. The mouth hung open in a toothless scream. Its eyes were open in an expression Heather recognized, though for a time she could not place it. She bent closer, trying to read them. What did they say? Where had she seen them before? Then the moon shifted or the clouds did. The shadows crept away, and she saw her own reflection in the water staring up at her as if she were a different person, an underwater person, sharing the same body and personality and memories as her normal self. This underwater person, though, knew all the secrets. And finally she knew where she recognized the eyes. They belonged to the girl staring back at her. The look, she understood now, was simple confusion and fear. Nothing so confusing and frightening as being born into death.

She made herself look away.

An arm fell around her shoulders. Jeremy knelt beside her, pulling her close. Together they gazed down at the creature.

"Is it an alien?" he said at last.

"Yeah," Heather said, seeing them all in the water now, the baby, Jeremy, and herself. "It is."

37

HALLOWEEN COMES TO
COUNTY RD. SEVEN

Doug settles back down on the couch with a fresh beer, as Martin starts another porn flick. Doug doesn't say anything, opting to drink his beer in silence while Martin adjusts the volume. A girl saunters onscreen, her silicone implants rigid, her shorts so tight they might as well be painted on.

The sex starts without preliminaries. It's cruel and mean and soulless. Doug focuses on the trees outside Martin's trailer, and thinks today might be the day to leave.

Two weeks ago, Doug was fired from his job at the Honda plant because the shift foreman smelled alcohol on his breath one time too many. When his wife found out, she told him not to bother coming home until he had another job. He's been with Martin ever since.

He looks over at Martin, high as the cow jumping over the moon, grinning stupidly at the television. Martin, whom Doug has known since grade school, lost his job three years ago and just look at him—a sack of shit, true, but a happy sack of shit. He lays around most of the day, taking hits of crank, then doing something asinine like shooting a hole in the side of his trailer or running laps around his above-ground pool. Sometimes, after a few hits, he just sits and picks at his toenails for hours, mutilating them until they look like tiny, bloody faces, leering back at him. Once he got scared and tried to cut them off, but Doug managed to talk him down. Mostly, though, Martin just sits on the couch, watching porn, raving about some whore he's done or wants to do, waiting for the doorbell to ring. The doorbell rings, he gets up and answers it. Trades little homemade baggies for government-issued green. Saturday nights, he might shower, go to a bar, pick-up a twenty-three-year-old in high heels and a mini skirt looking for some free crank.

Doug and Martin have an agreement. Doug can stay indefinitely as long as he is willing to help out when some fellow named Snakeskin shows up. Doug isn't even sure if Snakeskin is a real person or just another one of Martin's drug-induced delusions.

"Snakeskin's going to be by one of these days, and when he comes, he's coming to kill me," Martin told Doug a week into his stay. "That's when you'll earn your keep, Dougie. You'll know it's him by the sound of his truck. It's geared low, so you'll feel it in your gut."

Unable to deal with more porn, Doug leaves Martin alone and escapes through the back door to light a cigarette on the tossed-together deck. The air out here smells good. Another downside of living with Martin: his trailer smells like chemicals and stale beer. Not that the happy bastard ever notices. Doug glances back over his shoulder and is grateful for Martin's darkened windows. Sheathed in black trash bags, the windows remind him of something. Today is Halloween. He thinks about his daughter, Maci. Is she old enough to go trick or treating? Probably not, maybe next year.

He stands, watching the afternoon sky. There's a good

breeze, but it's cold, too cold for late October in Alabama. Winter's coming and it's going to be a bitch. Especially without a place to stay or a job. He tries to convince himself that he can find work again. Tries to believe he can patch things up at home. Tries to imagine how next Halloween will be: Maci waiting for him to come home from work. She'll be standing in the driveway dressed as Tinkerbell or some princess. He likes this image. He wants to go back home.

As he starts back inside for a beer, he stops, frozen by a loud rumbling out on the road. He waits, hoping it will pass. When it doesn't, he feels torn between going back inside or taking off for the woods where his truck is parked.

The trailer shakes as the truck eases up the gravel drive.

"Doug. Hey Dougie boy," comes Martin's voice from inside. "It's show time."

He could run up through the woods and be at his house in no time. He could convince his wife to take him back. He could help Maci make a costume and together they could go trick or treating.

Where would they go?

He laughs at the prospect of coming to Martin's door. What would he put in Maci's bag? A joint? It's not funny, though he has to laugh anyway.

And just before Martin swings the door open, Doug feels it. A burning inside of him to get the hell away from Martin. Back in school, Doug always managed to get wrapped up in Martin's stupid schemes. The door is open. Martin stands at the threshold.

"Shake your thang, man. It's time."

Doug hesitates, maybe even steps away from Martin.

Martin's smile vanishes. "You aren't thinking about bolting, are you?'

Doug doesn't speak, his eyes down.

"Hey, there's nothing to it. I need your help, Doug. Just

like you needed mine."

Doug steps back inside.

"Take this gun," Martin says, opening a drawer that contains several dirty needles, a pair of women's underwear, and the biggest handgun Doug has ever seen. "Go to the lab and—"

"Lab? I—"

Martin holds his hand up. "The fucking closet." He motions to a door with the gun. "Flip the vent up so you can see. If Snakeskin makes a move, shoot him right between the fucking eyes." He holds out the gun.

Doug looks at it but nothing else.

"You think I'm fucking with you, Doug?" Martin shoves him hard in the chest. "You think I've just been letting you lay on my couch and drink my beer for free? Take the gun. Now."

Doug hears someone outside fiddling with the gate. A coldness grips him, and all of the beer he drank today feels like it's in his bladder. He reaches for the gun.

Doug doesn't know guns. The one in his hand is so heavy, the barrel so thick, he is sure it can destroy a man, obliterate him, change his face to pulp, from something that's recognizable to something that isn't.

The "lab" is dark and smells like ammonia. He finds and opens the vent enough to see out into the room where Martin is taking a final hit before facing Snakeskin.

Doug doesn't want to shoot anyone, but the second Martin opens the door and Snakeskin walks in, he knows that he may not have a choice.

He wonders sometimes if he has ever really had a choice. Martin reminds him of better times, and better times is all he's got. He wishes he could forget Martin completely, but he feels powerless to do so. His life seems like a series of inevitabilities, like he is rolling down a hill, continually picking up speed. One of these days, he knows that the bottom will come and when it does, all those inevitabilities will crush him.

From the open vent, Doug watches Snakeskin come in. He is a small man, but muscular. His complexion is dark, as if he has spent many days in the sun. His dress is minimal—a white tee, blue jeans that fit tight around a trim waist, a pair of shit kickers that look at least a size too big. Doug unconsciously raises the gun to the open slat.

There are hundreds of men just like Snakeskin all over the county. He looks not unlike Doug himself, perhaps a little more muscular, his clothes a little tighter. The real difference is in the eyes. They look wild. Reckless. Doug knows those eyes. They belong to men who have stopped caring a long, long time ago.

Snakeskin exudes a confidence that sets Doug on edge, and he grips the big gun a little more tightly, lifting it closer to the open slat.

Behind Snakeskin comes a tall razor blade of a man. He's younger than Snakeskin, but only his flesh shows it. His eyes look tired, so lazy that they are intense, so unconcerned that they are hard.

Snakeskin asks Martin how he's been doing.

Martin, nervous, jumpy Martin, manages to say, "Life's good, man. Who's your friend?"

Snakeskin frowns at the floor. Then thrusts a thumb at the tall man. "This is Rodney. Rodney, this is Martin." He looks at Martin eye to eye and adds, "The one I told you about."

Rodney barely glances at Martin and says, "The one that sells good shit or the other one you were telling me about?"

Snakeskin says, "The other one, man. The other one."

"What I thought," Rodney says.

Martin glances quickly at the closet door and says, "Fellas,

I'm just trying to run a lab here. If it ain't about crank, you probably got the wrong guy."

"Oh, I think we got the right guy." Snakeskin pulls a switchblade from his back pocket. He nods at Rodney. "Go get her."

Rodney bobs his head as if to some unheard music and says, "Hell yeah."

An awkward moment passes as Snakeskin keeps his eyes trained on Martin, and Martin shakes and fidgets like he needs a hit of something bad.

Rodney returns with a young girl, maybe seventeen. She walks in front of him, and he stares at her ass, barely covered by a pair of tight cut-offs. Prime jailbait, the type of girl who's been living a life unfit for any age, much less seventeen, the type of girl who wears her sadness underneath hard looks and snarled lips. She doesn't meet Martin's eyes, and Doug knows why Snakeskin is here.

"Martin, you know Emily?"

Martin shrugs. "I think I've seen her around."

"Seen her around." Snakeskin nods slowly. "Seen her around."

He makes like he is about to stroke his chin in a thoughtful manner with the hand that does not hold the switchblade. The blade is still unexposed, and he is twirling it between his fingers as if this might just be a nervous habit, nothing more. Then suddenly and with great force he thrusts the palm of his free hand out, catching Martin hard in the nose. Martin's head snaps back. He shakes it once and thick streams of blood pour from his nostrils.

The switchblade is open and at his throat. "You seen her around, huh? If by seeing her around you mean sticking your dick in her, then yeah, I suppose you've seen her around."

"No," Martin says. He's crying. "No, I ain't never fucked her, Snakeskin."

"Oh, am I mistaken? Let me check my source." He turns to Emily. "You and this fella ever do anything?"

Emily looks at Martin then. "Well, yeah," she says. "A couple of times. It was a trade. He gave me what I wanted. I done told you all this before, Snake."

"Yeah, but I needed to hear it again, baby." He looks at Martin. "You knew me and Emily had a thing going right?"

Martin doesn't respond.

"Answer me!"

Martin shrugs. "She offered."

"You should have said no," Snakeskin says and grins. A boyish grin. It makes him look younger, maybe less dangerous. This is only an illusion, a trick. "I'm not into sharing her. You think I get off on her being with another man?"

"I'm telling you, it was a fair trade. I didn't make the offer. She did. I didn't know you two had a thing. How could I have known that, man?"

Snakeskin turns to Rodney. "You believe this shit? First he didn't fuck her. Now he fucked her but it was just a fair trade. What's next? He going to ask me for a refund?"

While Snakeskin's eyes are on Rodney, Martin looks in Doug's direction. He nods his head quickly as if to say, now or never.

Doug already knows this, yet he feels no real obligation to Martin. He doesn't even like him. Maybe he did once. A long time ago, when they were young. When the world was different. Somehow, Martin reminds Doug of that place, that youth, that happier time. Yet, he still considers briefly just letting Martin get what is coming to him. If he could get away with it, he might, though he realizes that the situation is more complicated than that. Snakeskin will likely cut Martin. In which case, Martin will scream for Doug to shoot them. In which case, they will come for Doug too.

So, it really is now or never. Martin glances nervously over at Doug again, his lip trembling.

Snakeskin says to Martin, "Rodney, we got us a little weasel here. A lying weasel. Know what that means?"

Rodney shrugs and scratches his ass.

"Means I'm going to have to cut—"

The sound is deafening, the recoil sudden and harsh and for an instant Doug thinks that the gun has misfired and he has been the one shot instead of Snakeskin. He sees Snakeskin's body jerk back, sees the blossom of blood soak through the white t-shirt, and Doug knows that the bullet has hit its target. It's like somebody presses a slow motion button. Snakeskin grimaces and lurches, tries to find where the shot came from. Doug feels like vomiting, but grips the gun tighter and squeezes off two more shots. One sails over Rodney's head. The next one collides with his mouth. For a second Rodney twists his face up as if he has only swallowed a bitter pill instead of a bullet. His mouth begins to leak blood. He falls down hard. Doug drops the gun, doubles over, and pukes on the floor.

Emily is screaming.

The next thing Doug knows, Martin is standing over him, ordering him to get up and "shoot the bitch." Doug shakes his head and throws up again between his knees.

Martin reaches into the puke, retrieves the gun. Doug hears the front door bang shut behind him. There is another blast from the gun.

Doug pulls himself up, wiping off his knees and hands.

Martin comes back in and tosses the gun on the couch. He pumps his fist in the air a few times and fumbles inside a chest of drawers for his stash of crank. He does a line, inhaling hard and shadowboxes the air, shuffling his feet, bobbing and weaving like some hick parody of Cassius Clay.

"We got to clean up this mess and hide the bodies!" He shouts and does a little two-step around the den. "But hell yeah, Martin lives on! Dougie saves the day!"

Martin does his little jig, flailing around like a man who has just won the lottery. His face is flushed, splashed with tiny beads of blood and sweat; his nose is swollen from where Snakeskin hit him, and it's still bleeding, staining his smile red. Doug sees the gun on the couch, blood and vomit around the trigger. It's time to act.

He has it before Martin even stops dancing. He aims it at Martin's head and waits.

It didn't have to end like this. There were places, bumps along the journey where he could have jumped off the Martin train. He simply chose not to because the ground looked too hard and rocky and the ride was just too much damn fun. So he had held on for this.

The gun is warm in his hand, his pulse like thunder.

This could work. The bodies, the drugs. He could put the gun in Martin's hand. He could be home in fifteen minutes, maybe less, leaving this part of his life forever. He could start over.

Martin still has not noticed Doug or the gun. He is jiving to some soundtrack in his head, oblivious to everything except Martin.

"Hey, Martin?" Doug says.

The soundtrack ends. Martin shimmies to a stop. He turns, sees Doug, sees the gun, makes a face like he can't believe Doug is pointing a gun at his head. Then he scoffs, making some half-assed noise in his throat, making it sound like he thinks it's funny Doug is pointing a gun at him.

"Stop playing, Dougie. We got some work to do."

"You shouldn't have gotten me mixed up in this, Martin. This wasn't any of my business."

"You got your ownself mixed up, Dougie. I didn't pull the trigger. You did that, man."

It's true, what Martin says, and somewhere below all of

Doug's anger and his shock, he realizes that the best thing to do would be to put the gun down and leave. But Doug's best is already behind him. He has reached survival mode. Here there can be no black and white, no right or wrong, just shades of gray, melting together to form something he can barely recognize.

There is only one way out now.

Doug pulls the trigger. The bullet hits Martin in the chest and he woofs loudly. Martin staggers and then collapses. Doug goes over and watches him gurgle and spit blood. Martin wants to say something, but there will be no more words from Martin. Doug aims again, this time at Martin's forehead. He fires once and then twice, ripping chunks of flesh from bone, obliterating his friend's face.

He drops to one knee and carefully pries Martin's fingers open. He almost puts the gun in Martin's hand before realizing there is a better solution. Wiping it clean of blood and puke, he slips it inside the waistband of his jeans. On the way home, he will toss it into the river.

He leaves Martin's trailer. The wind has picked up, howling through the bare trees, banging the back door of Martin's trailer. He steps over Emily, feeling sorry for her. She's just one more piece of debris caught in the windstorm he's been plunging headfirst into his whole life.

Out by the road, someone has thrown a pumpkin from their car, and Doug starts toward it, thinking Maci might like to have a Jack-O-Lantern to put on their doorstep. As he gets closer, Doug sees that the pumpkin's been smashed, and the orange pulp lay in glistening strings against the blacktop. It's gone rotten and stinks. Doug turns away and circles the trailer, beginning the walk into the woods where he has parked his truck, hidden away from a world where things so often go to ruin.

WALK THE WHEAT

Mama called the doctor when Cody's head wouldn't stop bleeding. The doctor, an old man who could barely sidle in through the doorway and kept hitching his pants up over his belly, looked at Cody's white hair and silver eyes for a long time before removing the damp cloth Mama had placed on his forehead.

You should've took this boy to the hospital. Gash is an inch deep.

No hospitals, Mama said.

The doctor frowned, the lines on his bald head furrowing into criss-crosses of light and dark.

I'll get my surgical stuff.

We waited as Cody stirred. Expression came back into his eyes instead of that scary, glazed look he'd been wearing. His mouth was no longer a flat line. His face no longer a dead, blood-streaked thing.

The doctor wiggled back through the door, carrying two leather pouches. He put them down, kneeling beside Cody, his large frame shifting the trailer with a loud creak.

This'd be a great deal less painful if you'd call an ambulance.

No, just do it, Mama said. Do it quick.

Fifteen minutes later, Cody had seven stitches in his forehead and was sitting up, drinking a glass of water.

I've got to ask, you know, the doctor said, mopping sweat off his forehead, how it happened this time.

He hit his head. Outside, playing.

The doctor turned to Cody.

Cody shrugged, his white hair sliding over his collar, his thin, pointed face, expressionless unless apathy could be considered an expression.

I hit my head. Like she said. Can't you tell?

The doctor did not look satisfied. He looked worried. He glanced from Mama to me to Cody and back to Mama as if trying to break the complex code that existed among us and decipher all the unuttered words we wished to speak.

I've been here too many times. And that last time. . . . He trailed off, as if unsure how to speak of such a thing, or maybe he was afraid to speak of it, afraid that saying the words out loud would make them true. Next time, he said, I won't come. Do not call me. Call the hospital. I wash my hands of you, all three.

Let me pay you, Mama said.

He waved her off. I shouldn't have come. Something is wrong in this place. You people have done something so wrong I can smell it. Don't call me again.

That night we lay in the cool dark of the room, the windows half-up, the blinds tied back, opening the night and the miles of wheat beyond like a story book except the words were written in a strange tongue.

Cody? I said. Did you really drown? Or did I just dream it?

Cody sighed. Just forget about all that stuff, Davy.

I can't. I mean, I try, but then you start bleeding again, and I want to tell Mama about what happened, but then I think she knows, but I'm not even sure if I know. It eats at me something bad.

Okay, he said. I'll tell you what I remember. But you can't tell Mama. I don't think she can handle it.

I promise.

He told me of the day just a few months ago when we'd gone to the rock slide up in the cove, where the water runs off the creek and slicks the rock and pools at the bottom. I remembered it well, going out with our towels and shorts, getting sunburned before we even made it to the cove, and then letting the big oaks shade our skin like a balm.

We found the place, a dark and magical oasis where the sun did not break through the forest canopy and the sound of water was in our ears like the sound of silence, deafening and impossible to hear all at once.

I'll go first, Cody had said.

Shouldn't we check the pool? I said. Cody had told me before never to slide down the rock until I was sure there were no logs or other debris submerged beneath the dark water.

I'm checking it now, he said, and slid, his feet flung up in the air, his arms spread out as if he were trying to hug the whole damn forest. Down he went, gray water pluming out from under his cut-offs, his body spinning round and round like a top. He let off one whoop of joy before hitting the water.

There was a splash and the whole cove got quiet. Even the noise of the water seemed to recede, and all I could do was wait for him to come back up.

But he didn't come back up. Not for a long time. And when he did finally emerge, his hair and eyes were silver, and his body looked put together wrong.

I think I broke my back, Davy, he said. A slight breeze wandered through our window and settled on my forehead.

There was pain, like my whole body screaming out at once, then numbness. Then I was trying to come back up, but I couldn't move. And then I couldn't breathe.

He shuddered.

You were down there a long time, I said.

You should have pulled me out.

I was scared.

Cody stood up and crossed the room. He sat on the edge of my bed and put his arm around me. I know you were scared. So was I. But I'm back now and that's all that matters.

What was it like? I asked him. When you were gone?

After I ran out of breath, I just closed my eyes, and waited. I couldn't feel anything, not even the water. It was like I was in a vacuum. And then I opened my eyes and it was just like darkness. Just pure, clean darkness. No noise, no light, not even smell. Nice. I liked it right away.

And then what'd you see?

I told you I couldn't see nothing.

Well, what happened?

Nothing. At least not for a while. Long enough for me to realize that I didn't exist like I thought I did.

He got off my bed, his long white hair hanging over his eyes and continued: I remember leaving the cove. I remember walking. Wanting to come home bad. There was a wheat field . . . like a maze. It was this wheat field— he said, pointing out the window —but it wasn't this wheat field either. I dunno. I saw things. Things I can't explain. Shapes and shadows and so many things that just don't have names. Then I heard your voice, Davy. I heard you talking to me and I listened hard and kept moving toward the sound. Next thing I knew I'd come out of the wheat and I was wet again, and my leg was stuck in something, some deadfall or something, and I jerked it free and it tore my knee up something awful, but I was alive again. And I swam to the top and saw you standing beside the pool, reaching out to me.

Mama shit herself when you came walking in that day. None of your bones fit right.

Yeah, he said, popping his shoulder in and out of place with a sickening crack. Still don't.

I'm glad you came back.

Me too, he said and began to cough. It was a shallow, sputtering noise and it sounded like there was gravedust in his lungs.

He went back to his bed and we didn't talk anymore. But I wondered why he'd come back and how long he'd stay.

The wind started blowing wide open outside the trailer and our beds rocked to and fro and the moon sat high and fat in the heavens, an unlidded eye that never slept.

A woman came to visit us the day after Cody's knee started bleeding. His kneecap looked crooked and there was a gash above it that ran the width of his leg. The woman said her name was Victoria. She was pretty, prematurely gray, and concerned.

Mama tried to hold her at the door, so she wouldn't see inside where Cody was bleeding all over the newspaper, but the woman pushed past her and into the house anyway.

Doctor Fitzsimons called me. I work for the state, family services.

She looked at Cody, the blood, the newspapers balled up in the corner of the room—stained so red they barely looked like newspapers and more like skins from some moulting demon.

She knelt beside Cody. Tell me what happened. Tell me the truth.

It just opened up and started bleeding.

And nobody touched you? Nobody at all?

No, not this time. Not anymore.

What do you mean, anymore?

Mama ain't never touched me. Then Cody shut his eyes and refused to talk.

She turned to me.

How old are you?

Fourteen.

Do you know what happened?

I nodded.

She smiled. You can tell me.

He just bleeds. These cuts open up on him and he bleeds.

He'll be okay. It'll stop in a few hours.

I see. She stood up, keeping her distance from the newspapers. She looked at Mama. I'll be back, Mrs. Langer.

I didn't see her again for a long time.

Cody sat up in the bed during the thunderstorm so suddenly I thought lightning had struck the trailer. Outside, the storm was brewing hell and bringing it down hard and relentless. The rain sounded unending, like the sound of being in your own skin, like a sound that had stopped being a sound and had become a wall, a physical thing that couldn't be broken or even shaped anymore beyond a single concussive drone. A thousand bees synched with one heartbeat.

What? I said.

He stood up and looked out the window. The backyard flashed in a photograph of blue-white lightning.

My knee stopped bleeding.

It did?

He lifted his leg onto my mattress and switched on the lamp between our beds.

See? There ain't even a scar.

I whistled softly. I reckon that's good since you seem to get a new one every time you turn around.

Yeah, Cody said, smiling. I reckon it is.

We listened to the rain some more, and I had the feeling that I was waiting on something, but I couldn't honestly say what. I was almost asleep, lulled by the distant thunder and insistent rain when Cody's voice brought me back.

I was supposed to come back, Cody said.

I'm glad, I mumbled, half-dreaming.

Some time later, the rain broke and there was a long silence followed by a flare of lightning and whipcrack thunder and the sudden smell of smoke. I joined Cody at the window where we watched a magnolia tree catch fire in the yard. Beyond that, the wheat formed a wavering line and I thought of Cody wandering there, alone. His body lying at the bottom of the rock slide under six feet of water, his leg caught in a deadfall. I pictured him walking down row after row of wheat, all jangled bones and bloody flesh, until he saw an opening, a door from that world back to this one. Did he hesitate? Or did he jump at the chance to come back to the world where the living do not understand the dead, much less themselves?

Bobby Jackson Jr. showed up at our door three weeks later. Mama met him at work and they'd shared some drinks and now, here he was, in front of our trailer, smiling a smile only desperate widows could believe.

Your mama around? He hooked his thumbs in his back pockets like he owned the place.

She died last week, Cody said.

Bobby took out some rolling paper, shook some tobacco from a tin, and began to build a cigarette. Funny thing, he said. Last night, she sure seemed alive. He grinned again.

Mama appeared at the door. Boys, please allow Mr. Jackson to come in. He's going to be staying with us for a while. He's come upon a string of bad luck, so we're going to be doing the

Christian thing and help him get back on his feet.

Cody and I stepped aside and Bobby Jackson Jr. came through the door and into our lives.

Bobby liked to sit on the couch and cut his toenails. He went at them with something approaching obsession, whittling them down until they were bloody and swollen. Toenail flecks littered the den. One afternoon, after flicking another nail onto the floor, he told me to clean them up.

I ain't touching those.

He laughed. All right. Little man has a mind of his own. I like it. Give me five, Peewee. He stuck out his hand. Foolishly, I slapped it.

His big hand closed over mine. He jerked me to him so hard my mouth slammed into his shoulder. His other hand came down on my head and buried my face in the sofa, crushing my nose until I heard it crack and felt warm blood seep over my upper lip. I felt an intense burning, and I resisted the urge to touch it, to feel how bad it was.

Now, I'm going to ask you again, boy. Would you mind cleaning up my toenails? He laughed at himself and let me up for air.

That's when Cody came flying in. He took off from one side of the room, leading with his forearm and clocked Bobby in the forehead. I watched as he stuck two fingers into Bobby's eye sockets. Bobby screamed and let go of me. I stood up, hacking and wheezing for breath.

Bobby punched Cody in the face, knocking him off balance. Then he found a heavy vase on the coffee table and broke it over Cody's mouth. Dropping to his knees he went to work, hitting Cody over and over until the only thing bloodier than his fists was Cody's face.

Then he was standing over me, his eyes crooked and scratched raw, a lopsided grin on his face.

I'm going to break you boys. Your mama's pussy is too sweet not to make the effort.

I flew at him, but his fist stopped me cold. I thudded to the floor and saw the room spin once, twice, and I was gone.

The war lasted three more weeks. It was an ugly war, full of unrepentant violence and malice so dark its causes were beyond the pale of discernment. By all rights, Bobby should have won. He was older, tougher, and a hell of a lot more mean. But Bobby had never fought anything that kept coming back the way Cody did.

Cody's injuries healed faster than ever now. And this, above all, seemed to vex Bobby. I frequently noticed him studying Cody, as if he were a puzzle he could put together if he could just see the bigger picture. And even when Bobby hadn't touched him in days, new wounds would appear all over Cody's body and heal the next hour.

Me, I kind of took my licking and fell in line. One fist to the temple had been enough to teach me. I returned violence surreptitiously. A shake of salt into one of his wounds while he slept; a toy carefully placed on the floor near his bed that might cause him to stumble; an upturned tack on the couch where he liked to sit.

Cody, though, was determined to kill Bobby. Either that or make him run. Out of some kind of twisted code of respect that I could not fathom, neither of them would fight when Mama was around. She surely knew it was happening. The tension in the trailer was so flagrant that ignoring it was like trying to ignore the sun on a cloudless summer day.

It happened on a Friday after Mama had gone into town for groceries. Cody told Bobby he needed to leave or he would kill him. Bobby told Cody to come suck his fat one. He wasn't going anywhere. Cody came for him with a switchblade we'd bought with the money we found after going through Mama's underwear drawer.

Bobby caught Cody before the blade could do anything. The two tumbled to the ground, shaking the trailer. They rolled the length of the trailer, fighting for control of the knife. It ended up in Bobby's hand and then in Cody's neck. The blood spilled out in a thick river of pulsing red.

And then, for the second time in Cody's sixteen years, his pulse stopped.

Get some towels, Bobby said. We got some work to do before your mother comes back.

We cleaned the linoleum, sopping the blood up with every towel in the trailer. I worked silently, aware that I was dying inside myself, losing touch with who I was, what I hoped to be, everything except the hate I held for Bobby Jackson, Jr.

We hauled him to the wheat field and dropped his body between the rows.

He'll come back.

Bobby looked at me like I had lost my mind.

You're in shock.

Maybe so, but he's done come back before. He'll come back for me.

You're a fucked up little kid. He took the shovel and raised it up high. He brought the sharp edge down repeatedly over Cody's neck until he had made a clean break between body and head. He kicked the head away. If he comes back now, he'll be in right bad shape, he said, laughing.

We buried the body in a shallow grave. Bobby took the head back with us and buried it underneath the trailer.

I didn't know what would happen next

Bobby told Mama Cody had run off after a fight.

Boy said he'd never come back here. Bobby shook his head.

Shame he was so headstrong. You gonna call the cops?

Bobby talked Mama out of calling the police, convincing her Cody'd come back quicker if they didn't make a big deal about it.

If Mama had doubts, she kept them to herself.

Eventually, Bobby got so cocksure he'd gotten away with it, he told me I'd be next. I believed him. Bobby was a lot of things, but I'd yet to know him as a liar.

I thought about going to Mama, but I was afraid. Not that she'd tell Bobby. I was afraid she would believe me. She would believe every word and do nothing. I was more frightened of the person my mother had become than anything else.

One morning while Bobby slept, I saw her crying. She was cradling one of the little dolls Cody had slept with as a baby. She held it tight to her breast like a woman suckling a child, and I wondered how she lived with herself knowing that the man she slept with every night had killed her oldest son.

I watched her in silence for a moment, before slipping out to the storage shed to look for a shovel.

Digging his body up was the easy part, but after that I had to think of a way to get his head from under the trailer and out to the wheat field. I settled on an old pillowcase. Placing the head inside, I tucked it under my arm like a running back carrying a football.

Once I had him out of the ground, I tried to remember what, if anything, I'd done while standing in the cove near the rock slide, waiting for him to emerge. I seemed to recall a prayer.

Lord, I know it ain't natural, but I need him.

I need him real bad.

The morning clouded over and I couldn't tell if it was a sign or maybe just a front moving in. It started to rain, a hard rain that tore at Cody's flesh, and made the stench even worse.

Nothing happened.
I went home, determined to kill Bobby myself, if necessary.

Mama was waiting for me in the den, a half-smoked cigarette in her mouth, an overturned whiskey bottle beside the couch.
Where you been?
Out playing.
In the Goddamned rain?
Wasn't raining when I went out.
Cody's dead, ain't he?
The silence in the trailer was as heavy as the rain outside.
Yeah, Mama. He's dead.
How'd it happen? Tell me right now.
Bobby . . . Well, they was scuffling.
Fighting?
Yeah. And Cody pulled out a knife.
And Bobby had to defend himself right?
No, it wasn't like that—
Yes, it was. Subject's closed. She hesitated, as if she wanted to say more.
The rain pounded the trailer, sounding every bit like an angry god.
It wasn't never natural, she said. The way he would bleed . . .
I didn't say nothing to this. Instead, I went over to the window and pulled the blinds apart. The day had grown dark, like somebody had thrown a caul over the sun. Shadows squirmed in the front yard and I looked for Cody, but all I could see were miles of wheat, waving in the darkness like some great undulating beast whose secrets I could never grasp.

That night the rain stopped suddenly and the silence woke me up.
Cody sat across from me on his bed.

I came back for you, Davy.

He was no more than a shadow, silhouetted against the window and the moonlit fields beyond.

You going to stay this time?

He stood and went over to the window and opened it to the night. The smell of wet grass and wheat sifted in.

I ain't supposed to be here, Davy. There's another place I'm supposed to go. He gestured to the wheat field. Some place out there. Something's coming for me, and when it does, won't be nothing I can do to hide anymore.

He came over and sat beside me, putting his arm over my shoulders. I've learned a few things in the wheat. It's powerful easy to get lost between here and there, there and here. That goes double on this side. Mama's lost her way, Davy. She's so tangled up in stuff she won't never find her way out. You're right there on the edge. And if something don't give, you're gonna fall into the same pit she's in. And once you're there, it ain't about climbing out. It's about just seeing your way through, keeping the muck from your eyes and the mountain vines from wrapping you up and holding you forever. What I'm saying is you got to get in touch with that Victoria lady. Tomorrow.

He stood up. I was dead a long time, Davy. It ain't like last time. I shouldn't stay.

No, I said. You gotta stay. Please, Cody.

He nodded and the moonshine came in through the window and fell on him. I saw how his head wasn't on right, how it hung over to the side, how the hole gaped on one side of his neck like a wordless mouth.

I ain't much to look at, he said.

I don't care. Don't go.

So he didn't. We pushed our beds together like we used to do when we were little kids and got scared of the wind in the wheat. We lay for a long time, talking of death and Mama and how she always ended up with guys like Bobby. We talked about the path Cody'd glimpsed in the wheat and how he felt sure he was bound to walk it, one way or the other.

You ain't going to kill Bobby? I asked.

Bobby'll kill himself eventually. On the other side, you can see how things that make sense among the living are really foolish. Revenge can't fix nothing. He seemed to think for a minute, then added: If I knew it'd fix you, I would, Davy. I'd kill him. But it'll make things worse on you. That's the nature of this world. That lady, Victoria. She's your ticket.

In the other room, I heard Bobby snoring. A night bird twittered outside and somewhere far away, thunder boomed like a muted explosion. I reached out and put my hand on Cody's arm. He felt still. And cold. But I kept my hand on him until I fell asleep. That night, I dreamed dreams only the dead could fathom.

First light and I turned to see Cody gone. The bed was still there where we'd pulled it snug against mine. I got up and pulled on my clothes, aware that this day might change my life.

I made it to the front door before I heard Bobby's voice.

We need to talk, Davy.

I turned around. Where's Mama?

Don't worry about her. Me and you need to talk.

I slung the door open and tried to dart out into the yard, but before I could, I heard the click of a hammer being pulled back.

I'd slow down, Peewee.

You gonna shoot me? I said, trying to make it sound like a challenge.

Matter of fact, I might. Come sit down.

I pulled myself over to the table where Bobby had been eating eggs and sausage links and chasing it down with Wild Turkey.

You and your mama been talking?

Huh?

Don't huh me! He sprang from his chair, knocking the table and all of the contents onto the floor. He had the gun in one hand and the bottle in the other. He stuck the gun against my forehead. Where was you going just now?

To school.

Bullshit. It's the Goddamn summer and you know it.

He was pushing the barrel against my forehead so hard it hurt.

I was going to talk to the coach down there about football next season.

That's a damned lie. You was going to tell somebody about what I done wasn't you? I ain't no fool. Well, guess what, Davy boy? I'm going to cancel your plans. Come on, we're going to the wheat field to do it this time. I don't feel like cleaning up the blood.

I'd never been so deep in the wheat before. We walked and walked until the outside world receded like an obscure dream. The real world awaited now—a place that destroyed the senses and made reality an endless series of swaying wheat stalks.

Somewhere above us, the sun beat on our backs and great blackbirds swept across the sky like chiaroscuro brushes.

Bobby told me to sit on the ground and look at the wheat.

I did as I was told, settling onto the soft soil, letting the breeze rattle through the wheat and flow over me like baptismal waters. I was ready to die. It would be over soon, and I would be up and walking, gliding like an unmoored stalk of wheat, searching for Cody.

But Cody came to me.

I saw him first in outline, as the wheat parted and bent, sketching my brother.

As he materialized, I reached out to him. Cody ignored my hand and stood in front of Bobby. He looked good—healthier than he'd been in life. He looked wise—ancient somehow— but most of all he looked happy. Even with the gun pointed at the back of my head, I found myself overcome with grief and love and awe. My brother had given all for me. He'd come back for me, died for me, and somehow come back again.

You ain't here, Bobby said.

It's you that ain't here, Bobby. You've come too far into a place you don't understand. You can't hurt me anymore, Bobby.

You ain't real.

Cody extended his hand to me. I grasped it, surprised at how substantial it felt, and he pulled me to my feet.

The gun went off, once, twice. Two dimesized holes appeared in Cody's forehead. A sliver of blood leaked out before both were filled with new, unblemished flesh.

Bobby dropped the gun and ran.

I picked up the gun, but when I turned back to see Cody, he was gone, disappeared among the wheat, as if he'd never existed at all. I stood there, the gun heavy in my hand. I watched the wheat bristle beneath a clandestine breeze and knew I would never see my brother again. Not on this side of the wheat anyway.

I caught up with Bobby, as he was getting into his truck. I felt calm, more in control than I'd ever felt, and I walked slowly to the rear of the truck and put a bullet in both back tires. Bobby clambered out of the truck, tried to run, but tripped. He fell onto his stomach and rolled over on his back to face me.

He's dead, Bobby said. He's dead.

So are you, I said. My finger actually tightened on the

trigger. I had every intention of shooting him, but then Mama's car came down the road and pulled into our gravel drive.

You see? You see your boy? Bobby said. What he's going to try and do to me?

Mama got out of her car. She was crying.

Davy, baby, she said. Put down the gun. You're not like this. Please, don't be like Cody.

At those last words, I spun around, aimed the gun at her. Don't be like my brother? He's the only one I'd ever want to be. He killed Cody, Mama.

I know, baby. I know.

And I'm going to do what I have to.

You ain't got the damn guts, Peewee, Bobby said.

Yeah, and Cody wasn't going to come back either, was he?

That wasn't real, he said, but his eyes told a different story. They looked haunted. They looked like they had seen something that would forever float before them even when the lights were out and his eyes were closed. Especially then.

I aimed the gun at the space between his eyes, right above the bridge of his nose. I imagined the bullet tearing through his forehead, little bits of bone and flesh scattering across the front yard like hayseed. Imagined Mama screaming, crying, losing it, losing it all.

And I remembered Cody, sitting on my bed last night, telling me that Bobby was already dead. And I wondered if I'd be dead too if I shot him.

Slowly, reluctantly, I lowered the gun. I heard Mama let out a groan of relief.

Bobby struggled to his feet, the tension in his face draining away.

Give it to me, he said. Give it over.

I turned toward the wheat field and slung the gun as far as I could across the road and into the swaying stalks.

Mama was crying and I went to her and we embraced. She

held me tight and for the first time since I was a little boy, I allowed myself to cry.

Mama asked Bobby to leave that afternoon. He left us with a shower of curses and threats. After he was gone, she took my hand and told me things were going to be different. I wondered if she'd climbed out of that hole Cody had told me about. I wanted to believe she had, but I'd known Mama for too long to drop my guard.

A week later, Bobby was back, grinning like nothing had ever happened. Mama mumbled something about a fresh start, a new beginning. I didn't argue. Instead, I started out through the wheat and made my way to town where I found the Family Services Center and a woman named Victoria. I told her about my mother and her boyfriends. I told her about Bobby and my brother.

I spent the rest of my teenage years with foster parents. Like most foster kids, many family situations I found myself in were less than ideal, but I hung in there, reminding myself nothing could be worse than Bobby Jackson, Jr. And when I felt like giving in, I thought about Cody and how he'd come back for me. It kept me going.

I'm fifty-seven now. I have a wife and three kids. I have cancer. Terminal. The kind the doctors like to call efficient. I won't see fifty-eight. But lately, when it rains, or when I see a wheat field on the television, or when someone mentions a young person who was willing to sacrifice themselves in a way far beyond their years, I wonder where Cody is, and what I'll say to him when I see him again.

THIS IS WHERE THE ROAD ENDS

2010, Texas

They'd finished eating lunch when Wanda excused herself
and went into the diner's restroom. Jonas pushed his plate
away and looked out the window at the dirt parking lot,
which was inexplicably almost full with cars, trucks, and
a row of motorcycles that clearly belonged to the group of
men dressed in heavy leather at the counter. He could be out
the door and gone before she came back. He'd leave the keys
on the table, hitch a ride with some trucker. Lose himself
somewhere. It was a damn big country. Big enough to live
with himself and what he'd done? He had his doubts about
that, but he'd try. What else could a person do?

The other option was to tell her. It had been on his lips
since New Orleans when they lay in the dark of the motel
room, his hand on her newly swollen belly, his heart beating
against her shoulder. Telling her was just as bad. It was as if
he stood atop a tall skyscraper and somebody was ordering
him to jump. He could jump left or right, but the result was
always the same: smashed on the concrete below.

He rehearsed the words in his head. *Once, three years ago, I was drunk—*

You don't drink, he could hear her say. *You've never been one to drink.*

He chuckled because *that* was funny. The kid in the booth next to him—the same one that had been bawling his eyes out during most of their meal—caught his eye and grinned a huge grin. A Marcus grin. No, no, don't start thinking like that again. It was a kid's grin. No more, no less.

See, I used to drink. Before I met you. Everything changed when I met you.

She'd smile then, crinkle her eyes and give him the look. The look that said, *you can do no wrong in my eyes, Jonas Withers.*

That's the problem, he thought. That's always been the problem.

The door swung open. He held his breath. He hadn't made a decision yet. Not good. Putting it off was unacceptable. He'd been doing that for the better part of three years. He waited, frozen by the decision that sat like a lump in his chest. A waitress came out. He let out a breath. The damn waitress. She was the blonde, pretty one with the narrow hips. Probably never had kids. He envied her that, even though he'd never actually been a father either. The baby was coming though, and then there was Marcus.

"Time is running out," he said under his breath. The kid in the booth looked at him like he was crazy. Kids have a sense about these things, right? He supposed he'd have to admit that they did.

2006, Alabama

Jonas hit the kid on a warm fall afternoon, the sun flattening out over the horizon in a spectacular crush of gold.

Sometimes, especially late at night when the house was quiet and he'd gone out to look at the stars, he almost convinced himself it was that sun, not the seven beers he'd had over lunch with Bryant Keith that had caused the accident.

The worst part was that Jonas had been expecting him, bracing for him even. How many times had he made the turn by the Mitchell farm and seen the fat little kid trudging home from his bus stop? Dozens, at least. Probably more. The kid had always had the common sense to stay on the left, out of harm's way because even a fat little kid knew the turn was as blind as Stevie Wonder. Sometimes, he'd even wave, but most days he'd just huff and puff his way on past, like the little kid that could, trying to make it home from his bus stop in time for a glass of milk and a bagful of cookies before the reruns on channel eleven started at four. Once Jonas saw him on his knees, investigating a dog carcass. It was the only time he didn't look comical, like the little fat kid you see in the movies that doesn't run because he waddles, the kid that got all the bad genes and all the bad luck. But even then, poised above the dead dog like a prayerful Buddha, he had been on the left side of the road.

The day Jonas hit him, he was on the right.

Jonas tried to brake, but all that did was give the kid time to look up from watching his feet. Their eyes locked for a long second and then there was a sound like you hear when somebody sits on your hood and the sheet metal pops. Then the kid was airborne, and somehow one of the boy's feet got snagged on Jonas's side mirror, and his body twisted violently before the foot was wrenched free. Jonas felt his seatbelt lock as the car came to a hard, tread-burning stop.

What followed was silence. This was the moment that could still make Jonas a blubbering idiot. He could think about all of it now, all of it except that one moment when he had to actually make himself get out of the car. Make himself see what was left of the kid.

When he did get out, he was blank. Can the mind ever be completely blank? At that moment, climbing out of the car, his was. It was as if his brain was in the process of rebooting itself, of clearing the old memory, deleting programs that would no longer be relevant, and getting ready to adapt to a new operating system, one that came with viruses and malware, and an impossibly steep learning curve.

After the blankness, when his mind started working again, the only thing he could think was *it isn't real. There is not dead boy on the road. There is not an impending 911 call.*

He was lying just off the side of the road, a lump of breathing flesh. His sweatshirt had gotten twisted around his neck and his bare belly was exposed. Jonas watched it heaving for a full twenty seconds before he realized what this meant.

The kid was alive. That meant Jonas had to move. Fast.

Jonas's mind knew this, but the signal wasn't getting to his body. He kept walking, his pace leisurely, if a not a little crooked. At any moment, he might fall down. He did not want to look, to see what his drunkenness had caused, but he knew he was being a coward. He quickened his pace and knelt beside the boy, steeling himself for the worst.

The kid's face was implausibly alert despite one eye that kept looking off to the left at a gnarled stump, as if it were something constant, a way to deal with his shattered fate. Jonas fumbled for his phone. Dropped it. Picked it up again. Pressed 911. Waited. There was nothing. The kid was sucking in air like a great steam engine, eating it up in loud, painful snorts, but he was alive, wasn't he? That was something.

Why wouldn't his phone connect? His head hurt. Hungover. What did he expect? Jesus. He looked at his cell. 811. He'd hit eight instead of nine. He cancelled the call.

The kid took a great suck of air, like an anteater clearing out a hill, except, he wasn't taking in ants, he was taking in air, the last he'd ever take.

Jonas pressed 9—

And then waited. Silence. A squirrel running out to the end of a branch, the creak under its weight. A breeze.

He waited for another breath. It didn't come. His thumb was poised over the one. His hand quavered and he dropped the phone. It landed on the kid's face and slid off into the grass where brain matter and blood had begun to coagulate in the dirt. Jonas reached for it gingerly. His thumb touched something wet, and he dropped it again.

He stood up. The boy was dead. The boy who he'd passed dozens of times on his way home from work—when he'd had a job—and dozens more times since he'd been unemployed and on this latest drinking binge. He'd hit the kid and killed him, and there was nothing anybody could do for the dead. Death was one of those things that made everything else too late.

Except there were stories right? Miraculous surgery room recoveries. The body gets lighter as the spirit leaves. Spirit sees its old body from a bird's eye view and comes back in. Ten minutes later a man comes back alive, a young girl calls her mother's name, an old woman recovers from flatline to live ten more years, extolling the virtues of clean and right living to anyone who will listen to her story of the light at the end of the long, black tunnel.

Jonas reached down for the phone again. This time he rubbed it across the ground, scraping the congealed brain matter off before opening it and dialing the number quickly.

"911 dispatch," the voice—female—said. "What is the nature of your emergency?"

"I . . ." He looked at the kid. A fly landed on his nose. His face was peaceful now. His spirit probably already gone, watching Jonas from somewhere in the trees. He felt an absurd urge to lift him, to check his weight, to see if he weighed less than he should.

"Hello? Please state your location. Sir?"

"I . . ." Jonas was frozen. Immobilized by fear, maybe shock, a hangover now pounding in his head like a volcanic pulse. "I dialled the wrong number."

The operator said something then, but Jonas was closing the phone and couldn't hear.

He took the boy's hands in his, amazed by the warmth in them, the way they felt just like living hands and pulled him away from the road into the trees.

Afterwards, when he had time to think about what had happened, Jonas realized that he'd almost acted unconsciously. He was drunk or at least still feeling the effects of alcohol. He'd already had his license suspended once, a year ago, and before that, he'd done a seven week community service stint for reckless driving. None of this came to mind exactly, but it was all there bubbling under the surface. What did come to mind was one thing: *you can't help the dead.* Over and over again, a litany in his head. Call it shock, whatever, but Jonas couldn't make his mind think clearly.

At first, he sat beside the boy and cried. This would be one of the things he left out if he decided to tell her. The crying part. Not because he was embarrassed about showing emotion, but because of what was causing him to cry. Not the dead boy. He cried for himself, for the pestilence that had been dropped on him like a Biblical plague. He was like a little kid—scared out of his mind—and he couldn't even make himself think. So he just cried. Finally, he remembered the Mitchell farm and the little barn that was situated on the south end of the pasture. There would be tools in there, a shovel, maybe.

Still, he couldn't get up. He had a plan now, but he found himself transfixed by the boy's peaceful face, the way the top of his head had been torn off, the vividness of the blood, the blue of his eyes like you always imagined blue eyes when you heard about them in a song, the fat, blubbery cheeks, and the way his mouth was stuck in an elongated o, seemingly still trying to suck in that one last breath. Maybe it was because Jonas didn't really know death, had never experienced death this close before. He'd missed all the wars—too old for the Gulf war, too young for Vietnam. Both parents still living. He'd even had good luck with pets. His one childhood dog had died when he went away to college, so he was spared even that. Spared death, but not heartache, he supposed. Up until this point, his life had been a series of disappointments, filtered through the lenses of weekend binges and dead sober resolutions that made life seem dry and pointless and devoid of anything meaningful. In short, death had never concerned him because he was too busy dropping the ball that was his own life to think about it. Now, faced with death, he wanted to live so much it paralyzed him, and he sat for a long time just thinking.

Sometime later, in the dark, he made his way up to the Mitchell barn. When he'd been a kid—maybe sixteen—he'd worked for old man Mitchell, but when Mitchell had a heart attack, his son, Porter Jr., refused to rehire Jonas the next summer. It had been a good job too, the only one Jonas had ever loved. Jr. had let the property go, focusing on Sr.'s other real estate ventures as a means of supporting himself. For these reasons, Jonas had always held a kind of irrational loathing for Porter Jr.

What he had remembered as a barn, looked more like a shed to Jonas now, and he began to doubt he'd find what he needed inside to bury the body. The entrance was overrun with kudzu, and he had to tear the vines apart just to get inside.

Twice, he remembered the boy—his body twisted and inert, so vivid against the grass in the shade of the trees—and twice he had to stop and put his hands to his face, taking deep breaths to calm his nerves in order to go on.

There was no shovel, just an old hoe, which he took. He'd return the hoe when the boy was buried.

He felt sick because of what he was doing, worse because he knew he was going to get away with it.

This end of the county had been dead for twenty years or more. There were signs that it had once been thriving—the half-crumbled gas stations and convenience marts that hadn't opened their doors since the eighties, but still stood, resolute, haughty even, despite the ravages of time. Kudzu was the thing out here. It ran over trees, and buildings, and cars if they sat still long enough. Sometimes, Jonas liked to walk the road from his house out to the highway and just look at all the shapes the kudzu had made as it swallowed everything in its path, rolling relentlessly on.

Out here, he could bury the boy underneath the dirt, but there would be a second burial when the kudzu rolled over him, and this was good. Out here, things would stay buried.

He began to work methodically, chipping away at the ground. Occasionally, he stopped to look at the boy, to make sure he was still dead. He was having an argument inside his head now because he felt like maybe he wanted him to stay dead, that this was actually easier. But then some other part of him—his conscience?—kept reminding him how truly sick that was. So he just went back and forth until he finally spoke the question out loud to the surrounding trees: "If he woke up what would you do, Jonas?"

"I'd call 911, get him some help." This helped settle him down. Of course, he would. He wasn't a murderer. But the boy was dead. The dead do not wake up. Nothing in this world for the dead.

When it seemed deep enough, Jonas bent and put his hands on the boy's shoulder and waist. He paused because this seemed like one of those moments of no return. Was this what he wanted?

There were only two options, right? And neither one of them were any good for the boy. He was still dead no matter what Jonas did. One of the options helped Jonas. Hiding the boy meant he'd escape a messy trial and possible prison time. He'd made a mistake, sure, but this was enough to keep him from ever doing it again. Lesson learned.

As he began to push on the boy's shoulders, another thought came to him. The family. The kid would have a mother, a father probably. Maybe even brothers and sisters. Weren't they owed the truth? Didn't they deserve to know their loved one was dead, not missing? Shit, he hadn't thought of that.

His hands ached to push the kid into the hole, but he pulled them away. Couldn't he make it up to them? Yes, he'd find out who they were and be like a guardian angel. Dedicate his life to making sure theirs was as perfect as possible. Behind the scenes, just little stuff that could be meaningful for them later. He could do that. It was better that way because he'd still be able to live his life—to turn his life around, actually, something that he needed to do badly. So, when he looked at it the right way, this was the only choice.

Feeling more settled—or at least pretending to be—he tried to roll the kid over into the shallow grave, but he was too heavy to flip over without Jonas straining his back. Dropping to his knees, he pushed him to the lip of the grave and then over. The kid landed face down in the dirt. It didn't make sense, but Jonas felt like he needed to turn him over, to give him a proper burial. After rolling him over so that the boy's glassy eyes reflected the starlight, he began throwing dirt over the body.

He pushed fertile soil over the boy, covering his face and then the rest of him with a thin layer of dirt. He felt better now that he could no longer see those eyes, those fat cheeks.

The boy coughed. At first, Jonas ignored it because it wasn't possible. He scraped more dirt into the hole using the hoe like a rake. Another cough, this one lung-rattling and wet. Jonas stopped, the hoe dangling from his right hand, and listened. It was like being awakened at night by a strange noise that you know has to have a logical explanation, so you lay there very calmly to see if it happens again, but even while you wait, you know very well that when it comes again, you will say *aha! The icemaker, or the air conditioner, or the fucking dog*, but it will always be *something*. Then a hand, milk white and pale, rose from the dirt. The boy was reaching up, trying to claw his way out.

Jonas dropped the hoe, a good thing, at least in retrospect because his first instinct (and maybe he was still drunk) was that the kid had come back as a zombie. Jonas staggered back as if struck. A tree broke his fall, and he stayed there, braced against the tree trunk, ready for anything.

In a way—a very real way—the thing that came out of that hole was a zombie. The only thing you could say for the poor kid was that he wasn't dead yet. He climbed out of the hole, still oozing brain matter and blood. His eyes shined like the eyes of a feral night cat, one that you glimpse skulking around your yard at midnight. He tried to stand, but his legs couldn't do much; they wobbled and he teetered like a heavyweight after getting pummelled with one too many shots to the jaw. Still, he maintained his balance, and Jonas saw how twisted his body was now, that his legs did not align with his torso, and his neck seemed limp, unable to hold his head on straight.

Jonas slid down the tree, ripping his shirt and scraping his back on the bark. He hardly noticed. His eyes never left the boy, who was now losing his battle to stand. Just before he toppled over, Jonas broke his paralysis and rushed forward. He caught the boy and held him up. Something wet fell on his arm. He refused to consider what it was. The boy's head lolled up at him, his blue eyes flashing, reflecting the stars. The boy's mouth opened and closed. Jonas heard a wet sucking in his lungs and thought *blood, he's drowning in his own blood.* He turned the boy around and struck his back with the flat of his hand. The boy coughed and whimpered. He hit him again, harder and the boy fell limp in his arms. Jesus. Jonas lowered him gently to the ground.

"Stay with me, son. Oh God, stay with me." His voice sounded disembodied, like it came from above him, a wind through the trees that only sounded like a voice.

His eyes still seemed alert, but his breathing had gone all wrong again, like his lungs were full of broken glass. He tried to speak. The words died on his lips. He tried to sit up. He didn't get far. At last, he breathed a word. Jonas leaned in close, an overwhelming need to hear what the boy had said— he didn't know why.

The boy's breath tickled his ear.

"Mama."

2007, Alabama

Four months later, the news was still talking about Marcus, the eleven year old who disappeared walking home from his bus stop. CNN, Fox, MSNBC, the local news, Jonas couldn't turn the television on without seeing his face. One afternoon, he came in from work, turned the television on and there he was—that same forlorn picture they always showed of him looking away from the camera at something in the distance. He knew they'd chosen it for effect, those bastards because they were sensationalists, every last one of them. They imagined a million scenarios—kidnapped by a pedophile, taken by the stepfather (ex-stepfather), lost in the woods, abducted by a cult for God's sake—but he'd never heard any of the so-called experts theorize the truth, that a drunk failure had mowed the kid down and just buried him a few yards from where he landed. Lately, he'd developed a certain anger towards these people, their assumption that Marcus was the victim of some deep and conspiratorial kind of evil. He wanted to shout at them that they could have done the same thing. It was a blind curve. He was drunk. Not evil.

Or was he? He knew—from the psychology classes he took in college, the few books he read in passing on the subject of guilt—that anger usually stemmed from being the very thing people accused you of being. Sometimes, he felt evil. Sometimes, he felt it right down to his bones, and had to fight off sudden and vicious urges to enact violence. He usually quelled these inexplicable urges by destroying furniture, the sheetrock in his bedroom, kicking his bed until both feet were numb.

"You don't fucking know!" he shouted and picked up his old RCA in his arms. The cord stuck in the wall outlet and he wrenched it free. It whipped around and struck his knee. It probably hurt, but in his rage, he couldn't feel pain. He carried the television out to his back deck. Propping it atop the railing, he surveyed the grass below for the point of greatest impact. A few stones surrounded a little area he'd started to dig for a fountain last year. He'd never finished of course. His life had stopped after Marcus. He slid the TV along the rail, digging out splinters from the unfinished wood, and then he shoved it hard toward the rocks. It fell in a slow arc, missing the stones completely and landing in the soft grass. This infuriated him even more. He could break a kid in half, but his television was invulnerable to his anger. He spit on it, threw both his hands up in the air, let out a guttural scream, not caring in that moment who the hell heard him (not that there were any neighbours to hear), and he went back inside for the shotgun he kept under his bed. He was halfway back, almost to the deck when he stopped in the kitchen, thinking *what a cliché. What a damned cliché I am. If I had any real guts, I'd turn the thing under my chin and let the real fireworks begin.* Shooting the damned TV. He laughed and dropped the shotgun. Then he dropped himself to the floor beside it and lay there for a very long time, thinking something had to change.

He started driving by her house, mostly late at night when he couldn't sleep, sometimes during the day too, if he'd called in sick to work because he couldn't get Marcus out of his mind. The warm feeling of his hands when he dragged him into the trees and kudzu—he should have known then that he wasn't dead—the glassy look of his eyes, the fat cheeks, his voice, oh shit . . .

Mama.

So he would get in the car and drive. It was his first instinct born from the memory of an old neighbour when he'd been a kid who kept odd hours and drove around the block late at night, listlessly, barely pressing the gas. That man had disappeared when Jonas was a teenager to little fanfare, just there one day and gone the next, but Jonas had later learned the man grieved for his child who had fallen out of a window left unlocked. Jonas never had to ask who had left the window unlocked. The answer was written in every late night drive around the block, and underlined when the neighbour vanished.

Jonas didn't have a block to drive, just winding county highways that meandered into dirt roads and sometimes less.

Sometimes, he enjoyed driving them until he couldn't turn around and the kudzu crowded his car. The roads out here eventually just stopped. A strange thing to think about, but he found some comfort in this somehow. He thought of his neighbour, driving until he found a road like this, and then just flooring it, going off road, slipping away from everything into a tilting darkness, a shadow world where you could leave behind the past like a discarded jacket. When Jonas found one of these dead ends, snowed over with kudzu and shadow, horizonless, he always backed out, inching slowly, his foot on the brake. Once he stopped for a long time and wondered how long it would take for the kudzu to roll over him, his car, everything that made up his world. He wished to be buried in a peaceful slumber like Marcus and when he sat long enough and the light from the moon was obscured by a scrim of clouds, he thought maybe the boy was better off being away from all this, taking an early exit.

That was the night he hit bottom. His soul felt like something foreign to him. He was cold and kept blowing on his hands. His mind reeled back to the day it happened. He had it all just so in the flashing images of his brain. The drunk turn, the moment of clarity when he realized what was about to happen, the squeal of the brakes—so useless—the pop, the boy in the air, foot snagged on the mirror, his body twisting, flailing before the car released him and he landed yards away at the side of the road.

Later, the dark, the promises he'd made to convince himself it was the right thing to do. Those promises to take care of the family—he'd learned since then it was only the mother, single, widowed, then divorced—had sounded so good to him. He'd barely thought of them since. What a selfish, evil bastard he was. Yes, that's right, evil.

He cranked the car, turned on the lights and started backing up. He knew where she lived. He'd go sit outside her house. Be a guardian angel, make damned sure she suffered no more.

She liked to sit near a willow tree at night. She'd wear a dress without shoes, and sit on a little picnic table while the moon rose and sunk in a sky so vast, Jonas felt dizzy looking at it. He always parked across the road, out in the cotton field, headlights off, and watched. He wished he smoked, but he didn't, so he kept the radio on low, listening to an AM station out of Chilton County that played old time country. Sometimes he cried, watching her. She seemed so lonely.

It was spring, nearly warm, when he saw her sobbing for the first time. At first she seemed to be talking, arguing with someone who wasn't there. Jonas had been about to doze off, something he did more and more on these nights because it was the only time he'd found he could sleep, but he sat up abruptly when he saw her stand up, lifting her arms in the air and shout. It was as if someone was in the willow tree, but he knew that was unlikely. No, he told himself, *she's yelling at me*.

The yelling lasted a few short minutes. Like Jonas, she had no neighbours to speak of. In fact, the nearest house was his own, two full miles away. She collapsed on the picnic table and he could hear her sobs.

He glanced at his watch. Nearly 3 AM. He cranked the car, watching her carefully for any sign of awareness. She lay on her back on the table, her face to the sky, her fists like little hearts by her sides, beating rhythmically at the picnic table.

Keeping his headlights off, Jonas drove through the cotton field, easing back onto the road. He drove away from her house until he was out of sight, then turned on his headlights and turned the car around. He came back by her house, driving slow, pretending to just be passing by, stepping on the brake near her front yard, cutting the window down.

"Are you okay?"

She turned around, the look on her face was shock and something more—hope?

She tried to answer but another sob came out. Jonas put the car in park and got out, leaving it running. He stood in her front yard, close enough to his car to feel the heat of the engine. He did not want to frighten her.

"My name is Jonas," he said. "We're actually neighbours. I've been meaning to come by, after the . . ." He trailed off, suddenly realizing how utterly foolish this was, acutely aware that his leg was just inches away from the point of impact, that first hollow pop before Marcus went flying.

She threw her hands up in the air. "It's okay," she said, and his heart flip-flopped due to the raw emotion in her voice, the nakedness she was revealing to him, the ultimate stranger. "I don't know what to call it either."

He looked at his feet, his own hands—they hung listless by his sides, his fingers trembling—and his eyes moved unconsciously to the bumper, the almost imperceptible ding that he'd been unable to buff out.

"Thanks for stopping," she said, the emotion and nakedness in her voice, now covered up by a suspicious reserve. This is how he'd expected her to be. She was ready for him to move on, not to stay, because staying would be too awkward, too weird, like a stalker, which he was.

"I . . ." he faltered, not knowing what to say, where to go. Like those roads, he thought. He'd hit a dead end. Then it came to him. "I lost a boy too. That's why I felt like I had to stop."

"Oh?" her voice was kind, but still not inviting.

"I see you on television, and I drive by your house, and sometimes I can't sleep at night because I remember what it feels like. Nobody can understand how much that hurts." Was he crying? He wiped at his face, and his hand came away wet.

She got off the table and walked over to him. "Stay and talk. I need someone to talk to."

"Okay." She touched his arm, guiding him over to the picnic table.

"Tell me," she said, "what happened."

He never hesitated. It was as if the story was his now. "I was twenty-four. My wife and I had been married for five years. Our boy, Jonas Jr., was four. My wife was always on me to take care around Jonas, to keep things safe, but I was a smoker, and sometimes I'd be too lazy to go downstairs. My wife hated me smoking in the house, insisted I go outside, but when she wasn't around, I'd open our bedroom window and smoke one or two. One day, I forgot to shut it back. Two days later, Jonas was gone."

He was surprised at the emotion he felt in telling this lie. It was as if on those nights driving to the dead end roads, he'd internalized his neighbour's plight without even realizing it.

"I'm Wanda," she said.

"I know."

2010, Texas

The lies he told her. Jesus, he just let himself talk. The worst, the one he'd regret later was about his parents. Texas? But, it had been a necessity. If she ever met his real parents, it would be blatantly obvious that he'd lied about Jonas Jr. But he never considered the consequences as he spoke, just as he'd failed to consider the consequences of what he'd done.

Now, he was faced with a new set of consequences. At any moment, she'd return from the restroom. He could smile at her, ask if she wanted dessert—she'd probably say yes because being pregnant had made her crave sweets, especially cobbler and pie. And this diner, this was definitely a cobbler kind of place. That was all fine. No problem, he could pretend like he'd done for the last three years. Except, it wasn't *all* an act because he did love her. He cared about her life, her happiness more than he did his own, and wasn't that what marriage was supposed to be about?

But—and this was the thing, wasn't it?—they were going to see his parents. He had no way to explain this lie. His carefully constructed house of cards was about to come fluttering to the ground. He reached for his keys, plopping them down on the table. When the bathroom door swung open, he was halfway out of his seat, his eyes fixed on the parking lot and the trucker readying his rig. Jonas froze, the instant seeming to draw out like an old reel to reel stuck on the same piece of film. Everything stopped.

Hadn't he given her exactly what he'd taken and more? She was pregnant with a child. He'd brought her through her grief, made her happy again. Did he owe her something more?

His legs twitched, anxious to move. He looked at the kid at the next table. Marcus made over. The kid waved. Jonas waved back and sat down.

Wanda came out of the bathroom. She was smiling.

He smiled back at her, wishing he could erase the past, and focus only on her smile, their future. That was impossible. Hell, he didn't even know how he'd explain about his parents, but he would do it without telling her about the fall afternoon over three years ago. She didn't deserve that.

She sat back down. "You won't believe what I overheard in the restroom."

He shrugged. He'd believe just about anything.

SHOEBOX TRAIN WRECK

I imagined Suzy running across a great expanse of prairie, hair swept back by the wind, mouth opened to a laughing smile. For the prairie I used cut grass from the yard, taking time to glue each blade to the inside of the shoebox. Above her, cotton-ball clouds hang beneath an orange-peel sun. On either side are the things she loved in life: Skittles; Barbie dolls, represented by tiny, colour cut-outs from *Girl's Life Magazine*; miniature plastic puppy dogs I found at a garage sale; and a beaded necklace, each bead painstakingly looped along a filament of thread no larger than a wisp of hair. Her hair, or so I like to imagine.

As for Suzy herself, I found her at the flea market, a glorious little figurine at the bottom of a box of toys. I knew the second I saw her. Something about the eyes, the smile, the windswept hair. It was Suzy.

I found the others in much the same way. Oh, not all of them were ready made like Suzy. I had to piece Samantha together from old action figures, but eventually, I got her right.

When I started them, three years ago, just after the wreck, I had plans of calling the parents, the families, inviting them over to my room, showing them what I'd done, how hard I'd worked to denounce that day, to make their children alive again. I imagined them impressed, murmuring to their significant others, pointing at the level of detail, marvelling at how I seemed to get everything just right. There would be tears, of course, but I'd wrap them up with hugs, and the tears would never hit the ground. Instead I would soak them all up in the folds of my shirt, so that when they left, I could hang it in my closet unwashed, and touch it each day, another reminder of what I'd wrought.

Today, I stand inside my room and survey the six shoeboxes, wondering what might be done. I can think of nothing new, so I go to them, one at a time, starting with Michael, ending with Suzy, Adriana, Phillip, Adam, and Samantha in between, the order I see them when I dream. I listen, their voices welling up from deep inside the boxes, soft sounds, like murmuring wind. Leaning closer, I mould the sounds into words and they become a chant I cannot understand. Later, when the house is silent, and I'm in my bed, drifting freely from sleep to waking and back again, I'm able to just make out what they are saying:

The dead do not haunt the living.

I thought about moving. By the time I got around to putting my house on the market, I'd already started the shoeboxes, and I needed to be here on the south side of San Antonio to finish them. Not that anyone has ever bothered me much about it. Most people assumed that the bus driver, Jake Crowley, was at fault because he put a shotgun in his mouth three hours after the wreck and blew off the top of his head.

Nowadays, if people talk about the accident at all, they speak of phantom trains and ghostly images of Crowley prowling the crossing at Buck's Creek with a lantern looking for all the children he lost. There's also a widespread belief that parking your car on the tracks where the accident occurred will cause the spirits of those six children to push your vehicle to safety. Teenagers like this last one. It's common enough to see them heading by the carload out to Buck's Creek with six-packs of beer and bags of Gold Medal flour to sift like dust over their back bumpers. Drunk enough, they can convince themselves of anything, even that the demarcations in the flour are the prints of angelic fingers rather than where moths have landed, drawn to the warm glow of the taillights.

And even though I haven't touched a drop of alcohol since the day of the wreck, I can believe it too.

Inside Phillip's box I have laid smooth strips of hardwood, oiled and polished to a shine. Over these, I've painted lines and erected miniature hoops. Phillip would be a senior now, if he had lived. He would have been a varsity basketball player, a good one, according to his coaches. The article the newspaper ran after the accident quoted the varsity coach as saying that Phillip was one of the middle school players he had already pegged for a college scholarship.

When I stare into his shoebox, I can almost hear the crowd behind him, rooting him on, insisting he live.

And sometimes I can lose my hold on this world, like roots slipping through the soil. When this happens I see him move. I see him play. And for a time, he does live again.

The thing that pleases me the most about my dioramas is they represent an ordered place where violence cannot intervene. Here, I keep the children safe through diligence and attention to detail. They are invulnerable here, impervious to the awful winds of fate. Here, trains do not run, nor buses stall. Here, towns are not consumed by grief.

☐

I've slept a dreamless sleep when my eyes open and look at the blinking clock beside my bed. The room is dark, and it must still be hours before morning. Heaving myself out of bed, I go to the window and see that the yard is a wasteland of trash and tree branches. Earlier in the night, a great elm in my front yard cracked in two, and one side has fallen against a power line causing random electrical sparks. They look like silver eels, whipcracking in a black sea.

I hear a knock at my front door. A moment later I'm peering through the peephole at James, my brakeman at the time of the accident.

Like me, James had been drunk the day of the accident, and like me, he'd been able to act sober enough at the scene of the wreck, when everybody was shouting questions at us. In fact, he'd been the first one to come to my defence during the inquiry. "Wasn't anything Arch could do. Everybody knows that the county commission should have put a crossing arm at Buck's Creek a long time ago. In my opinion, no engineer could have avoided that accident."

James and I fell out of touch after the wreck, mostly due to my own guilt and anger. Also because there seemed to exist between us a kind of physical knowledge, an unspoken bludgeon. Whenever we were together, it hurt. I stopped answering the phone when he called. Once, I met him on the street on the way home from the library. We both pretended not to see the other. It was an unwritten pact, and we understood the parameters: suffer alone.

Now, he's outside my door, having braved a thunderstorm in the middle of the night.

I'd heard he was sick with cancer, but even that doesn't prepare me for the way he looks. His body is smaller, his collarbone protruding out and around his neck like some obscene bone scarf. His hands are crossed in front of him, clasped together like clusters of hooks that have become accidentally entangled. His arms droop like fishing line, so skeletal and long, I wonder how he moves them, as the muscles are so deteriorated, they appear to have vanished. When he speaks, his teeth—what's left of them—smile of their own accord, a crooked pumpkin grin.

"Arch," he says. "Can I come in?"

I step aside and he shuffles past into my living room.

I sit down, gesturing to the couch for him.

Outside, a rush of rain begins again, so loud against my tin roof, I wonder how I slept through it the first time.

"I got some things to tell you, Arch."

Lightning flashes, making the room go white and then black as my power goes off for good. It's so dark James is nothing more than a shadow across the room.

"What we did, getting drunk on the train. . . . You feel like a murderer. But that's over. For the longest time I wanted to go back to the day I lied and take it back. I wanted to go to jail. Die there. But I couldn't. You understand?"

"Yeah," I say. "I understand."

"Those kids down at the tracks. I talked to them. They want me to tell you something."

"Don't do this, James."

"They want you to understand. They're not still here because they want to be." He speaks calmly, oblivious to my rising anger.

"It's because I put them there, right, James? You were only the brakeman, ultimately not responsible for any of this. Isn't that the deal?" I'm across the room, reaching for him before I know what I am doing. Grasping his shirt in my fist, I try to pull him to his feet. But he's heavy, way too heavy for a man his size. A flash of lightning lets me glimpse his dark eyes; they're inexpressive, calm.

"Let them go, Arch."

He seems about to say more when a barrage of lightning lashes the house, illuminating the room in a series of repeating flashes as if a million cameras are being snapped in an instant. When the room goes dark again, James is gone; I can't see him at all. His shirt is still balled in my fist. In desperation I pull hard on it, trying to find him, trying to pull myself back to him, but it's no use. His shirt rips. My fist holds something, but I can't see what. My head aches. Thunder pounds around me. The room spins, and I lose my grip on consciousness.

The next morning, sun streams in my window so brightly I can barely keep my eyes open.

The clock next to me blinks 12:00 AM. I shade my eyes and peer out into the yard where the elm is split open. The power company is there, already working on the broken line.

I feel wasted, tired beyond all reason, as if I did not sleep at all. James's visit is still etched in my memory. What had he wanted to tell me?

A dream, I decide. Then I realize something is clenched inside my fist. Opening my hand, I find a solitary button.

I confirm James's death with a quick phone call. According to his wife, Beth, he died last night in the midst of the storm.

"I'm sorry for your loss," I say.

"James told me the truth, Arch. He told me about being drunk."

"Beth . . ."

"I hated him. I wanted him to go to jail. Then the next day I wanted him to be with me forever. Back and forth like that. It was a long time before I forgave him. Even longer before he forgave his self."

"It wasn't his fault, Beth. It was mine."

"Nobody can carry that by themselves."

"Ever wonder who decides?" I ask her.

"Decides?"

"Decides which kids are due to die? Which bus will stall on the tracks? Before the accident, I'd been drunk dozens of times on that train. None of those mattered."

"Arch . . ."

"And how many children's deaths had I heard about before the wreck? Hundreds at least. All you have to do is turn on the nightly news and you'll get your fill. But you know what? I shrugged them off. Paid them no mind. It was like they didn't matter. But it changes. It all changes when you're driving the train that hits the bus. They're not just children anymore. They're your children."

I begin James's box the next day. I construct James out of a clothespin and spindly bits of wire. His head is the button I managed to keep from my dream-like encounter with him.

Painstakingly, I build a little train and popsicle stick tracks. Placing James inside without me feels strange, but I do it anyway. I create a grayscale sky and dot the landscape with trees made from of old bottlebrushes. Finally, I fashion the school bus from an old Cheerios box and place it on the tracks, just ahead of the train.

The day of the accident, in a shoebox. I feel like God, except powerless to stop the past.

A few days later I hear a whistle blow. I step outside on my back deck and study the trees behind my house, as if they are somehow responsible for the noise. I know somewhere behind those trees are the tracks where the accident occurred, though miles away, too far for me to hear a train.

Yet, I can't deny the sound. I go back inside into my sanctuary and sit in front of my dioramas, waiting for the calm feeling to come over me, the feeling that lets me believe

I am in control and the children in these boxes are not dead.

Still I can hear the whistle. If anything, it's louder, more insistent, blaring, demanding that I do something.

Closing my eyes, I try to go back to the night I dreamed of James.

What did he want? What had been so important?

Let them go, Arch.

"They won't let me go," I say.

Then another voice. A voice from my dream. A child's voice. The dead do not haunt the living.

"Yes, they do," I say. "They haunt me."

The train whistle is louder.

I remember the day of the wreck, watching the trees as they scraped the sky. They looked like claws; the earth trying to peel back heaven.

That's what I was looking at when the 100-car payload I was pulling began to wrap itself snakelike around the blind curve, and I saw the school bus stalled out on the tracks. One minute I had been drunk, perfectly content with the world, and the next I was cold sober and stricken with such bone-numbing panic I felt helpless, stuck inside my own skin.

If I even considered blowing the whistle, I don't remember it. What I do remember is thinking I had to stop the train. This thought was followed closely by the cold realization that I couldn't stop it, not in time to avoid a collision.

I never thought about bailing. Though it's nothing to be proud of, I did stay with the train.

By the time I engaged the brakes, the train was on top of the bus.

There was a ground-shaking smack followed by the rending of metal on metal, the sickening scrape of steel, and then a single scream, which died almost as soon as it rang out, extinguished like a snuffed match. The train kept going, barely shuddering as it bisected the bus, sloughing off the front and back like great rocks tumbling from a precipice. When it was over, one thing stood out. I never blew the whistle.

But someone is blowing it now.

Later that evening, I take my pick-up truck out to the tracks, to Buck's Creek where the accident occurred. In back I have a bag of flour.

When I arrive, another car, a convertible, full of teenagers, is already there. They've parked on the tracks, powdered the bumper with copious amounts of flour, and now they wait, throwing back beers and laughing, pretending to hear noises behind them. They ignore me.

I wait too. An hour passes and the evening drops a veil over the sky, creating a hazy glow as silver as it is black. The stars are above me in draft, barely bright enough to be seen. Off in the woods an owl hoots, marking time, until the moment comes when the last inches of daylight are shooed away by shadows, and I see them gleaming in the almost darkness, six shapes, rising out of the earth. So slowly it's as if they've choreographed their movements with the setting sun.

By full dark, I can recognize them all; they line up in the order I have set for them in my room: Michael, Adriana, Phillip, Adam, Samantha, and Suzy. Suzy is not smiling. Phillip does not look pleased or full of athletic potential as he does inside my shoebox. Michael, Adrianna, Adam, and Samantha all look tired.

The children reach out for the car in front of them, their fingers barely grazing the bumper. They don't push as much as touch and the car, already in neutral I suppose, rolls off the tracks. The teenagers inside laugh out loud. Somebody snorts and spews beer all over the others. A girl says, "Oh, hell no. That did not just happen." A big kid with long straight hair and a beer in his hand jumps out and runs around to the back. "Holy shit, guys! Holeeee shit! Come look." They file out to look at the flour and the fingerprints of the children I killed. Yet, they cannot see the children who stand on the tracks as if they are unsure what to do with themselves now.

One of them, Suzy, turns around and seems to see me. Her face is distraught, shining silver like the face of the moon on a clear night. Her eyes meet mine, and I hear the voice again. Her voice: The dead do not haunt the living.

Slowly, they reform their line in the centre of the tracks. They stand, resolutely facing east, waiting for the train that will kill them all over again. Within seconds I spot smoke, snaking in thin columns over the tree line. The acrid smell of diesel fills my lungs. The earth beneath my feet begins to thrum.

The train appears, heaving forward like some hound unleashed from hell. The children are erased, obliterated, sent back to the soil from which they rose, sentenced to re-form and live again, however briefly the next night and the night after that and on and on until . . .

I let them go.

Driving away, into the shadowed dusk, I finally understand. The dead really don't haunt the living. The living haunt the dead.

I'll build a fire. Let the flames lick the bottom of the pines and watch the smoke curl heavenward. Then one at a time, I will bring them out, toss them into the fire, turn away as they burn.

Last, I'll come to James's box. Keeping his button in my hand, I'll burn the rest. The fire will give off the sweet smell of death and no more lingering, a final scent, like the odour of chrysanthemums after a long rain.

Breathing in the air, I'll take a moment to think how the world never gives you what you expect. Like ghosts. Me keeping them around. I'll laugh at this thought and try to take some lesson from my anguish and the way it results in more anguish, an endless cycle, forever rolling over on itself until there is no proper way to tell where the cycle begins or, much less, where it will end.

After I've stood for a long while, I'll open my hands, palms up and stare down at the button. I'll consider keeping it, one last token, one more way to hold on. I'll want a drink. Ignoring that desire, I'll close my eyes, and in the tilting darkness, cast the button into the fire. When I open them again, all of this will seem half-remembered, a fever-dream of little worlds. I'll turn back to my house, and when I go inside, I'll begin the real battle of living with myself and what I've done.

THE BEST PART

Danny and Truck are tossing horseshoes outside Mom's trailer when Truck says he's got a moneymaker. "Surefire," he says and underhands the horseshoe in a practiced arc toward the rusty pole.

"Surefire, huh?" Danny says.

"Sure fucking fire."

Danny doesn't believe in surefire, though his lack of belief is less a matter of principal than it is experience. He *wants* very badly to believe in surefire. Surefire would be so much simpler than the chaos the world usually offers. Still, he's willing to listen. Moving in with his mother last month has made him willing to listen to a good number of things.

"Last time you told me something was surefire, I ended up in the state pen for twenty months."

"I was stupid then. That was insane. This is smart. A clean job."

Smart and Truck are not two words that ever belong in the same sentence, but Danny finds himself curious, despite his better judgment. "What are we talking about?"

"Savannah Ridge, baby."

Danny nods. "That's where Darrin lives, right?"

"That's the one. They're building a new section just behind Darrin's house. He's already got some new neighbours behind him."

Danny knows about the new construction because a few days earlier, he borrowed his mom's Intrepid and drove out to the site to ask about a job. The foreman all but laughed at him, said there were grown ass men he'd had to lay off, why would he want to hire a skinny kid?

Danny hasn't mentioned this or any of his other efforts to find honest work to Truck. As far as he knows, Truck hasn't tried to find a job—a real job—since they got fired from the landscaping crew last fall. That had been a good gig. Hard work, but the money was cash and the boss paid every Friday. Truck hadn't liked working with the Mexicans, but Danny suspects that Truck wouldn't like working with anyone.

"So, here's the plan, Danny-boy," Truck says, picking up another horseshoe and swinging it a couple of times, as if to test its weight. "Darrin says these new neighbours are some rich pricks. Says they work all the time, up in Birmingham at some uptown ad agency. The husband drives a Beamer. The wife—Darrin says she's fucking fine—drives one of those gas guzzling SUVs. Wears big jewellery, like she's a fucking hip-hop star or something. Bling bling and shit. Darrin says there's no alarm system, no dog, nothing except a dead bolt lock on the front door."

Darrin is Truck's drug friend. He's a few years older than Truck and Danny, which means he dropped out of high school around '03 while Truck and Danny both quit in '06. He married the first girl he got pregnant whose grandfather died a month after they got married and left her sixty-three acres of land on the southside of Wilton. They sold to the highest bidder, and then she died in a drunk driving accident. The kid—a boy Darrin named Shaun—laid in the ICU for four weeks before *he* died. After a whirlwind five months, Darrin wound up with no wife and no kid, but about eight hundred thousand dollars for the land sale, and that wasn't all. He also got a ninety thousand dollar insurance check for his dead wife. All this explains how Darrin not only affords Savannah Ridge but also why he sits around the house in his boxers all day downloading porn and getting baked.

"If it's so surefire, why doesn't Darrin just do it? Why involve us at all?"

Truck tosses the horseshoe. It's a good one, clanging against the metal pole before catching and sliding to the ground. He smirks and leans his head back on his neck, exposing a huge Adam's apple that makes Danny think about a turkey he saw his father kill once. His dad had big hands and when he laid hold of something, those hands were going to do what they meant to do, and that turkey didn't stand a chance. Danny remembered being surprised that the bird didn't call out in pain, but now realizes it had died too fast to even scream. This realization fills Danny with a sudden and fierce sadness that he can't explain.

"Any dumbass knows you don't steal from your neighbour."

"Well, what's the difference? He's helping us do it."

Truck laughs, and the Adam's apple works like a bobber on his neck. "He's just letting us know that it's there if we're interested. He's helping out his friends. You know how much money a good haul like that could bring in?"

"No idea. A lot probably."

Truck spread out his hands, a gesture that seemed to say, *Now you're catching on.*

"Darrin's an idiot. He's too high to know how to spot an easy mark."

"Jesus, Dan. Just listen for a second. I haven't even gotten to the surefire part yet."

Danny bites his lip and waits. He doesn't want to hear

the surefire part, or maybe he does. Truth is, he's found work so hard to get lately, if something did come along that was surefire—not that he believes in such a thing—but say something came along that was pretty good odds, then he'd be tempted to consider it. He wants to move out of his mom's trailer and go back to school. He'd have to get his GED first, but that can't be too hard. Then he can get his own place and enrol in some online classes. Mom's friend, Shannon, takes them and she says when she finishes, she'll be certified to be a court reporter or a legal assistant. Danny doesn't want to do those things, but he wants to do something. Maybe take art classes. That's what he's always loved, seeing something and making it come alive on paper. There are angles and shadows he sees all the time that he frames inside his head and wants to get down on paper just right, but he's usually with Truck who scoffs at art, or if he's not with Truck he's laid up in the bed trying to sleep off one of Truck's marathon benders he'd been foolish enough to participate in. Seems stupid really. The one thing that gives him joy, the one thing he loves to do, he mostly just remembers doing a long time ago.

Truck is talking again, and Danny forces himself to listen. There's no surefire, he reminds himself, but maybe that works both ways. No surefire failures either. Just listen, he tells himself.

"There's a vacant house for sale across the street from the rich fucks. Darrin says there's a window in the back that's not locked. We sneak in there and case the place from across the street. You know watch the neighbourhood, learn their schedules. When we've got it down, we make our move. They've got a garage, so once we break in, we just need to get Chet's van inside, and I figure we can have at least four or five hour—"

"Hold it," Danny says. "When did Chet get involved?"

"When we needed a van. You got a van?"

"No, but Chet will do something stupid. Chet will get us caught."

Truck pauses, and Danny knows it's because of the truth of what he's said about Chet. Chet is just like them. From the trailer park, a drop-out, a kid whose future has seemed pretty bleak since the time he could walk, but Chet is also different than Truck and Danny. When Chet kept getting fired from jobs after dropping out of school, he started finding other ways to make money. He would often get people to pay him to do things they didn't want to do. When part of Gray Pierce's trailer collapsed and pinned his golden retriever, Sally, to the ground, the aluminum siding almost cutting her in two, he paid Chet twenty-five dollars to shoot her and fifty more to clean her body off the siding. More recently, Chet has found his true calling, doing stupid, dangerous stuff that people around here seem to think is hilarious. Danny had seen him eating grass until he threw-up while some woman stood by with her baby on her hip, urging him to eat more and more. Another time somebody paid him to let them hammer a nail through his cheek. He had to ask Truck along for this one to help him get the nail out after he got paid his seventy-five dollars. But the big money came from jumping off the bridge out at Moss Rock. The high school kids would pool their money, and he sometimes made up to three hundred dollars a jump, which was at least half as much money as Danny had ever made in a week working landscaping.

Inside the trailer, he hears his mother's alarm going off. Five-thirty. She has an hour and a half before her shift at the Waffle House begins. He needs to get rid of Truck soon to avoid a lot of yelling.

"I'm in if Chet is out," he says.

"Negative. We need his van."

"Forget it. Either me or Chet. You said it was surefire. Chet is not surefire."

"How we gonna haul everything off without a van?"

"Pay him to use it. If this haul is as good as you think, we ought to be able to cover that."

"You think?" Truck says, his face twisting up in that perplexed look Danny had seen so much back in Algebra class.

"Of course. You said they were rich, right? Tell him we'll give him fifty bucks and a full tank on return."

"Shit," Truck says. "You think it'll work?"

This is Truck. Something starts as surefire, and five minutes later, he's asking Danny if it'll work.

"We won't know until we watch the place for a few days."

"Okay," Truck says. "Now you're talking." He laughs and claps a heavy hand on Danny's back.

Danny wants to pull away. The weight of his old friend's hand there makes him feel trapped somehow, like he's being bound and gagged and shoved into a closet or the trunk of a small car. The world will go on all around him, but he will be stuck in the darkness, alone.

Like everybody he knows, he wants to get out of this town and start his life all over again. That was the thing he thought about more than anything else when he had been landscaping, mowing or pulling weeds or blowing leaves across somebody's lawn. He would imagine himself in a new place away from Mom's ratty old trailer, away from Truck and Chet and the ex-girlfriends that broke his heart, not because he'd loved them, but because he'd loved them young and now he sees them fat and lethargic, toting around toddlers with dirty faces and shit-heavy diapers, left alone by husbands who in one way or another had learned to abandon everything— including the boys they once were—as a matter of principal. But lately, he thinks of moving away less, and instead sees his life as an airplane that never flew too high but always managed to stay a notch or two above the clouds. Until recently. Now it has begun to lose altitude at an alarming rate and seems to be heading directly through the clouds into a full tilt nose dive. Danny can't shake the idea that once the clouds do finally clear, it will be too late, and the ground will rush up and eat that airplane alive.

A week later, after forcing open a downstairs window, Danny and Truck sit in lawn chairs in the den of the newly finished house, running the air conditioner full blast, drinking cans of ice cold Schlitz. Another case waits, unopened in the refrigerator, which they have turned to the highest setting in order to ensure that the beer is as cold as possible.

"Never had beer this cold," Truck says as he drains the last of his can and tosses it with the other empties beside the window.

They've been inside this house, watching the one across the street for three days now, and while Danny still doesn't believe in surefire, he is beginning to think they can pull this off. The couple across the street do not vary their schedule. The wife leaves first, always before seven. The husband strolls out an hour later. Truck calls him "the fat fuck," but he's not actually fat, just big, muscular even. He is a fuck though; Danny can't help but notice the way he walks, the way he brushes the slightest speck of lint off his suit, the way he pauses just for a moment after opening the door to his Beamer, as if to say, look at me, world, look at what I've accomplished.

This last part is good because Danny still has qualms about stealing from people, even rich people. When they started breaking the law, four or five years ago, both he and Truck used to worry about the ethics of it all. Even Truck, after they took that lady's purse at Wal-mart, kept going back and forth about returning it, maybe even turning themselves in. Sometimes, he still wonders about that lady, if their thievery had caused her any permanent pain or misery. He doesn't think so. As Truck has pointed out time and time again, the lady was rich. She was good looking. She would land on her feet. Besides, the credit cards had been cancelled within a few days.

It's gotten easier, though. Each time, they worry less. Truck has become completely immune to guilt in the last few months, since their last attempt at honest work had failed. Danny still has some issues, which in some ways, he supposes makes his own decision to participate in these kinds of shenanigans even worse.

This guy though, this fuck across the street, Danny is going to rob him without feeling a bit of guilt. No, that's not even true. The guilt will be there, but at least it'll be easier to ignore.

"Why not now?" he says, suddenly.

Truck is flipping through a skin magazine. When he hears Danny, he closes the magazine, keeping his place with his thumb. "What?"

"Why not now? It's nine thirty. Even if they did break routine and come back for lunch we could be out of there by noon."

"No way. We don't have Chet's van yet."

The plan they've discussed involves going to get Chet's van this afternoon and breaking into the house tomorrow.

"So, we can at least see what's in there. The chick will probably have enough jewellery that we can stuff our pockets."

Truck shakes his head. "Not a good idea."

"Why not? It's a great idea. Do it now and Chet won't be around to screw it up."

"I'm afraid it's too late for that."

"What are you talking about?"

"Chet's actually coming over today."

"That's not what we agreed on."

He shrugs. "It'll be fine. We talked last night. Changed the plans. It's better this way, cause when he gets here, we can go ahead and do it right. Have the van and everything. Besides, he's just dropping it off. He'll probably hang out here, drink a few beers, whack off, whatever while we do the job. Then we'll all get out of here and divide up the loot."

"Divide up the loot?"

"Chet wants a share. For letting us use the van."

Danny groans. "This is stupid, Truck. Remember when I told you selling drugs at work was stupid? What happened that time? We went to prison. Chet's a timebomb, waiting to detonate."

Truck shakes his head, trying to stay calm, but Danny can tell it's getting to him. Truck has always hated to be wrong. Must be a miserable life, Danny thinks, because Truck is wrong more than anybody he knows. Which says exactly what about you, Danny?

There's a sharp retort from outside and Truck nearly falls out of his chair in surprise. "What the fuck—"

Danny's heart sinks. He feels a sudden, anxious surge run through him, like fight or flight, and he's leaning hard toward the flight part.

Outside the window, pulling into the driveway is Chet's van. The engine is loud enough to wake sleeping neighbours— had there been any—and the backfire that nearly knocked Truck out of his seat is the first of many more. Danny counts seven before Chet kills the engine and throws open the driver's side door.

"Scared the living hell out of me."

"This is a mistake."

Danny watches as Chet unfolds his muscular frame from the driver's seat. His feet hit the ground and he pauses to take a look at the house before rolling his neck thoroughly as if working out any residual traces of sanity from his head.

"It's a mistake," Truck says, his voice pitched high and whiny, mocking Danny. "Don't be such a baby, Danny Boy."

"The van is louder than a fireworks show."

"But there's nobody to hear it. See, that's the beauty. These fuckers made a mistake by moving into an empty neighbourhood."

Chet scares Danny. Always has. Something about his eyes, the bruises all over his body, the way he doesn't care about the future or the past, just living, just fucking staying alive in whatever shape that might be.

Close to the bone, that's the phrase he thinks of when he sees Chet. His whole persona is like a raw nerve that twitches wildly in the light of day.

He has the kind of face that says a thousand unspoken things and none of them make sense. I could draw him, Danny thinks. The knowledge thrums through him, giving him a kind of pure pleasure that is something akin to the afterglow of sex. I could draw him.

There's a knock on the front door and a loud, high pitched voice. "Little pig, little pig, let me come in."

Truck smiles and goes over to open the door.

Chet's wearing a tank top and shorts that hang down low enough to expose his ass crack. His head is shaved and nicked with every kind of scratch, like a bowling ball that has been dropped on concrete too many times. His face is pitted with scars and acne and beneath those are deep purple and blue and sometimes green bruises. He's missing teeth, but that's just part of his look. This guy isn't meant to have teeth. Or shoes apparently. He's barefoot, exposing grotesquely thickened and yellowed toenails.

"Nice," he says, looking the place over. "How's the shitter?"

He seems to address the question to Danny, but Danny is so totally unprepared for such a question that he only shakes his head in frustration while Truck answers.

"Clean as the inside of a virgin's cunt," Truck says, still smiling like an idiot. Danny has to resist the sudden urge to hit him right in the face. Why does he want to bring this asshole along?

"Time to deflower that bitch," Chet says, letting a cheek-rattling fart ring out.

Truck giggles like a second grader, slapping five with him as he walks out of the den and into the hallway looking for the virgin bathroom.

The reason Chet scares Danny is because he's not afraid of anything. Jumping off the bridge at Moss Rock has been done before, but not with the same reckless abandon as when Chet does it. There is only a sliver of safe water wedged between some of the most jagged rocks Danny has ever seen. The others foolish enough to jump take their time, measuring out each leap, their bodies tensing on the way down, tightening into a straight line, an arrow aiming for the bullseye because any slight deviation can mean a lot of pain. Chet lives for the pain, the deviation. He never worries about hitting the mark. He takes off at a dead sprint, thrusting his body off the bridge in such spectacular fashion that Danny can barely breathe as he watches. Occasionally, he cracks a knee open on one of the rocks, but mostly, he falls into the slip of water, a burning bundle of kinetic energy. Danny can only stand, amazed, as the water snuffs out Chet's fire. He thinks, no, never. He will not come back up. But then he does, rising from the river like the phoenix reborn, water hanging off his raw skin, gleaming white in the late afternoon sun, laughing about it. Laughing.

Goddamn.

"Does it hurt?" somebody called out once.

"Oh, fuck, it hurts," Chet said.

"Do it again."

And without a word, Chet's climbing the grass embankment, trotting on what should be broken legs back up to the bridge, back up to the guardrail, which he stands on top of like a crazed, wingless hawk perched on a precipice, and he jumps without even hesitating. That's the part that scares Danny. He doesn't hesitate. Sometimes, Danny dreams about himself standing on that bridge, arms raised up, readying to jump. He hesitates, not because he's afraid of dying, but because he's afraid of living with the pain.

Chet, though, he's not afraid of anything.

"Fuuuuuuck!"

"What's up?" Truck says to the bathroom door.

"No fucking toilet paper."

Truck laughs. "I had a blowout earlier. Forgot to restock. Hold on, there's some paper towels in the kitchen." He looks at Danny as if he expects him to retrieve them.

"Get them yourself."

Truck smirks. "What's up your ass?"

Danny grabs his arm as he walks by. "Chet, that's what. Sometimes, I think you want to go to prison again."

Truck shrugs him off and keeps walking. When he comes back with the paper towels, he pauses, speaking right in Danny's ear. "Sometimes, I think you wish you'd never left."

In prison, you wake up in the morning and know the day. It's not even a day, really, because day implies that there is possibility inherent in the hours that wait. In prison, there are no possibilities. You sit up, clearing your dreams from the night before, which is fine because with the dreams come the occasional nightmare of standing atop a bridge, hesitating to jump. There's breakfast and yard time and lunch and back to the cell for a few hours of sitting on your ass and thinking about how you'll change your life if you ever get out of those walls, even though there is a part of you that absolutely knows that change—real, fucking change in life—is about as likely as winning the lottery. Sure it happens to some people, but mostly it's a pipe dream people buy into for a few hours, maybe days, before being disappointed.

No disappointment in prison. You wake up in the morning. You know the day. Until you've done your time and you wake up, and you don't know what to expect any more and you realize, sitting on the edge of your narrow bed that your knees are shaking.

So maybe Truck's right. After all, Danny doesn't trust Chet, and yet he's here in the same house with him, about to go through with the next step, robbing some rich people and doing god knows what else next. It's not like prison, that's for sure. It's wilder, scarier even, a long drop from a bridge, with so many opportunities to land in the wrong place.

Before Danny can contemplate his situation any more, he notices a small green car pulling into the driveway right behind Chet's van. It looks like a Civic or Corolla or some similar compact Japanese car. The car stops, and he watches—feeling slightly mesmerized by the whole thing— as a woman steps out. She's attractive—not in the bling bling, fake tit way that the woman across the street is—but really pretty. She's got short brown hair, and big brown eyes, and nice legs, well toned legs. She looks straight at the house and then back to Chet's van.

By this point, Truck sees her too. He's standing next to Danny, shoulder to shoulder, looking out the window. The woman runs a hand down her skirt, straightening it, and starts toward the house.

"What the fuck is she doing?" Truck says.

Danny shrugs. "Maybe she's selling something." He's not

exactly afraid yet, but he feels a sense of unease begin to twitch in his stomach.

She passes the window and disappears as she reaches the front steps. Her heels click on each step. There are six in all. Danny waits, tensed, for the doorbell. Instead, he hears the rattling of keys, and a bolt turning, and it dawns on him—too late, of course—that this woman is a realtor and this is one of her properties.

The door swings open part way and she says, "Hello? Is there someone here? If you're here to finish the kitchen, it's about time."

He and Truck make a break for the hallway, passing the bathroom where Chet is probably figuring out that paper towels don't flush.

They bump into each other and curse and round the corner into the dining area, where there is some table and furniture, and—yes—a realtor's card with the lady's pretty face staring back at them. Truck throws it down in disgust. "Not good," he hisses.

Here it is, Danny thought. They had been so stupid. How many times had he walked through here in the last few days and looked at that card? Yet it had never crossed his mind that the lady would actually show up.

There are no doors to the outside in this room, only a bank of shuttered windows. Danny goes over and flings open one of the shutters just as he hears the woman's voice from the front room: "Is there someone in the house? Is someone in the house right now?"

Danny's lifting the window when he hears the falsetto reply: "Why yes, dear, I'm home. Just taking a shit. Be right out."

It's Chet. The toilet flushes. Truck spits out a torrent of profanities and pushes past Danny for the window. Danny lets him go.

The bathroom door swings open. Chet inhales loudly. "I

love the smell of shit in the afternoon."

The woman says, "I have a can of mace and a cell phone. Don't come any closer."

Chet laughs. "Hear that boys? She's got mace."

Truck doesn't hear it because he's out the window, tumbling in the backyard, grimacing from a longer than expected drop, but he looks okay. He's up on his feet waving at Danny. "Come on!"

Danny shakes his head and turns away from the window.

Before going to prison, Danny always heard people say that prison teaches a man. He'd heard his father say it when he was talking about Danny's uncle who went inside an alcoholic and came out four years later, stone sober and full of what he called the Holy Spirit. Another uncle, this one on Danny's mother's side, learned how to be violent inside. He'd always been as meek as a lamb until prison taught him that he could settle most anything with a pair of clenched fists.

Danny likes to think that prison taught him as well. He learned that there are limits to what he can—in good conscience—live with. He learned that living with a bad conscience is a way he can't live at all. He also learned that there is an area—a certain kind of grayness when a man's fears override his better judgment, and he finds himself doing the very thing he didn't think he would ever do. Then there's nothing for it except living out his days in misery.

This is what he fears. More than prison, more than anything. The gray area where things overlap.

In the other room, the lady screams.

Once it comes into focus—what Danny is looking at—he feels a little better, a little more like himself. He could draw this moment, frozen forever on a page, and get to the truth of something, Chet maybe, the lady too. If he is lucky, even himself. He'd use pencils and plenty of overlapping lines because that's how he sees them, all elbows and teeth, hands and hunched shoulders, fingernails and pinched lips. He doesn't know which one draws the eye more, Chet or the lady. No, take that back. It's Chet. Definitely Chet. He's got a rusty box cutter to the lady's throat, his other big hand resting on the nape of her neck, almost gently, like a lover, or a parent holding a child. His face, though, is a comic book parody of violence, jagged sneering lips, bulging maniac eyes.

The woman's face is a slate rock, pale white, devoid of any emotion except what's found in her tiny brown eyes, which are wet and quick and full of regret. She is murmuring something so low Danny doesn't realize it's her at first.

"You think I'm going to hurt you?" Chet says, his voice still strangely soft, high-pitched, loving.

The woman doesn't speak, but the answer is in her eyes.

He pops the back of her head with his hand. "Why do you assume I will hurt you?"

She whimpers. "You've got a razor."

Chet's eyes dart around, lively and full of manic energy, and for a second he reminds Danny of a bird, a tiny bird, pecking the ground for some food, its dark, sudden eyes wary and wild.

"Oh, how about that? I've got a razor. Good ol' box cutter." He swings those terrible eyes over to Danny. "Did you know I had a box cutter, Danny Boy?"

Danny is silent, but he nods slowly.

"I've already called the police," the woman says.

Chet doesn't appear to hear her. He leans in close to the woman, speaking low into her ear. "If I wanted to hurt you, I'd cut out your cunt and feed it to you. You ever eaten cunt?"

The woman—the card had said June, right?—looks like she's about to faint.

"It's a delicacy. When a woman's real wet, you know the cum, it tastes really good. First time I tried it, I wasn't sure, but you know it's one of them acquired tastes."

"Chet," Danny says. "You probably better let her go."

Chet laughs, a dry heaving sound, which makes him cough. "Don't worry, Danny. I'll share."

"No, nobody is going to share."

The dry laugh again, this time more like a cackle, and Danny remembers the first time he heard that laugh. Chet had been up on the bridge, his hands above his head, the wind blowing back his hair. "You people think I'm crazy. Maybe that's right, but at least I'm doing what the fuck I want to do." Then he went into the laugh, and it was a high, keening sound in the night, a signal to fly.

Which he did.

Danny breathes deep, filling his lungs with air, attuned to his chest expanding, trying to find a level of calm he does not yet feel, but he knows is there somewhere.

"Chet," he says. "You ever been to prison?"

"Juvie, but that doesn't count." He's running the blade over the lady's cheek, almost cutting the flesh, but not quite.

"I've been," Danny says.

"Did they fuck you in the ass?"

"Yeah, they did it all. But after a while, you learn how to avoid that kind of stuff. You look in people's eyes, you know? You see the ones who are capable and the ones who aren't."

Where is he going with this?

Chet nods. "Oh, I know. I see shit all the time in people's eyes. Mostly fear." He glances at the woman, as if to punctuate his point. "But I wonder, Danny-Boy. What do you see? What do you see when you look right here in these peepers?" He tilts his head and opens his eyes even wider, until they look like they might pop right out of his head.

"Ever see anything like this in goddamn prison? Go on and tell me the truth."

Danny hesitates. What can he say? He takes a step closer, his hands extended, as if he means to touch Chet, but why would he do that? He stops short, holding his hands in front of him, trying to steady Chet without touching him, trying to make the world stop quavering without actually grabbing it. "The truth is," he begins, "your eyes aren't like anybody else's. You might be afraid of something, but I don't know what it is. When I see your eyes, it's like looking in a mirror. All I can see is myself." Danny stops suddenly, realizing he has gone too far.

Chet leans forward, the box cutter still pressed against the woman's face. "Go on. When you see yourself, what do you look like?"

"Scared. Confused. I think those two are the same sometimes. How do you jump from the bridge like you do?"

The woman whimpers, but Danny has almost forgotten her. Chet is stroking her hair with one hand, holding the box cutter tight to her neck with the other. "The bridge? Shit, I could ask you the same kind of question. How do you go to a fucking job? How do you let somebody tell you what to do? The bridge is as easy as moving my feet. And then I fly. You ever tried it?"

"No," Danny says. "Never."

"It's fucking beautiful. That time in the air is the only time I don't feel like nothing can touch me. It's the very fucking best part of my life, man. And then I hit and just want to do it all over again." He shakes his head, remembering. "What's prison like?"

"It's regular. You know what's coming. Boring."

"I couldn't take that shit."

Danny says nothing. He thinks the situation over. Chet hasn't cut her yet. He hasn't raped her. They're talking, just having a conversation. If he can say the right thing, he might be able to convince Chet to let her go, to put the box cutter down. Then the woman goes for her mace. Her purse is still around her shoulder, and she reaches with one hand into the purse.

Chet reacts more quickly than Danny would have. He slides the razor across her face, cutting through her cheek, exposing tender white flesh that quickly disappears under the free flowing blood. With his other hand, he knocks the mace away. It rolls across the hardwoods into the foyer. He shoves her to the floor. She's screaming now. But it's actually good, he's let go of her, and she's going to live. Maybe it's over. Then Danny realizes what Chet means to do.

He doesn't even have to unbuckle his pants. He just shimmies his hips and they slide down to his knees. Danny looks away but hears the box cutter clatter against the far wall as Chet tosses it away. He tries to ignore the sounds of Chet working himself up—the grunting, the rubbing, the deep moan as he spills his seed all over the floor, but these things are impossible to ignore.

"This," Chet groans, "is what I think of you and this fucking house, bitch."

Danny turns back around. Chet has his pants around his knees, one hand still absentmindedly working his softening penis, the other hand useless at his side. His head is down, and the eyes, the same ones that seemed so foreign and unreadable just a few seconds ago, now look wounded, and amazingly, Danny sees a glimpse, just a flash really, of the scared little boy Chet used to be.

And strangest of all, that flash of insight breaks Danny's heart.

Chet looks up suddenly, catching Danny watching him. "Don't you fucking dare feel sorry for me."

Danny lifts his hands, a gesture of surrender.

But it's too late. Somehow, Chet sees him. In one instant, Chet has taken Danny's measure and he knows. Or maybe he always knew, maybe everybody knows. Maybe it's written all over Danny like a tattoo.

"You want to go back to prison, don't you?" Chet's grinning savagely now, as he walks over to retrieve the box cutter.

The woman has scooched across the floor, almost to the front door now. Danny nods her on. Hurry, he wants to say, get off your ass and get out of here.

Sirens whine in the distance. Probably out on the highway, heading this way. She really did call the police.

"Here," Chet says and Danny turns to see the box cutter flying at him.

He catches it and looks at the blood already congealing on the orange casing.

"Police are on the way. You want to go back, Danny-boy? Well, then do some damage."

The sirens are closer.

Danny looks at the woman. She's so afraid. He doesn't blame her. There's no end to it out here, the fear, the confusion, the wild ass world that keeps coming at you no matter how much you might need a break.

Danny's afraid too. He takes a deep breath and imagines a canvas, unblemished and clean. He's sitting in front of it, his pencils laid out neatly, ready to make something that matters. Then he picks one up and he presses down.

It breaks.

Outside, the police car pulls up to the front of the house. The fat fuck—apparently, he does come home for lunch sometimes—is standing in his yard, trying to look tough, like *look at me, I'll help out, bust some heads or something.*

A policeman gets out of the car and begins walking toward the house.

Fat fuck calls out to him. Policeman turns around. Fat

fuck is pointing at the van, shaking his head, and moving his fat fuck mouth.

"Go on," Chet says. "Cut somebody. It's like flying, the best part."

Two days later, Danny and Truck are throwing horseshoes in the early evening. The light still lingers but the air is cooled. The yard is shady and crickets buzz from the hidden places.

"Nice one," Truck says.

Danny says nothing and goes to retrieve the horseshoes. He comes back and hands them to Truck.

Truck takes them, makes like he is going to throw one and then stops, putting them down on the grass.

"They got Chet."

Danny nods, wishing Truck wouldn't talk. Why ruin the silence?

"Pulled his ass out of bed. I heard from his sister that he went apeshit. Took like five cops to hold him down. I heard they beat the absolute fuck out of him. Heard he took a night stick to the eye that near about blinded him."

Danny picks up a horseshoe, weighs it, lets it fly. Wide right.

"What happened in there?"

Danny doesn't know where to begin, so he shrugs.

"Lady must have described him pretty well."

"Must have."

"You ain't worried she'll make you too?"

Danny shrugs again. He can't decide what would be worse, going back to prison or living out here where he is always falling, speeding toward the next crash. He has decided one thing since leaving out the back window with Chet still telling him it wasn't too late to find out about the best parts of life. He's going to leave this place. If he's going to fuck up, it won't be here anymore. He hasn't told Mom yet, but he plans on leaving tonight after she gets off work. She'll ask him where he's going and he'll tell her he doesn't know, which will be the truth.

"I thought he was going to kill her," he says. "Rape her."

Truck shrugged. "You can't never tell with Chet."

Just then, a car turns off the highway and onto the dirt road about a half-mile away.

Danny ignores it. Tosses another horseshoe.

Wide right again. Shit.

One more. He picks this one up, feeling it perfect and solid in his hand. He can make it count. One more chance. If he concentrates, throws it just right, it'll be dead on. Surefire? No, not surefire. But a good chance. That's all he's ever asked for.

Truck whistles low and soft. "You see what's coming down the road there? Shit. I'm gone. You got any sense, you'll head for the woods too."

But Danny isn't listening. Instead, he's focused on the little pole in front of him, his arm already in motion.

He lets it go.

SLIDE

We pulled into my cousin's gravel drive and saw my uncle's truck, its windshield splintered into a spider's web of cracks, glittering white in the moonshine. I was thirteen, and sleepy in the backseat from the long drive, but I sat up straight when I heard my mother gasp. Dad slowed the car, eased up alongside the mess. The passenger side window was gone except for a few jagged shards of glass that clung resolutely to the seal. The rest lay on the ground, tiny seeds among the rocks.

Mom glanced at me in the back seat and then over at Dad. He put the car in park and got out. Easing the door shut, he walked over to my uncle's truck. For a very long time, he just stood there, staring at the windshield as if he could read the tenuous latticework of anger that had been left across it, much the way an archaeologist might read the history of an artefact from the long-forgotten past.

He came back to the car and opened the door. "Stay here," he said.

My mother said, "Bill—"

But he was already gone, heading for the house.

□

My uncle had several nicknames—Budgie, Whip, Bo. I always called him Rusty. I don't know how he earned it or why it stuck, but I do know it fit him, and he wore the name with a kind of rugged grace I very much admired as a young boy. My first clear memory of the man would have been when I was seven. Dennis—Rusty's son—and I were playing with baseball cards in the basement at Rusty's house. Somewhere upstairs, we could hear the pleasant murmurs of our parents talking about the price of gas and Jimmy Carter.

When Rusty came down, he went to a refrigerator on the far side of the basement and opened the door wide. Inside was Pabst Blue Ribbon beer—cases of the stuff. He pulled a can out and popped the top.

He stood there, surveying us, one hand in his pocket, the other working the can up and down as he took long pulls from it, his face going fuzzy, a light smile playing on the corners of his lips.

"Can I have some?" Dennis said. He glanced at me, almost as if he wanted to see if I was paying attention. He shouldn't have worried. I was riveted. At seven, I must have had at least a vague idea of what a beer was. My own father drank them from time to time, though I'd never seen him attack a can with such obvious pleasure before.

"A sip?" Rusty said. "Sure. Have a sip."

Dennis walked over. He must have been nine, maybe ten at the time. He stood next to Rusty, and they looked nothing like father and son, what with Rusty's long lean build next to Dennis, who was short and dumpy like his mother, my Aunt Gloria. Rusty smiled and held the can out. Dennis, smiling too, took the can and turned it up, taking a huge gulp.

"Easy, Cowboy," Rusty said.

Dennis swallowed, winced, and handed the can back to his father. Rusty looked at me sternly. "I'll let you try it too,

Will, if you promise not to tell your mother."

Even at seven I had been promising not to tell my mother things for as long as I could remember. Mom worried about rain or sometimes even clouds. You couldn't cross the street without making her anxious.

"I won't tell."

And then I had the can in my hand, felt the cool aluminum on my lips. There was a strong odour, and I remembered thinking it smelled like Rusty. I let the tangy liquid slide over my tongue and almost spit it out.

"Get her down," Rusty said.

I made myself swallow.

"What'd you think?"

I looked at Dennis. He looked at me expectantly.

"Pretty good," I lied.

Rusty slapped me on the shoulder. "It's a man's right, Will. Beer. Don't let nobody ever tell you any different."

The rockslide in the mountains near Rusty's house was just that, a big slab of slick, moss-covered rock, tucked beneath a trickle of a waterfall. The slide must have been at least thirty feet from the top to the deep pool at the bottom. When we were really little, we would slide down in our underwear, spinning like tops as the sky pinwheeled above us, a carousel of blue interspersed with the green leaves of summer. Mom would be up top, wringing her hands, while Dad waited below, stripped down to a pair of cut-off blue jeans to catch us. Rusty sat on the tailgate of his truck, a beer in his hand, smiling as we splashed into the water so many times the moss from the rock turned the backs of our legs green.

The rockslide was hidden in the most secret of places, a mile or so off the dirt road that traced an almost invisible line up the steep slope. I remember Rusty having to coax his truck over giant stumps and through rocky ravines,

but he always got us there. Some of my best—and worst—
memories happened on that rockslide, and even today, I can
still picture the kind of details that usually fade with time:
the patchwork of tree branches above us; the claw marks left
by a black bear on the bark of a sycamore; the mud, thick
on Rusty's truck after hauling us up and down the mountain
for the third time in a week; the faint sliver of moon in the
late afternoon sky. Most of all, I remember the faces of the
adults: Mom, Dad, Aunt Gloria, and Uncle Rusty, pleased
with themselves at finding such a perfect spot, at providing
this safe place for their children. And later, the worry, etched
so deeply in the folds of their skin that it was easy to miss or
misconstrue. I realize now that at least some of them were
frightened about how it would all end.

Wanda, Dennis's little sister, was two years younger than I
was, so she would have been about eight when she told me
she wanted to die.

"Why?" I asked her.

We were out in her front yard, under the biggest tree
I have ever seen. A white oak, so thick that together, four
grown men couldn't wrap their arms around it. Wanda was
in the tire swing Rusty had put up years ago.

She shrugged and let her feet dangle over the unmowed
lawn. Her toes scraped past stalks of dandelions, destroying
their blossoms and spreading achenes over the ground. "I
don't know. I'm just tired of living."

"That's dumb."

"Is it?"

"Yeah."

I gave the swing a push.

"You ever think about heaven?"

"Heaven?" I heard her fine, but the truth was, the thought
of heaven scared me almost as much as hell.

"You ever wonder exactly what it will be like?"

"I don't know. The Bible says there's gold streets and mansions and singing and . . . stuff."

"Yeah. I hope it's not that."

"Me too," I said. "Be boring after a while." I was a little surprised we agreed on this subject. Wanda scared me sometimes because she always seemed to focus on apocalyptic stuff like when Jesus was coming back and all the sinners would sink into a giant crack in the earth and burn forever in the flames of hell.

"I hope it's like the rockslide," she said.

"Dumb again," I said. "Why would you want heaven to be like the rockslide? Even the rockslide would get boring after a while. Anyway, we can go to the rockslide any time. I want heaven to be a place I can fly or do anything."

Wanda shook her head and looked at me. Her eyes were so large and deep and full of a silky green colour that I almost wanted to look at them forever. I remember thinking she was lovely at that moment. It wasn't sexual. I was still too young for that. The longing came from somewhere deeper. A longing for something true and steady.

"No," she said. "The rockslide. When I die, I hope it's the rockslide."

"And if it isn't?"

"It will be," she said and closed her eyes.

I pushed her again. The oak limb creaked. Above us, in the high leaves of the towering tree, a wind breathed.

I was twelve. We rode up the mountain in the back of Rusty's new truck, one he'd brought home, according to Dennis, last spring. "He won it in Las Vegas. He told me he can win every time."

"You can't win every time," I said. My pre-algebra teacher, Mr. Bozeman, had spent a day that spring telling us about

Vegas and the way they make sure to always get their money.

"He can."

"Bull."

I let it go. Arguing with Dennis about his dad was dangerous. Once he'd slammed my head into his bedroom wall. The wall took the worst of it, but Aunt Gloria had been very upset and come upstairs with some putty and paint to fix it before Rusty got home. Anyway, I wanted to believe if anybody could take Vegas, Rusty could.

When we made it to the secret road, the one that was little more than a slip between the trees, Rusty revved the engine and attacked the rough terrain. He swung the truck around a blind curve, narrowly missing an eight point buck running for deeper woods. We were slung side to side in the back; Wanda hit her head. It bled instantly, a scarlet V forming above her right eye. Dennis landed on me and I pushed him off. A cooler of beer turned over and ice and cans slid across the truck bed.

Somebody up front screamed. It sounded like Gloria. My dad said something, but it got cut off as we flew into the air. For a brief second everything was airborne, nothing was stable or in place or safe. The world changed.

When we hit the ground, the beer was gone. The cooler was gone. Bits of ice lay melting in my hair. I couldn't breathe because the wind had been whoofed out of me and I just lay there, letting the vibrations from the truck bed shake my stuck lungs.

My world became the simple need to breathe. Later, Mom told me that Dad climbed into the truck bed, lifted me up, shook me, turned me upside down.

He must have slapped me on the back because my breath came, rushing through my lungs and the world slid back into focus. There were trees again, and my father's face, voices saying words I couldn't understand, and beyond that the gurgling of the rockslide.

"You could have killed him," Dad said.

I turned. Rusty was off aways, behind the truck. He'd found one of the beers.

"Or my own," Rusty said. "It was an accident. I didn't know the deer was going to be there."

I looked around. Next to me, Gloria held the hem of her sundress against Wanda's forehead. There was only a little blood now.

Dad said, "Give me the keys."

"The hell I will," Rusty said.

Gloria began to cry.

Mom stood over Dennis. She turned to my father and touched his shoulder. "Maybe," she said, "since we're here. We should just make the best of it. Dennis is okay." She looked at me. "Will just got the wind knocked out of him—"

"I'm fine," I said.

"Wanda?" Mom said.

"I'm okay."

Gloria was still crying. I looked at Dad. He looked away.

Once at the slide, I was amazed how quickly the tension evaporated. Mom, who rarely participated, went first, primly easing herself down the slide, but she lost control near the bottom and her legs flew up and she flailed helplessly, as she splashed into the cold water. The kids laughed. Rusty opened another beer. Gloria stopped crying and smiled a little. Dad, however, sat on a rock by himself and said nothing.

The slide was fast that day. We went down it head first, feet first, sideways. Mom and Aunt Gloria laughed. Rusty, who had collected all the beers, leaned against his new truck shouting encouragement.

As the day wore on, I felt myself getting angry at Dad, still perched on his rock at the top of the slide, doing his best to remain aloof. Why couldn't he loosen up? Why couldn't he just let it go? Rusty had said it was an accident. Did Dad think he could have done any better if he had been driving?

The brightness faded, the trees making it almost dark beneath their heavy boughs. Rusty asked Dad if he wanted a beer. Dad told him no. Rusty looked confused. "There's plenty," he said. "Just a short walk down the path." He grinned.

"I'll be damned if I have one of your beers."

Rusty laughed, a deep wide open kind of laugh. "Well, suit yourself."

Dad shook his head, ignoring a glare from Mom.

Rusty finished the rest of his beer and threw the can in the bed of his truck. He jogged over to the top of the slide where Dennis and I were getting ready for another trip. Rusty cut in front of us and jumped onto the rock. His blue jeans smacked against the wet slab and he went down, screaming with joy. When he hit the bottom, he disappeared into the water with barely a splash.

The water went still.

We waited and waited. No Rusty.

Dad and Dennis moved at the same time. Dad leapt off his rock, sprinting toward the pool. When Dennis attempted to slide after him, his foot got hung on a root and he fell onto the rock, slamming his head. Rather than slide, his body bounced down the rock. I watched as Dennis's body was wracked time and time again against the long flat slab.

Dad reached the water at the same time as Dennis, and for a moment, he seemed confused about what to do: go in after Rusty or try to help Dennis. He chose Dennis, hauling him up out of the pool and laying him out on solid ground. Dennis whimpered. The side of his face had been smashed by the rock and his leg looked unnatural on his body, like an appendage belonging to someone else.

Dad turned back to the pool just as Rusty emerged from the water. He wore a grin three sizes too big for his face and seemed confused when he saw Dad coming for him.

Rusty never realized my dad was going to hit him until the second before it happened. At first, he just smiled that stupid smile, pleased at how long he'd stayed under, how much he'd made us wonder. Then the smile faltered just a little as Dad sprinted toward him. By the time Dad hit the water, the smile was gone, replaced by the wide eyed look of a man who knows pain is coming and there is very little he can do about it.

Dad hit him in the nose.

The blood came fast. Rusty crumpled back into the water. Dad swam to the side and pulled himself out.

I could hear Mom praying softly under her breath. Gloria and Wanda were crying. I just stood there at the top of the slide, filled with a newfound sense of things, the way moods and tensions were like fast approaching storm winds and from this moment on, we would always be part of the storm.

Until we weren't. And on that day, the rockslide would dry itself and the smooth surface lined with algae and moss would harden and grow rough beneath our fingers. And I would try to understand. And try. And finally admit there was no understanding anything except what used to be and what was now. The slide is too fast. You reel too much. You hit the water and everything goes dark.

Somehow, as if by force of will, we all survived. Dennis survived. His leg was broken. His nose never did look straight again and he spent the next several months in pain as he recovered.

Nine months later, Rusty bought him a Kawasaki for his birthday. We made our usual visit, though Dad grumbled the whole way, and when we arrived, he kept his distance from Rusty.

By the end of the weekend, the two men were talking again. Something had changed about Rusty. I noticed it the second I walked into their house. Rusty did not have a beer in his hand. "Dad stopped drinking," Wanda said.

We were out in the woods behind their house, having ridden bicycles behind Dennis as he put the new dirt bike through its paces. Tired, Wanda and I had stopped under the shade of some pine trees.

"I noticed," I said.

"It won't last."

"Why do you say that?"

She looked at me, something like a smile in the corners of her eyes. "You don't get it, do you?"

"That Rusty likes beer?"

She laughed.

"Okay," I conceded, "he's an alcoholic. Is that what you wanted me to say?"

"My dad isn't happy without a beer in his hand. He can't function."

"So why not drink? It's every man's right."

I realized instantly I had said the wrong thing. Wanda stepped away, out of the shade as if struck. She said nothing else. Picking up her bike, she climbed on and began to pedal back to the house.

Rusty and I had the talk just before my thirteenth birthday.

We were in his truck, just the two of us. I don't know why. I don't know where we were going. Sometimes, I try to remember, but I can't.

He did not have a beer in his hand. Both hands were on the wheel. His face was set in a hard grimace. He watched the road as the scenery on either side of us peeled free like loose skin.

"Your mother tells me you like to read."

"Yes, sir."

His fingers tightened on the wheel. He usually smiled. He wasn't smiling now.

"Don't lose that."

"Okay."

He took his gaze off the road and looked at me. "I mean it."

I nodded.

"She says you've got talent. You're smart. Creative even."

I said nothing. The air seemed thicker. I could feel it on my skin.

"Do you drink?"

"No, sir."

"Don't start."

"But . . ." I wanted to tell him it was my right as a man.

"But nothing. I used to have an imagination. Now, I can't think of anything new. Just the same old stuff."

"But you made the woodsplitter, Rusty. Just last winter. That was new."

"That was shit."

I looked away. It hurt me to see him like this. I made up my mind that after the car ride, I would forget it ever happened.

"If drinking would make you feel better, why don't you just drink?"

He allowed himself a thin smile, all lips, curled open to reveal almost clenched teeth.

"There's no figuring it out," he said. "I just don't want you to make the same mistakes I made."

"What mistakes?"

He rubbed his eyes with the back of his hand and reached into the console for his cigarettes. Outside, it had started to rain. We were about three miles from his house.

He lit a cigarette and cracked the window. Rain came in on his sleeve and one side of his face. He let the water hit him. Didn't flinch, even though it must have been cold.

"What mistakes?" I said again.

He exhaled deeply and blew the smoke out into the rain.

"So many, no one can count them. So many, they bury you."

He tossed his cigarette out the window and waved his hands, letting go of the wheel. A delivery truck loomed ahead of us, gleaming in the rain.

I felt myself draw up. My fists clenched into tiny stones, my pulse beating out of them hard. My eyes scrunched themselves shut and for a second I felt the collision. A jarring smack spun us sideways and made me see in a rush that image of Dennis tumbling down the rockslide, somersaulting over the silent slab and onto the sharp rocks. I saw us splayed out upon the side of the road, glass in our mouths, eyes, nostrils; bodies immobile, crushed by pavement, just as Dennis had been crushed by the rocks.

Then the moment was gone and I opened my eyes. The road ahead was clear. Rusty had both hands on the wheel.

"Just promise me you won't end up like me, Will."

I couldn't promise. I couldn't say anything.

Perhaps I sensed even then that promises are just empty sounds. Maybe I already knew that, eventually, we all slide. And when you hit bottom, there's nobody there to catch you.

I watched as Dad disappeared inside my Aunt Gloria's and Uncle Rusty's house. I had a sense of what had happened though I didn't want to admit it to myself. So I sat very still and looked at the shards of glass that hung in the smashed out passenger side window instead.

"Get down," Mom said.

"Huh?"

"You heard me. Get down in the floorboard."

I did as she asked, crouching in the dirty floorboard, my bare knees hot against the rubber floor mats. The engine ticked, cooling. I turned over so I could see the moon through the backseat window. On the way over, I had watched it. Sometimes I felt like we were chasing it and then it was chasing us. I could never tell.

I can't say how long Dad was gone exactly. When he came back, he said nothing, only settled in behind the wheel and turned the ignition. The noise from the engine shattered the calm night, made me cringe. I almost called out for him to shut it back off, but then I realized I was being foolish and said nothing.

We were halfway home before Dad broke the silence. "Was a sledgehammer."

Mom sucked in a breath. "Not a gun?"

Dad shook his head.

"Thank God."

"Rusty decided to take apart Dennis's motorcycle so he couldn't drive it anymore."

Mom nodded as if this explained everything.

"I don't understand," I said.

"Your Uncle Rusty's an alcoholic, honey," Mom said.

"But he said he quit. He's never going to drink again."

The front seat was quiet, as the tires rolled over the road and the moon slipped past us again, and for the first time, it occurred to me adults don't understand the world any better than their children do.

The rest of the way home I watched the moon, wondered if there was some heaven behind it, some breathing place that would never change. I thought of Dennis. Of Rusty. Mostly, I thought about Wanda, what she must have been thinking when her father finally stopped drinking and her brother took the sledgehammer and all those bits of glass exploded in the night. Where had she been? Had she covered her ears to block out the sound? Had she pulled her covers up over her head as Dennis yelled over and over that he hated his father and Gloria had begged them to stop? I tried to imagine her, but always came back to the rockslide, an early crescent moon in a blue afternoon sky, three children sliding fast for the bottom, while the adults tried to pretend all was well and the rockslide would always be smooth and gentle and, most of all, solid, a place that would not change.

SAVING DOLL

The day Missy turned sixteen her brother gave her a new pair of track shoes. The old pair, the ones she was wearing when Danny found her out back, running sprints between Momma's Ford and the apple tree, were coming loose on the bottom, and they didn't fit right, making it necessary to wear two and sometimes three pairs of socks to avoid blisters.

Her brother stood, watching her, arms crossed, nodding his head.

"You'll take regionals," he said.

Missy slowed up. "Not unless I get faster between now and Friday. Jasmine Lopez is running for Cedar Oaks. She's faster than me. At least she was last year."

Danny shrugged. Ten years ago he'd run the 100 meters in Birmingham. Missy had been too young to remember, but she knew the story by heart. He missed winning the championship by three tenths of a second. Changed his life. He never said that, but it was in the lines of his face, the way he held himself, the way his eyes wouldn't look at her when he talked about it. Then, he'd been a skinny eleventh grader. Now, he was at least seventy-five pounds heavier, and walked with a limp from a wound he'd suffered shortly after dropping out of high school.

"Don't you have some work to do or something?" Missy said.

Danny laughed, shaking his jowls, showing an almost feminine red tongue. He had the smallest eyes, almost like beads, but they were sharp, and always found a way to look at you, no matter how much they might pretend to get buried under all that unshaven flesh. "Momma's already closed the fruit stand down for the day. I wanted to talk to you about something."

Missy turned back to her makeshift track, ready to do another sprint. "I don't want to sell," she said.

"Give me some credit, okay? You got a future. I understand that."

"So what, then?" Missy turned to make another sprint.

Danny opened the door of Momma's Ford and pulled out a shoebox.

"Now I'm not asking you to sell. And I'm not asking you to give up your dreams like I did, but—"

"That was your choice."

"Bullshit it was. You don't know nothing. Sometimes you don't have a choice."

"There's always a choice."

Danny nodded his head, smiling slightly. "You keep on thinking that. One day reality is going to slap you in the face. You wait and see."

Missy shrugged and broke into a sprint. When she made it to the apple tree, and rounded for the turn, Danny was still there, holding the shoebox, watching her with what Missy hoped passed for pride.

She made three more hard sprints from the apple tree to the Ford and back again before slowing to a walk. Hands on her hips, she took in deep lungfuls of the late afternoon air.

"Like lightning, girl," Danny said. "Does my heart good to see you run like that. Hell, if you don't win state, it'll be a disappointment."

He held the shoebox out.

Missy didn't reach for it. "What's the catch?"

"Catch? No catch. Take them. They're yours."

"I don't believe you," she said.

"The shoes are from me. Call them a sample of the way things could be if you listen and cooperate."

"Cooperate?"

"Yeah. There's a guy I know. He wants to meet you. He's harmless and—"

"Forget it," she said. "I don't want the shoes."

Danny smiled and dropped the box on the grass. "Nah, you keep them anyway. You'll come around."

Missy watched as he limped back to the house. When he had disappeared inside the storm door, she kneeled beside the box and removed the shoes. They were new and expensive for sure. She tore the tissue paper from the insoles, so she could look under the tongue to see if they fit. Size 9. Perfect.

Kicking her old shoes off, she quickly tried the new ones on. They felt good. She was about to give them a test sprint when something else in the box caught her eye. It was a receipt. $127.89.

Grimacing, she wadded the receipt into a little ball and tossed it into the high grass out beyond the apple tree.

Missy was warming up at track practice Monday afternoon when Coach Hudson called her over.

He'd been a high jumper in college and still looked the part. He was tall and long and angular, like something made out of toothpicks glued together to resemble a man.

Coach Hudson wiped sweat from his brow and peered out over the practice field at some of the boys goofing around with the javelin. "Your mother called today."

"My mother?"

"She says there's been some trouble at home, Missy. That you can't practice today." Coach spread out his large hands in a gesture of empathy.

She felt herself turning bright red. Her mother had no business calling here, interrupting her life.

Coach put a hand on her shoulder and squeezed. "Want to talk about it?"

"No."

"You better get going, then."

"No. I'm staying. Whatever it is can wait."

"Missy, you know how I feel. You take care of your family, your grades, then track. Go home. Take care of the problem. Rest. Regionals aren't until Friday."

She knew he was right. Momma might have fallen or worse. Something might have happened to Danny. Surprisingly, even the thought of Danny getting hurt made Missy sad.

"You've got my number," Coach said. "Call me if you need anything."

"I talked to Danny this morning, Missy. He told me some things."

Missy put her hand out to steady herself on the peach table and turned to face Momma. Peaches had been good this year, big and soft and spotted with red the way they get when they're almost perfect.

Missy forced her hand to let go of the table. She stood up straight and said, "About what, Momma?"

Momma wheeled her chair over to the table and ran her hand over the grapefruits, checking them for bruises and nicks. She decided on a dull, yellow one. Turning it in her hand, she gave it a once over, before producing a pocketknife and quartering the fruit in two quick strokes. Pink juice dribbled over her fingers. The knife disappeared as quickly as it had come, and Momma bit into the ripe flesh.

She spit out a seed and repositioned her wheelchair, making room for a customer to squeeze by. "About you."

"Momma, I don't know what he told you, but . . ."

"But nothing. Don't talk. Listen. He told me about the trouble you got in with that Miller boy. He said you came to him and asked him what to do."

"He's a liar. Me and Tommy Miller haven't had any trouble. He used to call me sometimes. Then he made up some story about what we did, and none of it was true. Danny must be confused. It's not true."

"So you say." Momma looked Missy over. "I see what you can't hide underneath them big shirts and baggy jeans."

Missy looked at her feet, embarrassed. All she wanted to do was run because running made her feel like her problems couldn't keep up, like the wind that blew past her was just pushing all of those anxieties further and further away.

And she was fast too. Real fast.

"Look at me," Momma said.

Missy looked up but not at Momma. Instead, she focused on a table of half-ripe tomatoes near the house.

"You know how I feel about these things. I had Danny when I wasn't no more than your age. I don't want you to work yourself half to death like I did. I had diabetes before I was forty and my legs taken from me before forty-five. But I don't want that for you, Missy. Now look me in the eye. Are you pregnant?"

Missy couldn't look her in the eye. It was all so ridiculous, so unjust. She'd never done more than let Tommy kiss her and put his hands on her breasts. He'd wanted more, and so had she, but she thought about what a baby would do to her life. She thought about Momma and the wheelchair, the dead air beneath her knees where her legs used to be. She thought about these things and told Tommy no. Tommy didn't listen and kept on, reaching for the waistband of her shorts, pulling them halfway down her thighs, sliding his hand up between her legs.

"This don't feel like no," he said, sliding the flat of his hand over her wet panties.

She pushed him away from her as hard as she could. They'd been behind his trailer under the makeshift carport. The trailer park was dead, sleeping except for the occasional bark of a dog or screeching of a cat fight. Tommy fell back against his dad's Chevy and his head struck the windshield.

He lay there for a second, draped over the hood of the car as blood worked itself through his tangled hair and down the side of his neck.

"Oh Lord, I'm sorry, Tommy."

He staggered to his feet. "Put your clothes on and don't ever come near me again," he said.

As bad as that had been, this was somehow worse, facing Momma like this.

"I'm not pregnant because we didn't do anything. He's lied to Danny. Or maybe Danny just made it all up. He's trying to get me to go with some guy. He's behind this.

He knows I'll do anything to get to run track."

"Danny wouldn't lie to me. He takes care of me." Momma pointed to the wheelchair, a fancy, electronic number Danny had bought for her at Christmas. "How many sons would stay on with their Momma like this? How many would work the family business like he does?"

"The family business is drugs," Missy said.

Momma's eyes got small. She brushed a strand of hair off her forehead. "Come over here," she said.

Missy stepped closer.

"Bend down."

Tears dropped on Missy's new track shoes as she bent over.

When Momma's open hand hit her wet face, it sounded loud, like the pop of a firecracker.

"Don't you dare say that. Don't you dare." Momma's voice trembled.

"Yes, ma'am," Missy said between sobs.

"That boy has seen hard times. He's made mistakes, but don't you dare make it worse."

"I'm sorry," Missy said. And for some reason she did feel sorry now. Sorry that she'd told the truth. Maybe even sorry she knew it at all. Sometimes she wondered if life would be better if she just played along like Momma did.

Momma's voice softened and she reached out and stroked the redness on Missy's face.

"We're not going to think on the past, darling. I've been there once and all I want is to make sure you don't see the same places I've seen."

It was raining when Missy knocked on the door of the shed.

"Come on in," a voice called from inside the shed. "Get out of the rain."

Missy stepped inside. Once it had been her father's workplace, and she dimly remembered the tools that lined the walls, the cutting boards and skill saws. Her father had been a cautious, exact man. In pictures he stood rigidly, as if letting his shoulders slump or his neck bend were a sign of weakness. Her memories of her father were mostly pell mell, cobbled together from stories, pictures, and indefinable snatches of imagery: him holding his hands out for her after getting out of his truck, a boot heel propped up on the coffee table near where she played with her dolls, an elusive smell of aftershave and sweat and something else—perhaps the loamy scent of the earth.

Now the shed belonged to Danny. His own father had died in a tent in the mountains of North Georgia surrounded by cans of Pabst Blue Ribbon. Danny had managed to avoid his father's addiction, but had found a career in feeding everyone else's. He sold everything imaginable from the shed, which with some help from his friends, he'd extended by half, so they'd have a place in back to make the meth. In the front part, where Missy stood, Danny had set up some couches that smelled of mildew and urine. He'd run the cable from the house into the shed and put up a big screen television. A table with uneven legs leaned to the left between the couches. On top sat a jar filled with cash. On the wall to Missy's right, Danny had installed a two-way mirror, enabling him to spy on certain customers from the tiny closet on the other side.

Danny stood in front of her, holding the remote in his hand, flipping through the channels.

"Sit down," he said.

"I'll stand."

"Suit yourself." Danny turned the television off. "The more channels you get, the less there is to watch." He tossed the remote on the couch and reached for the money jar. Opening it, he reached inside and pulled a wad of cash out, dropping it on the table in a heap.

"Count it," he said.

"No," Missy said. "I came to tell you that you can't stop me from run—"

"Count the goddamn money, Missy." His voice sounded low and flat, so unlike the happy-go-lucky voice he'd used when he gave her the shoes. Missy went over to the table and began to count.

The bills were oily as she dropped them one at a time back into the jar.

"How much?" Danny asked.

"Ninety-seven dollars."

He shook his head. "You never could add. There was

ninety-three dollars there. That's all. How much do you think Momma makes with that fucking peach stand?"

"I don't know."

"Guess."

"I don't know."

"Of course you don't know. The thought never crossed your pretty little head, did it? You just go on along running track, never even thinking about chipping in a little, doing your part."

"I take care of Momma. Who's going to bathe her if I don't? Who's going to help her sit on the potty and clean up her diaper when she doesn't make it? Who's going to make sure she takes her medicine? If it wasn't for me, she'd be dead by now, Danny."

Danny's hand shot out and shoved the jar off the table. It flew over the couch and landed with a tinkling of broken glass on the other side. "Does any of that shit bring us money?" He bore down on her, gripping her shoulders and squeezing tightly. "Does it?"

"No," she managed.

He let her go. "Hell no." Muttering to himself, he walked over to the couch and began picking up the money. "Hell no," he said again.

She waited, willing herself not to cry.

After he'd gathered the money, Danny stuffed it in his shirt pocket and turned back to her, his face different now, sad, almost loving.

"I want you to run track, Missy. I want good things for you. But I've got to put food on the table. So all I'm asking is for a little help."

She nodded.

"It'll be over before you know it. I promise. He'll be behind the two-way mirror. All you've got to do is give him a little show. You won't even know who it is. In fact, you can just pretend nobody is there at all. Or maybe imagine somebody else. Then, you can go win state."

The next day, Tuesday, was hot. By the time she finished warming up, Missy could smell the scent of her own sweat as it broke out over her skin, but as Coach lined them up for their first series of sprints, Missy pushed herself even harder, ignoring the sun, the humidity, the tiredness of her flesh. She thought only about Friday. About Jasmine Lopez, and soon she found the sweet spot, the place where her body left her and she was centred and numb, bearing down on the track like a locomotive. Her mind was clear now, her heart thudding in her chest, beating time and blood to the body that was no longer hers to feel. Nothing else mattered. Nothing else could matter because her mind began to run too, racing along with each step, sinking farther and farther into the sweetest oblivion she had ever known.

When practice ended, Coach called her over again.

"You're looking good."

"Thanks."

"I've watched you grow up out there, Missy. When you started in the seventh grade, you were just a baby. Now . . ." He spread his big hands apart, framing her between them.

Missy felt herself blush.

"All is well?" he said.

She looked at him, confused.

"At home?"

"Oh. Never better."

He touched her arm. "Don't lie to me."

"I would never, Coach."

"You better not. Remember, if things get tough, Missy, you've got my number."

"Right."

He nodded contemplatively. Then his face brightened. "I may come by for some peaches this week. I heard the first crop was pretty good."

She smirked. "You heard wrong. They're losers this year."

At dusk, Momma wanted to go into town. After Danny helped Momma into the passenger seat, Missy slid behind the wheel and started the Ford.

Missy pulled away from the house, leaving the gravel driveway for the pavement of the main road. Momma rolled down her window and grunted for Missy to do the same.

The light was fading, and the "milky time" was coming, a time Missy knew was Momma's favourite. That was what Momma called it when the sun disappeared over the horizon, when the light stayed and the summer air cooled enough so your sweat felt good against your skin and there was a murkiness that made the whole world soft and sometimes time seemed to last forever and you could forget the hot day and the harsh brightness of life and all the world weary stuff that had come before and would come after. Momma always drove with the windows down, and Missy could smell the "milky time" sifting through the windows. She breathed it in deep and let it out slow: honeysuckle, cut grass, and azalea blossoms.

"Momma?"

"Sssh." Momma pointed at the road ahead. She didn't like to be interrupted during times like this. Sometimes she would just sit for the whole trip like this and not say a word until Missy pulled into the Piggly Wiggly parking lot. Other times, as they neared town, Momma would grow expansive and talk about the past, about her sisters, her parents, and sometimes even about Missy's father.

Tonight, she remained silent, and Missy couldn't blame her. The night came in through the car windows and seemed to settle on her skin. In a strange way, it made Missy sad, but it was a sadness she never wanted to let go of. In this moment, Missy knew her life was changing, beginning a shooting star's journey across the sky, angling for extinction, yearning to be snuffed out against the spinning whorl of the heavens.

"Momma." This time she spoke firmly. You will listen to me.

"Yeah, darling?" There was a drugged quality to Momma's voice.

"You're not going to believe me, but I'm going to tell you anyway."

Momma turned her gaze on Missy. "Don't," she said.

"Don't what?"

"Don't tell it. Sometimes, baby, things are better left unsaid. Whatever it is, don't think on it. Think on something good instead. God made a whole world of good things—" she gestured to the landscape outside her window, "—but people always want to think on the bad stuff."

Missy shook her head, determined to speak. "No, Momma. Sometimes the bad stuff gets you even if you don't think about it. Danny has this man that I'm supposed to meet Thursday night."

Momma kept her eyes fixed outside the window. "Your brother is doing the best he can. He's the closest thing you've got to a father now. If he thinks this boy is good for you . . ."

"He's a man, Momma, an adult. He wants to see me with my clothes off. Is that what a father is supposed to want for his daughter?"

"I don't want to hear anymore."

"You've heard enough. Are you going to just let them get away with this? Danny is holding track over my head. He knows I'll do anything to get to run."

"Sometimes you've got to let things work themselves

out, Missy. Nothing is as bad as it seems. And sometimes anything you do is bad. Sometimes, you just don't have a good choice. But that's part of growing up. Now I don't want to hear another word about it. You're spoiling a perfectly nice ride."

Every Wednesday night, Coach Hudson held a team dinner at his house. He lived a few miles from Missy, so sometimes, when the weather was nice—like tonight—she'd jog over.

He greeted her at the door, smiling. "Such dedication. You know there is such a thing as overdoing it?"

Missy smiled back. She liked Coach Hudson; he had a way about him, easy, yet firm. Sometimes, she liked to think her father would have been like that.

"How are things at home?"

"Better," she said. "Don't worry. I'll be able to run Friday."

"That's what I wanted to hear."

He ushered her on into the house where several of her teammates were already seated and laughing at an old video of Coach high jumping in college.

"They called me 'Stick,'" he said.

"More like pogo stick," one of the girls said as the twenty year younger version of Coach flung himself over the bar.

Mrs. Cindy, Coach's wife, made spaghetti and meatballs and told stories about her husband's stuttering attempts to ask her out.

"He was soooo nervous," she said. "He couldn't ask me out directly. He had to go through my brother, if you can believe it." All the girls laughed.

Later, they watched more videos. Coach talked about runners from the past, mentioning Danny, saying he was "darn fast."

She was halfway home that night when she felt the warmth of headlights on her back. She turned and saw it was

Danny. He eased alongside her and spoke through the open window. "Get in."

He drove slowly, as if he wanted to put off arriving at the house as long as possible.

Finally, Missy said, "Tell me who it is."

"I can't do that. It's not part of the deal."

"Then tell me the deal. Tell me something."

They were nearing the gravel driveway that would take them to the house. Danny pulled over to the shoulder of the road and put the truck in park. "There's nothing to it.

He'll be behind the two-way mirror. You won't even know he's there. We'll have some music on. You can even pick it. Dance. Take off your clothes. Show him what you've got. He's paid for an hour." Danny sighed. "Look, if it makes you feel any better, this guy won't try anything. He's harmless like that. We go way back."

Missy couldn't imagine anyone who would pay to see a young girl as being harmless.

"You'll be fine. And once it's over you can go take the regionals and then state."

"I told Momma."

"You did what?"

"I told her what you were planning."

"Are you stupid? That's the sort of thing that would give her a heart attack. She can't know about this or anything in the shed. You understand?"

"She already knows," Missy said. "But you don't have to worry. She's good at ignoring the truth."

Danny exhaled heavily and shook his head. Rain began to fall, thumping on the roof of the truck, lazily at first, then with growing urgency.

"What was my dad like?" Missy said.

"Huh?"

"What do you remember about him?"

"Your daddy?" Danny shrugged. "I remember him taking me on his tractor out into the field. He'd let me drive sometimes." He stuck his hand out the window, letting the rain soak it. He smiled, as if remembering a particularly long lost memory. "When there was a tornado once, in the middle of the night, he took us all into the bathroom. I was so scared I didn't even care then that he wasn't my real dad. I wanted him to hold me. But instead, he was holding you, rocking you and Momma. I sat across from you guys, in the tub, trying to act tough. Shit." He laughed. "You weren't more than five and you had this doll you carried everywhere. Name was Tina or Katrina or something stupid. Later, when you and Momma and Dad had all fallen asleep and I could hear the wind blowing outside and it sounded like the world was going to end, I took that doll."

Danny paused long enough to produce a cigarette and light it. He blew a stream of smoke out into the rain.

"I took that doll and opened the front door. The sky was so black I felt like the world had disappeared. I could feel the wind shaking me from side to side, but I went out into the yard. The trees were bent over so far, I could nearly touch the tops of them with my hand. Behind me, I could hear the house shaking, but at that moment, I didn't care. I didn't belong, and I was mad at you because you did. I threw Tina into the air and watched as she flew over the trees and out into the woods."

"Did I know? I mean, did I miss her the next day?" Missy asked, speaking low, afraid she might break the spell that Danny seemed to have inexplicably fallen under.

Danny flicked his cigarette butt into the rain. "Nah. I felt like shit the next morning and went to go get it. It was wet, but you didn't care. The worst part was you thought I was a hero or something because I saved your doll."

He lit another cigarette and cleared his throat. "I haven't thought about that in a long time."

"Now, I'm the outsider," Missy said.

Danny screwed his face up and looked out at the rain. He puffed his cigarette twice before turning back to face her.

"You think there are always choices. But here's the thing: sometimes the choice you have is rotten no matter which way you go." He drummed his fingers on the wheel and then put the truck in gear. "I think you understand that now."

She started to respond, to ask him why he couldn't take it back this time, just like he'd done when she was five and he had been the hero, but the words wouldn't come out, or if they did, they were swallowed in the sound of the tires crunching over the gravel drive, the tattoo of rain on the roof of the truck, and some other noise—one that might have been the hiss and snarl of the past trying to reconcile itself with the present.

"He's here."

Missy looked up from her science book. Danny stood in her doorway.

"Let's get it over with."

Mechanically, Missy closed her book and stood up. She watched Danny's feet as she followed him outside and through the backyard, past Momma's Ford and the apple tree, to the shed.

He held the door open for her and winked. "Nothing to it. Just pretend Brad Pitt is behind that glass."

Missy felt sick.

"Well, if you're not a Brad Pitt fan, picture somebody else."

"I get it," she said.

Danny held his hands out in surrender as Missy stepped past him into the shed.

"When he's finished, he'll knock on the glass," Danny said. Immediately, Missy felt the presence behind the mirror. Someone was back there.

She was about to ask Danny if he had any music, but before she could, he pushed the door closed, leaving her alone with the man behind the mirror.

Missy focused on her own reflection staring back at her. Momma was right.

Sometimes anything you do is bad.

Still this is the best choice, she told herself. Maybe not the right choice, but she had to run track. It was that simple.

Missy took a last glance at her face in the mirror, trying to memorize the way it looked, especially her eyes because she knew, no matter what, she'd never see those eyes again. Then she stepped away from the mirror and began to remove her clothes.

She'd barely pulled off her panties when the door opened. Her back was turned to the closet, and she tried to turn around, but a hand fell on her shoulder and drove her forward into the couch. She screamed, and her open mouth struck the cushion. She tried to turn around, to see who was behind her, but he'd moved his hand up to her head now, and pushed her face in the couch. The cushions reeked of stale beer and cheap perfume. She couldn't breathe. Her nose felt smashed, flattened into her face, and then she felt his other hand, rough and hard, prodding her, exploring, penetrating. She pushed back from the couch in an effort to breathe, but she couldn't gain any purchase; her forearms slid between the cushions and her fingers grazed coins and moisture and paper clips. And still, she couldn't breathe.

Then her fingers grazed something else. It was cold and hard and buried deep under the cushions. She stopped pushing back and let him crush her into the couch. She got her hand around what she'd found, and it felt like freedom. It felt like a choice.

The barrel faced out, and best she could tell, she had a decent chance of hitting him somewhere in the groin area. She pulled the trigger.

The noise itself seemed to free her. The shed welled up with it, and it was like a sharp line in the history of her life, a signal flare that woke her from a deep sleep and thrust her into the present.

The roughness she'd been trying to ignore behind her went away. The man cursed under his breath and fell on her, burying her under his weight, driving a sharp elbow into her back, making her gag in pain. At least now, she was able to squirm away from him, even as she felt the warmth of his blood running out on her own leg.

As she tried to get up and face her attacker, a hand clutched at her arm and yanked. She nearly lost the gun, but only juggled it instead of dropping it completely. Whirling around, she fired again.

This time the bullet hit her attacker in the face, opening his cheek like a bloody, second mouth.

Coach Hudson tried to speak, maybe to curse her or tell her he was sorry for the way things turned out, or maybe just to ask for help, but words got lost in the blood. He began to gag and spit, and the red ran off his chin like someone had smashed a tomato against it.

Missy wanted to say something to him, something vengeful and profound, something that would let him know just how betrayed and hurt she was, but no words could convey those feelings, so she tossed the gun back on the couch and began to dress.

□

Danny arrived first, surveying the scene for a long time before speaking. "Son of a bitch. Did he hurt you?"

Missy pulled on her socks. "He tried."

"We got to clean this up," Danny said. "Right now."

Missy shook her head. She felt like the world had crystallized around her, slowed down somehow, become a place she could see for the first time. She didn't doubt herself now, even in the face of the violence and all the uncertainty that might follow.

"First we've got to get rid of the body," Danny said. "We'll load it into my truck and take it down to the river. Dump it there. Then we've—"

"No."

"—got to get rid of this couch . . ."

"No," Missy said again.

Danny turned away from Coach Hudson's body and faced Missy. When Danny saw the gun, he grinned. It was a stupid grin, the kind you give a child who you haven't quite learned to take seriously yet. "What the fuck are you doing with that?"

"Aiming it at you."

"What for?"

"We're calling the police."

"The hell we a—"

Missy fired a shot just past Danny's midsection. The two-way mirror exploded, glass glinting, spreading over the couches and floor and Coach Hudson like shiny, little seeds.

Danny's mouth hung open, frozen in midsentence.

"Call the police," Missy said.

Danny held his hands up. "What are you going to tell them? You're the one whose prints are all over the gun."

"I'm going to tell them about you, Danny. How you set this up. How Coach Hudson paid you."

"I'll tell them different," Danny said. "Me and Momma

will tell them we knew nothing about it. You'll go down. And anyway, this would kill Momma. You know that."

"Maybe," Missy said. "But if it doesn't, she'll finally be able to live again."

Just then there was a sound at the door. A knock. No, not a knock. It was the sound of something bumping against the doorframe. Missy turned and saw the wheels of Momma's motorized chair edging open the door. Missy dropped the gun to her side as Momma rolled into the shed.

No one spoke as she surveyed the situation, her eyes half-shut, as if she wished nothing more than to close this scene out completely, to wipe it clean somehow from her sight, from her memory. But then she surprised Missy. She opened her eyes completely. She looked. First at Coach Hudson and then at Danny, her eyes registering nothing as they passed from the floor to Danny and finally over to Missy. Her gaze lingered on Missy, as if seeing her for the very first time. Then she turned to Danny and spoke.

"Call the police."

Missy forfeited sectionals because she spent Friday afternoon at the sheriff's office, answering the same questions so many times, she reeled them off like answers on a history test. Because that's what they were, right?

History.

Momma was in the kitchen when she came in, and when Missy saw her, she started to cry. Waving her over to her chair, Momma embraced her and whispered in her ear. "Don't think on it anymore. Just close your eyes and think about something good."

So Missy did. She thought about the future, lining up on the starting block, a fine sheen of sweat already laying cool on her skin, hair pulled back in a ponytail, muscles taut, twitching with anticipation for the starting gun. And when it sounded, she would fire off the block, eyes on the finish line, her heart alive, a winged muscle in her chest. She'd hear her teammates urging her on, cajoling her to go, go, go, go, and somewhere in the midst of their cacophony, she'd hear her mother's voice at last, clear and strong, confident and unafraid. She'd hear her saying the things she said in Missy's dreams, and those words would be the ones more than any others that would keep Missy running.

ON THE MOUNTAIN

I was up watching television, drinking beer, waiting for the night to give way to morning when I heard the horses. I went to the kitchen window and saw three riders. Fetching my shotgun from the mantle, I turned on the porch light, and went out to meet them.

It was my sister, Kate, her husband, Pete, and his brother. They called the brother Sonny.

I waited for them to come close enough to see me. The porch light shone in their eyes.

Kate hung back, staying at the edge of the gravel road; her mare, a beautiful, charcoal-coloured animal, stomped nervously on the rocks, crunching and scattering them beneath her hooves.

Pete and Sonny tied their horses to a gum tree. I waited on the porch.

When they got near enough to make me out, I said, "Howdy."

Pete wore only blue jeans and a pair of boots. He kept at least ten yards between us. He carried a holstered pistol on his hip, and he glanced back and forth from Kate to me, as if trying to understand how the tenuous connection between us might have led him to my front yard. If he'd heard my greeting, he gave no indication.

Sonny wore even less: his blue jeans had been ripped into shorts. He was barefoot. He stood a foot taller than Pete and was twice as thin. The hairs on his chest were damp with sweat.

"I got a sick dog I can't shoot," Pete said.

"A what?"

"My dog needs shooting."

"And you came all the way down the mountain to tell me that?"

Pete ignored my astonishment. A truck went by out on the road. All of the windows were busted clean out. Somebody hollered "hillbilly," drawing the word out like a rebel yell. Pete bit his lip and waited for the truck to pass. Sonny glanced at the road and then back to the horses, as if they might be the ones offended by the insult.

"I've come close to it. I can't do what needs to be done."

I gestured to Sonny. "What about him? He can't fire a gun?"

"Sonny's come close to it, too. All of us have."

I looked at Kate. "What about her?"

"She don't handle guns."

"She doing all right?"

"She's making it."

I watched Kate, barely recognizing her as the little girl I once knew. She had changed so much, most of it willful, I decided, some of it just due to time. Her body hid inside of a shapeless jumpsuit that concealed her femininity. The paleness of her face made her seem ghostlike in the early morning dark. Even her body language had changed. She sat very still in the saddle, as if afraid that a sudden movement would betray her existence, causing others to remember her.

Only her hair seemed unchanged. It was as red and flowing and long as I remembered.

She did not look my way. Instead, she kept her head turned to the road, as if waiting for something. She had not spoken to me in years, and I couldn't imagine why Pete insisted on bringing her along on these trips down from the hills. Maybe to torture me, to show me that he had taken every bit of her, or more likely, he wanted to give me a visual reminder that he and I were kin, a subtlety that most folks wouldn't give him credit for.

I wasn't buying this shit about the dog.

He gestured at Kate, awkwardly. "She's had another baby."

"Boy?" I said. She already had a girl.

"Naw."

"What's her name?"

"Don't have one yet."

I nodded. A long time ago this would have angered me, but Kate had been with Pete since she was sixteen and that was nearly twenty years ago. I might get sad if I thought about things up on the mountain enough, but that's just it: I kept my mind clear of Pete and Kate. Or at least, pushed them to the back. Otherwise, well, otherwise nothing would make sense, and I'd have to think all types of unpleasant thoughts.

"You going to help?" he said.

"I don't have a horse." I knew that my truck, any truck, would never make it as far into the hills as we would be going.

"Sonny will stay. You can take his horse." Pete chewed on his lip. Sonny grinned at me. His teeth looked ragged like bits of chipped rock.

"No." I pointed at Kate. "Let her stay. I'll ride her horse."

Pete dug up my grass with the heel of his boot while he mulled this over.

"She don't leave my sight," he said, and there was a challenge in his tone.

If I had been dealing with anyone else, I would have told them to go to hell, but Pete was different. You didn't bluff him. You didn't tell him to go to hell, not if you planned on turning your back after you said it. So I tried to reason with him.

"I don't leave strangers at my house. He might steal something."

Sonny's grin flattened out. His eyes looked drunk, and I found myself wondering if I'd ever heard him talk.

"Sonny ain't a thief."

"That's what you say. I know Kate's not a thief."

"That ain't her name." Pete kicked the grass and rubbed the back of his hand across his brow.

He whistled and Kate guided her mare over. She kept her head down and did not meet my eyes.

I felt some of the old anger stirring inside me.

"Kate," I said.

She kept her eyes on her saddle pommel.

"I won't have her speaking to men," Pete said.

"Hell, I'm her brother." I came off the porch like I meant to rush him, but pulled up a couple of feet short. He watched me without flinching, unsurprised by my explosion.

"We got different ways on the mountain," he said.

"Goddamn, Kate," I said. "Would you at least look at me?"

Her head did not move; her eyes remained fixed.

"You going to help?" Pete said. "Cause you can ride her horse. She can stay. Maybe she could watch your place—" He glanced around my yard. "—weed your garden. You know, make herself useful."

"Shit," I said and spat in a flowerbed.

I didn't want to help this bastard. He talked about my sister like she didn't exist, and in a way, I wondered if he didn't have it right. She had always been rebellious. As a teenager, she listened to death metal and stuck safety pins in her ears

155

and nose. She dated questionable characters—rednecks, druggies, abusive types. My mother and father thought she'd eventually outgrow the need to rebel, to shock. Except, as we discovered when she'd met Pete, it was never about shock or rebellion, as much as it was about debasement, about an erasure of self. That's why she found Pete and his mountain persona so attractive.

"Yeah," I said. "I'll do it."

I didn't want to help him, but I did want to see my nieces. I decided there might not be many more chances.

He whistled sharply, and Kate dismounted, turning away from me as I climbed onto the horse. Pete and Sonny stood out of earshot, so I whispered to her: "You say the word, and I'll get you out of there, Kate."

I turned around and saw that Sonny and Pete were already back on their horses. The sun was up. "Hold on," I said, and spurred Kate's horse to the porch, where I reached for my shotgun.

I had known Pete since he was a boy. My family had tried to get him and Sonny enrolled in the public school. Several of the mountain men were waiting on my father when he went up with a sheriff's deputy to try to enforce the law. The men had shotguns and nobody seemed to doubt they'd use them. The deputy came back, swearing he'd never pay visit to those folks again. Dad said little. The next morning, the sheriff came by to see my dad and informed him that those on the mountain could stay on the mountain. As long as they stayed there, he reasoned, they couldn't cause any trouble.

He was mostly right, but how could he have envisioned a sixteen-year-old girl running away to the mountain? Dad had gone up and brought her back the first several times she tried it, but she just kept going back. The last time he went up for her, four or five men waited for him with shotguns.

They informed Dad that Kate's marriage to Pete wasn't going to change. There was nothing my dad could do to bring her back, short of violence, and the men made it clear that violence would be fine by them.

We didn't see her for eight years, though we got reports from Gerald Hand who would go up from time to time to trade with the families on the mountain. Gerald never said much except that Kate appeared to be in good health, and that as near as he could tell, she wasn't in no prison, meaning she could come home any time she liked.

My mother died first, and then Dad a year or two later. Kate didn't come to either funeral. As far as I knew, she didn't know they were dead.

I saw her and Pete once maybe twice a year, coming off the mountain on horseback. Usually they just went right on by my place, but occasionally, Pete would stop and ask for a favour—little things, help shooing a horse, a broken plough, that sort of thing. I always helped him out, even though I despised him. She was my sister.

It rained hard on the way up the mountain. So hard that the ground in front of us was covered in a dirty white mist that made it impossible for our horses to navigate the rugged terrain with any speed. It was a slow, wet crawl, and we passed it in silence.

After a point, I realized I was deeper into the wilderness than I had been before. I lost my bearings, settling for a vague feeling that we were going somewhere *different*, and the rest of the world was below us, spread out like the view from an airplane window.

The rain slacked up as we came upon a little wooden structure. It looked like something hikers might use as a shelter, but I couldn't imagine anyone hiking up here. Pete and Sonny passed it without comment.

After a while, Pete got ahead, and Sonny and I were side by side. I looked over at him, and he grinned back at me.

"What's the deal with this dog?" I said, not really expecting him to answer me.

"Ain't no dog," he said.

"No dog?" I started to say more when Pete turned around.

"Get your ass up here, Sonny."

Sonny grinned at me again as he spurred his horse on. I followed them for a long time.

At some point, a little boy ran across the trail screaming. Sonny laughed at him. The boy disappeared into the tree line only to reappear a little further up the trail with another shriek. Pete told him to shut up. The boy, small, with elf-like features, shrugged his naked shoulders and tugged on Sonny's bare leg. Sonny scooped him up and set him on his horse. The boy settled in behind Sonny and turned to stare at me. His face was dirty, caked with mucous and grime, and he watched me unabashedly. I smiled at him. His face remained neutral.

And, suddenly, we were there.

They lived in a clearing that would have been beautiful if not for the trash and the junk and the little shacks that leaned off into the woods and the half-starved dogs that roamed amongst it all, sniffing and grousing for something that might resemble sustenance.

Sick dog, my ass.

There were pigs and two cows and an overgrown garden. And surrounding it all were little shanties without windows or doors. Their roofs were caved in and their walls sagged.

I liked the cool feel of the shotgun barrel in my hand. I couldn't imagine what Pete really wanted me for, but I felt good knowing I had my gun.

A woman—Sonny's, if I had to guess—leaned against one of the shanties. Inside a baby screamed.

Pete ignored the woman as he dismounted and brushed past her into the shanty. I looked around and saw Sonny grinning at me.

"Somebody shoot you with happy gas?"

He kept grinning. "Ain't no dog."

"You already said that."

He smiled and smiled.

I climbed off Kate's horse and started into the structure that Pete had just entered. The woman in the doorway grabbed my pants leg. "No," she said, and I saw for the first time how emaciated she was.

"He asked me to come," I said.

"He'll be back out." Her head lolled to the side and she fixed me with bloodshot eyes.

"You're sick."

"Ate up with it."

"You need a doctor."

Her skin was a bright red, and I thought it would be hot to the touch. But I kept my hands on the shotgun.

There was a whistle and the woman looked away quickly. Sonny had seen us talking. He slid the boy off his horse, and spurred the animal over to where I stood. Without warning, he drew back and swung at me. His aim was bad, and his knuckles barely grazed my chin, but I had my shotgun up just the same.

"You son of bitch, don't you ever try that again," I said, aiming the shotgun at his stomach.

Sonny studied me carefully, and I swear I felt like he was trying to come to a decision, and that scared the shit out of me. Sane people didn't contemplate decisions at gunpoint. He didn't say anything, he just looked me over, his gaze tracking every inch of me, his jaw clenched, the muscles in his shoulders and chest tense.

"That's my woman," he said.

"She's sick," I said.

"Like I don't know it." He relaxed. "You going to see sickness." He climbed off the horse and led it over to a tree where he tied it down. "Ain't no dog," he said. Then he went over to his woman and pulled her to her feet. "We going home, baby." They walked arm and arm to another shanty and disappeared inside.

I was alone.

I looked around and saw that Sonny's boy had even disappeared.

The baby, who I could only guess was my niece, screamed.

I wondered where the other girl was. She would be seven or eight now.

Pete came out. "Don't do it with your gun," he said. "Use this." He handed me a pillow. It was pink and someone had sewed a purple teddy bear on one side.

I took the pillow and stepped inside.

The pillow belonged to Kate. She used to carry it around the house when she was a little girl. I could remember her crying when I tried to take it away from her once. Afterwards, Mom had made me hug her and tell her I was sorry. Even after my apology, she had cried for a very long time.

But she didn't sound anything like the baby that was crying right now.

I didn't want to look at it, so I looked at the pillow instead. The purple teddy bear had been sewn back on recently with black thread. The pillow was dirty and faded. It looked like flesh in the darkness of the room.

The baby kept crying.

I looked around. The place was deserted. Just a chair that leaned to the left because the legs had been cut unevenly, a collection of empty beer bottles, a dresser without drawers, a handmade baby crib.

Ain't no dog, I heard Sonny say.

I leaned my shotgun against the chair.

I forced my eyes to see what was in the crib. My niece. Kate's daughter. She was red, so red I could almost see the heat shimmering off her in waves as she bawled. Her mouth, an open O, sucked in air only so she could scream it back out. Her eyes were squeezed shut. She stank of shit and urine, and I gripped the side of the crib to keep from falling down.

I stayed like this for a long time, and I guess part of me contemplated doing it, and I began to think about things. Things that I hadn't allowed myself to think about in a good while. I thought about Kate and what Pete must subject her to up here. I thought about how I'd like to kill Pete. I thought about doing it now. My hands did not want to burn with that baby's fever. I kept gripping the side of the crib. I kept steadying myself and talking to myself.

Once I regained my composure, I picked her up. She burned on my hands just like they knew she would, and she wriggled wildly, kicking me so hard in the stomach that I almost dropped her. Carrying her over to the dresser and peeling off the cloth diaper, I used the clean side to wipe away as much of the mess as I could from her bottom. She screamed at me. I could see her uvula vibrating in the back of her throat.

I picked her up again, squeezing her to me tightly and went outside.

Outside, Pete waited, gun in hand.

"Take care of it," he said. He raised the gun so that it was aimed at my head.

"She needs medicine. It's a fever. Some kind of virus."

"I know," Pete said. "It gets worse. Take care of it."

"You can't expect me to—"

"She's going to suffer." Pete was crying now. The gun shook between his fingers.

"I can get her help."

"I want that child to die on the mountain. Not in some hospital."

"This what Kate wants?"

"Who's Kate?"

"Your goddamn wife. Is this what she wanted?"

"Sarah said we should get you. I wanted to go away for a few weeks. Leave the sick to tend the sick. Go up in the cove. When we came back it would all be over."

Kate was behind this? And as soon as the question formed, I knew the answer. Yes. She wanted me to come for a reason.

Pete kept the gun aimed at my head. I nodded at him before turning my back and walking over to Kate's horse.

As I walked I tried not to imagine the bullet tearing through my back. I tried to think of Kate. I tried to remember her when she was young, before she changed, before she began disappearing. These thoughts were hard and unsettled me greatly, so I listened to the baby's screams fill the hollow.

I set her on the ground while I untied the horse. She flailed around in the dirt, and I remembered that she was naked. It didn't matter.

After untying the horse, I lifted her into my arms and climbed on. I started back across the trash littered settlement and saw that Pete was still aiming the gun at me. Sonny, meanwhile, had come back outside and was leaned against the doorframe of his house. He was grinning.

I thought somebody might say something else, but nobody did, and even if they had, I wouldn't have heard it over the screaming baby. I left them there, on the mountain and rode all day. When the darkness came, the little girl fell into a feverish sleep and in the silence of the night, I thought about Kate.

THE CECILIA PARADOX

We've been underground for 193 days when Henry sends his only begotten son, Ralph, to save us.

Ralph's like eighteen and wears two big, diamond studs in each ear. He's got a beard and long Jesus hair. His breath reeks of tuna fish, and don't let him touch you because his hands smell like they've been places hands are not necessarily meant to go. Once, when I made the mistake of giving him a high five after my team won the New World Relay Race for a Better Tomorrow, my hand smelled like ass for hours.

There are only six of us. Survivors, that is. Or dumbasses. Sometimes it's hard to tell the difference. In order of how much I like them, they are

Cecilia
Theresa
Frank
Theo
Marjorie.
I hate Marjorie.
All of us signed up for some government survey. It paid

one thousand dollars, which is pretty good money, or was pretty good money. Now money is something you wipe your ass with when Dominic forgets to refill the toilet paper dispenser. Oh yeah, Dominic's the custodian/muscle down here.

So Ralph trots around all day, speaking in parables and turning water into wine—"You have to use your imagination!" he says when Theresa points out it still looks like water after he's muttered some mumbo jumbo over it—and raising little roaches from the dead. The roach thing is almost cool. After touching them with some holy water, he slides them across the concrete floor, and it's almost as if they scurry, but their legs aren't moving.

"So when's the big man going to show?" Frank wants to know. I like Frank all right, but he's a man, so I have to rate Cecilia and Theresa in front of him. Frank is the vocal leader of a group who believes this is all fake and we're on a reality show.

"But how can it be a reality show if it's all fake?" I ask.

"Exactly," he says. "One day one of us is going out that door and when we do, we'll see that everybody in the real world has got their damned TV's tuned to channel 3, laughing their asses off."

The others either pretty much agree with him (Theo, Theresa, and Marjorie) or pretty much think the whole concept is bogus (me). Cecilia doesn't really have an opinion.

She just likes to sleep around.

I love Cecilia.

So what do you do when you go to an underground room that smells like an abandoned whorehouse/methlab and a screen comes down showing you footage of your family dying from some airborne disease? What do you do when the screen switches and shows people all over the place dying the same way? What do you do when it looks real? More real than any of the movies? What do you do when a disembodied voice named Henry—who tells you right up front you should call him God—announces the old world is over and the new one has just begun? What do you do when he tells you, anyone may leave at anytime, the door is unlocked, but by doing so, you will be sacrificing his free gift of salvation and you will choke to death like the rest of the world he has chosen to forsake? What then?

Long answer: you agonize about the door, the world outside, the family that may or may not be dead, depending on how much technology this asshole has. You debate the merits of worshipping Henry (he is after all the man in charge) versus raging against him, and end up with a passive-aggressive stance, much like how a surly seventh grader would treat his pre-algebra teacher. You try to hook up with the girls. You fail. You meet Cecilia. You screw her twice before you find out she did Dominic four times and Theo (he's missing an arm) once. You fall into an emotional abyss, driven to the depths by grief and guilt. Cecilia comes by and makes you feel better with a blowjob. You love Cecilia and think how you and she will run away through that door together someday and whatever is there—good, bad, ugly— you'll find it together.

Short answer: nothing.

Originally there were eight of us. Sharon died when Henry showed her the footage of her son gagging on a pocket of bad air. His eyes popped out of his head and landed in his cereal. Sharon must have had a heart attack or something because she screamed once, swooned to the floor and died.

Then there was Freddie. Freddie's like the antichrist around here. We all worship him, but Henry tells us he's a false god and following him will lead to destruction and pain and our eyes popping out from all the bad air up there.

On the third day, Freddie rose from his tomb, amen. He asked me if I wanted to go with him. I told him I'd think about it. He promised to come back for us.

190 days later and no Freddie.

Marjorie asks me if I'm going to the Crucifixion later this evening.

"You're kidding, right?"

"No, Adam. Henry's serious about this. I think this may be the season climax."

"There's no one watching, Marjorie."

She twists her long black hair and looks at me with those stupid, pouty eyes. Getting caught down here is probably the greatest thing that ever happened to her.

"Then leave," she says.

"That doesn't make sense," I say. "If I think there is no TV show, it means I think there really was an airborne disease that killed everybody else in the world except us. It means I believe Henry is some kind of God or at least history's greatest scientist."

"Believe what you want. I don't care. Like I said, you should just leave if you're going to be so miserable. Go be like that idiot Freddie. I'll bet everybody's laughing at him right now."

"Bitch."

"Stupid fuck."

I snarl, about to say something else nasty when the fire alarm goes off.

Fire alarm?

Henry's voice booms over the loudspeaker: "This is not a drill. Report to the north exit immediately."

I look at Marjorie. She shrugs. "Maybe it's a ratings sweep.

We gather at the north exit, near the same brown door Freddie left by, months ago. Dominic hands out gas masks. I have to go to the bathroom.

"Hold it," Dominic says.

I smell smoke. We line up. Frank's behind me, saying he heard Ralph went nuts when Henry told him he was really going to crucify him and started a fire in the rec area.

"Henry told him he was really going to crucify him?"

Frank laughs. "Yeah. Henry is fucked up in the head. He really thinks he's God."

"And you really think this is a TV show?"

"No fucking question."

Dominic reaches for the door, resting his hand on the silver handle. "Get your masks on you two," he says, gesturing at me and Frank. He pulls his own mask over his nose and mouth, adjusting the valve.

"I want to see Henry," I say.

"Not possible," Dominic says.

"He's staying inside, then? With the fire?"

"He's the big man," Dominic says. "He calls the shots. Not you."

And that's that. I slide on my gas mask, Dominic opens the door. We shuffle out into the outside world. First time in 193 days.

They blindfolded us when they brought us to the survey. Top secret government bullshit. Just give me my cheque. I didn't care. Blindfold? Sure. You still paying me one thousand dollars at the end?

I've got a new perspective now. Like a man might have after being in prison for a long time. What's money? Shit.

Money's just paper or plastic. I want the air, the solid ground beneath my feet. I want the sun. These are the things that are real.

We're behind a pockmarked brick building with no windows in a little alley. It's dark out. I look up and see not a star in the sky, which would make sense considering all the bad air. Or it could just be cloud cover. The agony of not knowing is the worst.

Dominic looks like one of those guys you see in movies about World War I, holed up in his trench, waiting for the gas, waiting for the end.

"Face the building," he says.

"Eyes in front of you," he says.

"Keep those masks on. Stay together," he says.

"This is all a big fucking joke," he says. "But not, I repeat, not a reality show."

Okay, he doesn't really say those last two parts.

I'm trying to look around for something, anything that suggests people are still alive in the world. One good sign: I don't see Freddie's dead body anywhere. If he'd come out this door—which he did—his body would be somewhere over there by the end of the building. Hey, there is something over there. I crane my neck a little more for a better look and then WHAM. A big hand slaps the side of my face.

"Eyes in front. Face the building," Dominic says.

But what was that thing I saw?

The rumours are true. Ralph started the fire when he used one of his cigarettes to light a roll of toilet paper in the john. Funny thing is, he was taking a dump at the time, the dumbass, and after the toilet paper burned down to nothing, he couldn't even wipe.

This is our Messiah.

□

Henry announces it is time for the Crucifixion. We gather in the rec room wide-eyed and eager for some entertainment. Dominic stands, arms crossed by the double doors which lead into Henry's lair, aka Heaven, aka the promised land, aka some dumpy office with black construction paper shrouding the windows so none of us can see in.

"I Walk the Line" by Johnny Cash comes on over the loudspeaker. Henry is a devout old time country fan. We get treated to all the old timers: Hank Williams, Patsy Cline, Marty Robbins, and Willie Nelson before he discovered pot.

The volume is louder than usual, and we can tell Henry is trying to MAKE A STATEMENT. The doors next to Dominic fly open and Ralph comes out, dragging his cross on his back. He's wearing a pair of gym shorts but otherwise naked. Dark red lashes run the length of his thin frame, and this almost startles me a little.

"So he really lashed him," Frank mutters. "I wonder how much they're paying Ralph to do this." He whistles. "You think Henry spanked Ralph as a kid?"

There are so many responses I have for this question that my mind goes swimmy and I can't say any of them, so I simply shrug and watch Ralph drag what looks like a cardboard cross.

"You'd think with all the CGI effects they used on the videos of our loved ones dying, they'd be able to afford more than a cardboard cross," Marjorie says. "Very disappointing."

Johnny Cash reminds us it's because "you're mine" that he walks the line, and Marjorie shoves me out of the way when Ralph passes by. Dominic is behind him. Marjorie believes the TV camera is hidden somewhere on Dominic's massive body.

I drift to the back of our little group, where Cecilia puffs on a cigarette. She smiles at me. She looks hot. She's got on my favourite gray mini and the red sweater that makes her breasts kind of perky and pendulous at the same time. Her hair is pulled back and her forehead shines with a sheen of sweat.

"Hey," I say.

"Hey," she says, and it's a hey with possibilities in the tone, a hey that suggests another blowjob could be in the cards as long as I play mine right.

"You know," I say, "this Jesus stuff just isn't the same when his hands smell like ass."

"Fully God, fully man," Cecilia says cryptically. That's the other thing about Cecilia, the thing you forget about her because she's hot and capable of mind altering blow-jobs: she's really kind of smart. Maybe too smart to be here with the rest of us doofuses. Maybe Freddie smart.

"So what's that mean?"

She shrugs as Ralph climbs onto a stage Dominic constructed last week and lays his cross down on a chair. He looks dazed.

"Drugged," Frank says. He's in front of me and Cecilia. "He's been drugged."

"Fully God, fully man. It's Biblical," Cecilia says. "The Bible says Jesus was a paradox. Fully God and fully man at the same time."

Dominic is nailing the cardboard cross to the wall. Ralph watches him, red eyed and stoned.

Cecilia takes my hand. "I don't want to see this," she whispers.

"Nah," I say. "Crucifixions bore me."

We head to our spot, the third stall in the men's restroom. It's one of those handicap deals, so there's extra room and a bar for Cecilia to hang on to when I'm doing her from behind.

She locks the door and gets right to work, unbuttoning my pants and breathing all heavy.

When it's over, we both lay on the floor, exhausted.

Cecilia speaks first. "I really hate myself sometimes."

"Me too," I say, not catching the edge of seriousness in her voice, well at least not at first, not until it is too late.

Luckily she ignores me. "This sex stuff. It's an addiction, you know."

This time, I stay quiet and wait for more. She's quiet too. Finally, she sits up and pulls her sweater back on, sans bra which is still laying where I dropped it, on the back of the toilet. "He's probably dead by now, you know."

"Who?"

"Ralph. The Son of Man. Whatever you want to call him. He's probably already bled to death on the cross for nobody's sins but Henry's."

"Do you think Henry really killed him?"

She moves to the toilet where she sits to pee. "I know he really killed him. He's been talking about it for weeks."

"You talk to Henry?"

She tears some toilet paper off the roll and smirks. "Do you really think Henry's God, Adam? Of course, I talk to him. He's a man. You're a man. Think about it. As a man, would you not talk to me?"

I start to form an answer, but my mind is moving too slowly, trying to put it together. Cecilia and Henry. Henry and Cecilia.

She keeps talking instead of waiting for me to answer: "And me? I'm a sex addict. That's why I don't mind this place so much. All these men, young and old. No wives to get in the way." She pouts and pulls her panties and miniskirt up. "I hate myself."

"Why?"

She frowns, her brown eyes going serious and sad. "You're

just like the rest of them. You only want me for the sex. You don't even listen to me when I talk."

"No, Cecilia." I stand up, amazed a little by the intensity in my voice. It must catch Cecilia off guard as well, because she tilts her head to the side as if seeing me new for the first time.

"I do care about you. I want out of this place. Am I the only one who wants out? Do you want out?"

"I don't know what I want. I thought I wanted to have sex anytime I wanted it, with any man I wanted. I've got that now, sort of. You, Henry, Dominic, Theo. Frank."

"Frank? He's like seventy."

"I don't discriminate. Besides, he's a freak of nature."

"Come again?"

"Never mind."

I don't get mad. Not exactly. Just frustrated. Disappointed. Here I am thinking this girl likes me, but all she's concerned about is finding the next dick.

"I knew you'd get mad," she says. "If it makes you feel any better, I hate myself for being this way. I really do. And another thing. What we just did. Just a minute ago. It was special. More than just my addiction. I like you, Adam."

This is maddening. Maddening because I want to hate her but when she says something like this I can't hate her. In fact, I think I love her.

"You know what," I say, my voice rising. "You're a paradox. Fully slut and fully . . ." I hesitate, not knowing how to end it. From the look on her face, she is not hurt by the fully slut remark, so I reach for something else, some extreme that will satisfy both ends of her paradox, and settle on ". . . Fully slut and fully angel." It comes out silly sounding and sentimental, but she doesn't seem to mind. She softens, brown eyes doing this little flash before going all sweet.

She comes over and hugs me. "That's the nicest thing

anybody ever said to me, Adam." She holds me, not letting go and there is no sex vibe in this embrace, a first in all my encounters with Cecilia. She whispers in my ear. "You're different."

I whisper back, "I saw something outside. The day of the fire. I think it might have been a body."

They've killed him. Nailed him to the wall. He's still hanging there now. I would worry more about who is going to be next, but I think Henry has made his point. Today at lunch, he called for mandatory prayer time. Communing with Him, he said. We were supposed to lay prone on the floor and repeat some stupid mantra. I refused. Everybody else went down, the bloody spectre of Ralph hanging over them like a reminder that we may not serve God, but we serve Henry, and Henry is a vengeful, well, Henry.

Dominic comes over and grabs me by the scruff of my neck, nearly lifting me out of my seat at the table. I didn't even know I had a scruff on my neck, but Dominic obviously does.

"Get down like the rest," He shoves me hard to the ground, but instead of lying prone like the others, I bounce back to my feet.

"Leave him, Dominic," Henry's deep voice intones. "I would like to see him in my celestial office."

"Sure thing," Dominic says, cracking a big grin that suggests he knows what is about to happen to me and he finds it immensely pleasing.

Me? I'm scared shitless. I'm going to meet the only God I've ever known, and he's a loser named Henry who gets his kicks watching us squirm.

On the way back to that dark cubicle that is his celestial office, three thoughts run through my mind. The door to the outside, unlocked, beckoning is one of them. This is followed by a memory, just a flash, from the other day when Dominic had been shouting at us, telling us to face the building and I'd seen something by the corner of the building . . . what had it been? I try hard to pull a picture up, to rewind to that fleeting glimpse, but I can't. It was too fast. All I can remember is the sensation, the sudden gripping of my insides, a dizzy feeling in my head that whatever it was had mattered.

The third thought that enters my head on the way to Henry's idea of heaven is unrelated to the other two. Or . . . maybe it isn't. I can't tell. It is the realization that once again, Cecilia had not been among us.

Surprisingly, the door is unlocked. I walk right in. The room is bare except for a desk with a chair behind it and two chairs in front. The only other item of note is a long black curtain covering the back wall. Cecilia sits in one of the chairs, her legs crossed beneath her pink mini skirt, her hands folded in her lap. Despite this posture, her face tells a different story. Flushed cheeks, damp brow, languid eyes; she's been fucking Henry again. She looks at me and smiles and starts to speak, maybe to say sorry, maybe something else, when a voice comes from behind a curtain.

"Please sit, Adam."

I laugh, resisting the sudden urge to rush the curtain, peel back the veil and throttle Henry.

"Would you like to share your laughter with me, Adam?"

"Not particularly." I take the seat next to Cecilia and try to look relaxed. Now that I'm here, I can't decide if I'm afraid or simply amused.

"My son," Henry begins, and the curtain billows a little. I wonder if he's puffing it out for effect. "My son died on the cross for all of you, yesterday. I saved you from the Apocalypse. I fed you." His voice trembles with emotion. "I love you. Yet. Yet, you both dishonour me. You both choose to rut in the bathroom instead of witness the greatest event in the new history of your lives. Not that there is anything inherently wrong with rutting in the bathroom. That is one of the things I would like you to understand about the new history. The old God? He was a God of rules and of sin. That's not me. I actually encourage rutting. I need you folks to make babies if this new world is to survive. What I do demand is respect and fear. I demand you kneel when it is time to kneel. Or, if you don't like it, damnation, the new damnation awaits, ironically, above us now." The curtains shift, and I can almost picture a little bald man back there chuckling and scratching his ass. Anger boils inside me. I start out of my chair, but Cecilia puts her hand on my arm and I sit back down.

"Adam, my beloved, Adam," Henry says. "The door is unlocked. Please, if you would like to join Freddie in eternal damnation, go."

Cecilia's hand tightens on my arm.

"Well?" Henry says. "What will you do?"

Long answer: I see myself get up, go into the room where the rest of the idiots are still prone on the floor worshiping a man who doesn't have the courage to show his face. I tell them this is hell and I hope they're happy in it. I shout, "I hope you enjoy your reality show!" and dash for the steps, taking them two at a fucking time as I head up to the brown door. I wait, just an instant, just long enough to breathe a good gulp of air, long enough to feel it pour into my lungs. Long enough to know I've made the right decision, win, lose, or die. Then I turn the handle and step into a world without precedent, a world where it could all be true or a world where it could all be false. And I am not afraid.

Short answer: My imagination has balls, but I don't.

□

After we are dismissed, Cecilia and I go back to the others and assume the posture. My rebelliousness is gone, replaced by an apathy so profound I'm not sure I care about anything anymore. If the real God, the one who unfortunately has been as inscrutable as Henry in my own life, deems this to be my fate, then so be it.

The floor smells like sweat and piss and mildew, and I wonder if it has been cleaned since Ralph used to slide those half-smashed roaches across it. I try to think if I've ever seen Dominic with a mop before, and before I know it, I am asleep.

The dream is a simple one. Me, above ground, on a windswept piece of brown earth. There is nothing. Nothing at all around me except the same dull brown earth, hard packed and unforgiving.

The world is gone or appears to be. I'm left alone to wander this bleak landscape. But then I see it out of the corner of my left eye, a fleck of contrast, almost blinding in the drabness. I whirl and see a human body. It lays in the unnatural posture of death. I go over to it and am not surprised to see Cecilia, her face serene except for the deep cavities where her eyeballs used to belong.

I touch her skin, noting the smoothness, the soft texture, like velvet. I touch a strand of hair, moving it over one of the brooding caverns.

I sit beside her body for a very long time.

"We need to go now."

The wind keeps blowing. It's something. Better than nothing. And the body. Something about her body doesn't make sense. It's on the tip of my tongue.

"Now, Adam. We have to go, now."

Her skin is so new. The eyeballs are gone. Who took them? Her skin is so new, even in death.

The wind is clawing at me, pulling my shirt tight against my neck.

"Wake up, damn it."

And then I am awake. Eyes open, I see I am still on the floor, but the others have gone. I look up into Cecilia's face.

"Your eyes," I say. "They're still th—" But I trail off, assimilating the dream with what passes for reality these days. "Never mind," I add.

She stares at me, her eyes wide and earnest. She looks lovely. Not just sexy, but pretty, the kind of girl you fall in love with and leave underground shelters to face an apocalypse that may or may not have ever happened with.

"I know where the masks are. Do you want to go up? We could go look at what you saw. We could maybe learn something about the truth." She smiles. "You know, reality show or the end of the world. One or the other. Can't be both."

I smile. "Sure it can. If it's a paradox."

She takes my hand and helps me to my feet.

"What about Henry? And Dominic?"

"Taken care of. Even the Gods and their henchman must sleep, especially after a bottle of wine and a killer blowjob."

She says this last part without the least trace of shame, and I know now her addiction is separate from what we have, like an alcoholic who must get drunk, but still loves his wife. I decide I can deal with her addiction if it means I get to have her love. Besides, if things work out, it could be just the two of us in a new world, far above this godforsaken place. And for the first time, I realize my acceptance—no, my resignation— to the idea that the world is gone, and we are the last. I allow my mind to imagine, in detail, Cecilia and I rediscovering the world, mile by mile. The mountains, the oceans, the sky.

I shudder with pleasure as a new possibility strikes me: we would not only rediscover the planet, we would repopulate it. Post-apocalyptic Adam and, er, Cecilia.

"Coming?" she says. She's standing at the steps that lead up to the outside world.

"I'd follow you anywhere," I say. I am there when I realize it's true. I really would follow Cecilia anywhere.

As we prepare to leave the shelter, I say a prayer. Not to Henry's lame ass. Instead I set my sights higher, to someone or something more ancient than the earth, a master Creator who saw fit to let all us humans loose upon his sublime creation so we could fuck it up and fuck each other and fuck each other up. Perhaps I should be angry at Him for making us like we are. Putting us in a situation where our needs outpace our interests, where sex addicted angels like Cecilia are the nearest some of us will ever get to a prophet or a minister or even a person capable of true love. But I'm not angry. I'm only tense. Wound up with excitement of what could be, of what my life, so fucked up before, might offer around the next bend, outside the shelter, underneath a sky that just might have been made by a real, genuine God who loves us enough to suffer us, whether we be sex addicts or child-murdering pseudogods.

"It's a paradox," I say, talking in a low calm voice that, strangely, is completely representative of the way I feel, despite the possibility the world outside this door is gone and all that exists is the bleak landscape of my dream.

"What is?" Cecilia asks.

"I met the false god Henry and an angelslut named Cecilia. And now, I believe in God. You made me realize that. He's a paradox. Fully man, fully God. Once you've got that, everything else seems simple. Kind of like this whole experience being fully terrible and fully wonderful. Kind of

like Henry being fully genius and fully insane. A paradox."
I laugh with the joy of it all, thinking how there's one more
paradox I haven't considered. What if the world is gone? Yeah.
That would suck. But what if it's not? What if the thing I saw
is a corpse, but a corpse that has eyes and died some other
way than the disease? What if the world is still ticking along
just the way it always has, unaware of Henry and his God
games? Cecilia won't stay with me. There's no way. Out there
in the real world, a girl like Cecilia, a sex freak, won't give me
the time of day. I take her hand in mine. I want to leave, but
I want to stay; I want the world, but I want it gone, levelled
by the eyeball-popping disease and wiped clean. I want to
wander the bare, unpopulated earth with Cecilia, but I also
want to stay right here in this moment, one hand in hers, the
other on the door, a world of possibility on the other side.

"Are you sure about this?" she asks, as rain begins to fall
outside the door. It sounds wonderful, and I wonder if it is
cleansing the earth, washing away the disease, the hurt, the
addictions. And I wonder if it will cleanse us as well, so no
matter what is on the other side, we will be better than we
were before.

"I'm not sure about anything," I say, "but that's why we've
got to do this."

She nods. "If the world still exists, I'm going to do you like
you've never been done before."

"And if it doesn't?"

She tightens her hand on mine. "If it doesn't, I'll do you in
the middle of Times Square."

"Slut."

"Angelslut. Get it right."

"I love you," I say and open the door.

CHICKEN

I learned about defiance, real defiance, on a school bus. I was seventeen. That was the year I started drinking, the year my mother took my car keys away from me after I came home drunk. She waited until I was sleeping one off and hid them, knowing I wasn't about to give them to her, nor was I going to stop drinking. Not then. Becoming sober was still decades of misery away.

So I rode the cheese wagon, morning and afternoons, sitting in the back with a couple of delinquent ninth graders that looked up to me because I told them the sordid details of my life, embellishing most of them to the point of absurdity. And the more I embellished, the more the two boys, Davy and Ty-Ty, wanted to hear.

I told them that I was on the bus because some drug dealer associated with the Mafia took my car when I told him to fuck off. I told them that I had a sweet deal lined up with a guy who was going to sell me a brand new Dodge Viper. I'd be getting it in a couple of weeks. I told them about my brother, Steve, who worked in the pits at Talladega and how he always got me pussy when I went to visit him. I told them that nobody could tell me what to do, and I meant nobody.

"What about Champ?" Davy said. I looked up at our bus driver. We called him Champ, and I always assumed it was because he used to box, but perhaps I was wrong. Either way, his big forearms, thick black moustache, and scarred face always gave the impression that he was not one to be crossed. I'd only seen one kid try it since I'd been riding, and he was dealt with swiftly and soundly. Champ threw the bus in park, slung off his seatbelt and stormed back to the boy's seat. The boy cringed into his seat, terrified.

"Sure, he can tell me all he wants, but I'm not going to do it." And then for effect, I added, "I'm not scared of that old man," while in truth I was mortified at the prospect of crossing him.

Champ had one rule on the bus—stay in your seat. So it didn't surprise me when Davy called me on my big mouth.

"Stand up then," he said. "Stand up and we'll see how tough you are."

I smirked at the idea. "Why should I? I don't want to stand up. You and Ty-Ty can pull that pussy stuff, but I'm not bothering with it."

Davy snorted like he had blown my cover, but Ty-Ty just kept staring at me, his eyes full of something. Wonder? Disdain? It was hard to tell. It hadn't taken me long to figure out that something wasn't right with him.

I knew I was in danger of losing my audience. I had to act. I jumped up out of my seat and across the aisle at Davy. Grabbing him by his shirt collar, I pulled him face to face with me. "You little shit. You ever mock me again, and I'll kick your ass all over this bus."

"Okay," he said. "Okay."

I slid back into my seat and looked up at Champ. He hadn't seen. He was coming up on a stop and his attention was focused on the road rather than the rearview mirror. That's when I noticed that Ty-Ty was still staring at me with that stupid look of his . . . except now maybe I knew what it was. It was a snarl. A clear look of defiance. Maybe in my arrogance I had only assumed that he, like Davy, looked up to me. Now, he seemed much more menacing, and I found myself not wanting to meet his eyes. "Screw both of you," I said and turned to look at the window.

For the rest of the ride home that day, I ignored them, though I continued to feel Ty-Ty's eyes on me. They were like searchlights, covering my skin, making me feel naked and exposed.

The next day, I had found my bluster again after berating myself for letting some ninth grader get to me. I went straight to the back that afternoon (Ty-Ty and Davy didn't ride mornings) and settled into my seat. When Davy and Ty-Ty got on, I looked right at Ty-Ty, staring him down hard. Without changing his expression, he stared back, seemingly looking right through my eyes and into the back of my skull where I hid my true self, the one that was afraid. Again, I looked away.

I worked hard over the next few days to regain my role as hero to them. I told stories about flying private jets, screwing teachers, telling the principal he could go fuck himself. Some of the stories were loosely based on reality, but most were total fabrications, sprung from my mind to my mouth in hot seconds of inspiration.

"Either of you ever play chicken?" I asked one afternoon.

"Chicken?" Davy said.

"Yeah, dumbass, chicken."

"How do you play?" Davy said, sitting up.

"First of all, you need to have a car," I said. "So you two dipshits won't be able to play for a few years. But it's real simple. I used to play it all the time before my car got stolen.

All you do is drive right at somebody and fast. No matter what, you keep going. The first car to veer off the road is the chicken."

"You used to play?" Davy said.

"All the time."

"You never had a wreck?"

"Hell no. Wrecks are for chickens. I never chickened out. See, the game involves a very simple philosophy: make up your mind before you start that no matter what, you won't chicken out. The other guy always will even if it's the last minute. Never fails." I had never played chicken in my life. I'd only seen it in a movie.

Ty-Ty, who generally said little—how could he, with that scowl plastered to his face—spoke up. "What if the other person makes the same decision?"

"Huh?"

"What if the other person playing decides to keep going no matter what, too?"

"Won't happen," I said.

"It might," he said. "If I was playing with you it would. We'd collide with each other . . . unless you chickened out."

I shot a scowl back at him. "I wouldn't chicken out."

His snarl widened. "Neither would I."

The next words that came out of my mouth, I learned over time, to truly regret. Along with regret though I have learned over the years that some mistakes are irreversible.

"Ty-Ty," I said, "You wouldn't even play chicken on this bus."

He shrugged his shoulders. "I would too. But you got to tell me how to play."

Before I had a chance to say anything, Davy started in. "Ty-Ty, I bet you won't stand up."

Ty-Ty furrowed his brow. "I ain't scared."

I laughed. "Sure looks like it to me."

Ty-Ty shot up from his seat.

He stepped past Davy and into the aisle.

Seconds later, Champ was hollering: "Get back in your seat! Get back in your seat!" Ty-Ty gave no indication that he heard. The bus ground to a stop. Champ slung his seatbelt off and stomped to the back. "You got a hearing problem, son?"

Ty-Ty just stared at him, snarl stretching his face.

"I'm going to give you two options, son. Number one, you sit down. Number two, I sit you down."

Ty-Ty said nothing. He only stared.

Champ got really mad then. His face turned red and he seemed to grow larger. He towered over Ty-Ty, burning with anger, but Ty-Ty did not even flinch. That's when Champ began to look a little confused. He glanced at me and said, "What's wrong with this boy?"

I shrugged. He glared at me hard. I sat up and said, "I don't know."

He looked at Davy. "This boy related to you?"

"Yes sir. He's my cousin."

"What the hell's wrong with him?"

Davy studied the seat.

Champ turned his attention back to Ty-Ty. "One more chance, son."

Ty-Ty remained silent.

Champ picked him up and thrust him down into the seat. Ty-Ty popped right back up. Champ stared at Ty-Ty like a man might stare at a disaster. His face registered disbelief, and I could see beyond that there was fear. It seemed strange to me that a man like Champ could be afraid of a boy like Ty-Ty. Scrawny and short, Ty-Ty looked like a straw compared to Champ, but in that instant I saw that size didn't matter at all. It was a façade, a fool's way of judging the world, a mistake of the undetermined.

"You want to do this the hard way? Be stubborn? Son, you

don't know stubborn." He nearly ran back up the aisle, leaving Ty-Ty, scrawny, little Ty-Ty, still standing beside his seat, still snarling, still staring at the world through defiant eyes.

Champ snatched up the CB and put a call in to the school. He explained the situation and a voice said Ty-Ty's parents would be contacted.

"You tell them to get over here and pick up their son. He's not welcome to ride my bus anymore."

So we waited. Champ stepped off the bus and lit a cigarette, maybe to affect nonchalance, maybe because he was a damned addict like most of the male figures I'd ever known growing up. A few kids told Ty-Ty to sit down, so they could go home, but nobody really seemed to have their heart in it. There was something frightening about Ty-Ty standing there, braver than he had any right to be.

Finally, Davy said, "Your dad is going to be so fucking pissed."

"Dad can kiss my ass, just like Champ."

A few kids ooohed and aaahed over this. Most of them just looked out the window, perhaps wishing for Champ to get back on to keep this strange, stubborn boy away from them.

I closed my eyes, still trying to be cool, still trying to appear unbothered.

A few minutes later, I became aware of Ty-Ty's voice. "See, I told you I wouldn't chicken out. Me and you, we would crash in a game of chicken."

I opened my eyes and saw that he was looking right at me, grinning. It was the first time I had ever seen him grin, and it came off as more of a leer than a true smile. I had to play it cool: "I'd still beat you. You did all right with Champ, but you'd chicken out in a car."

The grin disappeared. He narrowed his eyes and seemed to study me, inch by inch. I felt my scalp tingle, my skin crawl. I was afraid of him, not because he was strong or imposing, but because he hated me, and, worse, he hated himself. I looked away, to the window. Outside an old Ford pulled up alongside Champ. A man got out. He was wiry and wore big shit-kicking boots and a belt buckle the size of a saucer. He pulled his sunglasses off and squinted at Champ. The two exchanged a few words, Champ obviously struggling to keep himself under control. He gestured at the bus, and Ty-Ty's father stuck his two lips together and nodded slowly. Champ led him onto the bus.

"Come on, Tyler," his father said. I was surprised by the calmness in his voice. I noticed his eyes, so set, so dead level, that I knew he wouldn't hesitate to beat the shit out of Ty-Ty later or now if necessary.

Ty-Ty didn't move. He still had the scowl of defiance on his face. He didn't look at his father.

"Boy, you got about four seconds to get your ass off this bus, or I'll throw you off."

Ty-Ty didn't move. His father didn't even wait half of the four seconds before he was rushing down the aisle, shit-kickers and all. He slapped Ty-Ty once before picking him up and tossing him over his shoulder. Ty-Ty kept his body stiff all the way back down the aisle. His father slipped on the steps, righted himself, and was gone.

Champ returned to his seat to crank the bus. In the rearview mirror, I saw fear on his face.

Ty-Ty was suspended from school for a couple of weeks and from the bus for over a month. During this time, I got my car back, got drunk, and wrecked it into a ditch at three in the morning. Mom didn't have to take the keys this time. The car was gone. I got lucky, at least that's what most people kept telling me. I had to get six stitches above my right eye and three more on my left cheek. The wounds healed and I thought the scars made me look tough. I went back to the bus bragging to Davy, who sat across the aisle from me by himself without Ty-Ty.

Ty-Ty came back quietly. Champ grunted something at him the first day back. It might have been, "That'll teach you," or maybe, "Son of a bitch," or even, "Oh Lord, here we go again."

And if he had said the last, he was absolutely right. Three days later, Ty-Ty stood up to open a window. Champ, who must have been waiting on that moment, roared at him to get back in his seat. Ty-Ty froze.

The bus stopped so fast that Ty-Ty fell over. He hit his head pretty hard on the floor, but popped back up like a jack in the box. His ear was bleeding. He waited for Champ to get there, lips turned in a crooked parody of a smile.

Champ picked him up and started to the door. "Your dad told me I was to leave you on the side of the road next time. And you know what else? You're done on this bus. Two suspensions equals no more bus riding!" He took two of the steps before tossing Ty-Ty out the door. Ty-Ty hit the ground and sprang back up. Too late. Champ had already slammed the door in his face.

Champ pulled off as fast as the old bus would go. I turned and watched Ty-Ty grow smaller as the bus left him behind.

I felt like Champ had won, and despite my own inert pseudo-rebellion, I was glad that order had been restored. Champ was supposed to be able to handle problems. The idea that he couldn't scared me. The idea that Champ had been scared frightened me even more.

I fell into the old routine of lying about my toughness. I beat up a college guy last weekend when he caught me with his girlfriend. I played poker with some of the men down at the City Bar, and won so much money they accused me of counting cards. They kicked me out on my ass, and threatened to shoot me if I ever came back. Was I scared?

Hell no, I wasn't scared. Most people talk a bigger game than they act, I informed my hapless listeners (Davy had been joined by a couple of eighth graders who listened with absolute, unquestioning awe). Last weekend, I had sex with Marci Crawford and Beth Smitherman on the same day. Beth squealed like a stuck pig. Marci was the silent type until I made her come; then her lungs opened up like a marching band at half time.

The boys listened to me while Champ drove the bus, grunting at us when we got too loud, scowling at us beneath his moustache, pointing fingers that worked like magic, causing us to scurry back to our seats. And I thought about Ty-Ty. How the magic of authority that Champ held over us, suckled us like infants; how we liked swaying listlessly beneath the yoke of his fingers, his scowls, and his inaudible grunts. How I felt like things were right in the world again. How I couldn't imagine what had caused Ty-Ty to become the scrawny, defiant ninth grader that he was.

"You ever see Ty-Ty?" I asked Davy one day when my other admirers had already gotten off the bus.

"I see him everyday," he said. "He lives with us now. His father's dead."

"Dead?"

"He got shot. Or shot himself. That's what my mom says."

"You're kidding."

Davy shook his head. He seemed a little disoriented by this line of conversation, especially coming from me.

"Is he any better?" I said. "You know . . . why does he act like he does?"

Davy puckered his lips. He looked like he had a headache. Squinting, he said, "Don't know. I guess because he was always getting beat up when he was little. He was so scrawny and all. And his dad liked to beat on him too." He shrugged his shoulders. "Hey, did you call that guy about your car?"

"No, I didn't call him."

"But you said you were going to call him and tell him that if he didn't have your car ready—"

"I didn't call him!" I exploded from my seat and shoved Davy against the window. His head thunked against the metal frame and he winced at me, tears streaking his face.

"What'd you do that for?"

"Tell Ty-Ty something for me."

"What?" Davy said, wiping snot from his lip.

"Tell him, I said he ain't no chicken."

Davy nodded and continued to cry.

The spring came, and the reality of being a senior hit me hard. I got depressed about having to ride the bus to school while most of my friends drove new cars. I got down about not having a girlfriend. Despite my lies to Davy, I had never even had sex. The closest I had ever come was junior year with Rebecca Sturgeon. Just before I put it in, I came all over her belly. I tried hard to get her to let me try again, but she wouldn't. After a while she stopped returning my phone calls, and asked Mrs. Morris if she could move to a new seat away from me in science class.

I thought about Ty-Ty far too much—his snarl mostly, and sometimes those level eyes—and it almost seemed as if I knew then that it wasn't over yet. A tragedy was spinning out before me like a spool of thread, and I was powerless to stop it.

I ran into Ty-Ty at school one day. I had been cutting English, so I was behind the gym, out near the dumpsters, tipping back a flask of Wild Turkey I'd filched from my mother. I had learned to hide my alcoholism pretty well by this point. I took a few nips between nearly every period. Whenever I felt like the coast was clear, I skipped English altogether and got good and numb before going on to sixth and seventh periods.

I was taking another slug when somebody walked up. I nearly dropped my flask trying to get it back into my pocket before I realized it was Ty-Ty.

"Hey," I said. "Have a taste."

Ty-Ty cocked his head at me and frowned, but he took the flask and drank some anyway.

We stood in silence for a while. I was drunk and didn't care. I took another drink. I said, "I'm sorry about your dad, Ty-Ty."

He didn't say anything for a while. Then he said, "You still play chicken?"

I shrugged. "Nah. I don't have a car. I totalled the damn thing. I never played that much anyway, Ty-Ty." I tipped the flask back again. "I'm just a damn liar."

"I've been playing."

"You can't even drive a car," I said.

"Been playing without one."

"You mean like you played with Champ."

"Fuck Champ. He's chicken of me, anyway."

I held the flask up. "Damn straight, Ty-Ty. Damn straight. But, you gotta admit, in the end he won."

"I'm not scared of him."

I nodded. I didn't doubt it. "Ty-Ty, does anything scare you?"

He seemed to consider this, a look of deep concentration covering his normally melancholy face. "Yeah, being scared scares me."

"You're a champion chicken player, Ty-Ty. A champion."

He reached for the flask and took another swallow. "I'll see you tomorrow," he said and walked off. I sat down against the dumpster and drank myself silly.

"I saw Ty-Ty yesterday," I told Davy as the bus lumbered off.

It was raining hard and steam clouded the windows. Champ was moving slowly, wiping the windshield with an old rag so he could see.

"He stayed home today," Davy said.

"Skipping?"

"Sick. Woke up throwing up. Said you gave him some whiskey."

I smiled. I wanted to ask if Ty-Ty was doing all right, if he was managing. Losing his dad the way he did had to be hard. I had lost mine a few years ago when he left my mom and me. I couldn't imagine what it was like to lose your father to suicide. I didn't ask because I knew that Davy or the other kids that gathered around me thought I was tough. And tough guys don't ask questions like that. So I sat in silence, ignoring the eyes on me, appealing to me to tell them more lies.

By the time the bus pulled up to Davy's house, the bottom had dropped out of the sky. Visibility was bad, and the only sound was the kettledrum rain on the roof of the bus. There were only a few of us left: Davy, me, a couple of seventh grade kids in the front, and Pete Turner, a sophomore nobody liked. Champ stopped and opened the door. A gust of rain blew in, soaking him. "Damn it," he muttered in his deep voice.

This was when I usually made my way to the front each day. My stop was only about a mile or two away, and I usually anticipated it by sitting in the front seat, waiting impatiently for Champ to get to my house. Davy told me bye, and I nodded to him. The seat nearest the door, where I usually sat was wet with rain, so I climbed in right behind Champ. Champ started to close the door when I heard him say, "Son of a bitch." He took his towel and rubbed the glass, though by this point the steam was not really a factor, the rain was. So I couldn't blame him for doing a double take when he saw the figure standing in the road.

Through the slashing rain, I could tell that it was Ty-Ty. He was just standing there, looking at Champ through the rain streaked glass.

Champ rubbed the window with the towel again. Then he turned to me. "Is that somebody in the road?"

"Yes," I said. "I think so."

He sat on the horn. "You'd think they'd have sense enough to get out of the rain not to mention the road."

I didn't say anything. I waited, holding my breath.

When Ty-Ty didn't move, Champ crept closer. "Motherfuck," he said beneath his breath. "That little punk." He stepped on the accelerator. Ty-Ty didn't flinch.

"He won't move," I said.

Champ barely turned his head. "Huh?"

"He won't move. He'll just stand there."

"We'll see about that," Champ said again. He floored the bus, and the wheels ground the wet asphalt for purchase. We lurched forward. Almost as soon as we moved, Champ slammed the brakes again. He whipped his belt off, set the emergency brake and leaned out of the door into the sheets of rain. "Get out of the way, you stupid kid!"

Ty-Ty shook his head slowly. Champ lost what little self control he had left then. "Kid thinks he can stand me down. I'll stand him down." He looked back at me. "He'll move this time, by God."

"No," I said, weak, barely audible, easy to ignore. I should have stood up and said it loudly and with swagger—that's how I'd told all my lies about being tough, but I said it softly, inaudibly even.

Champ didn't floor the bus this time. Instead he put it in gear and moved forward gradually, increasing his speed as he closed the twenty or so yards that lay between the bus and Ty-Ty.

As the bus got closer, I could see Ty-Ty's face better, how he was really only a boy with a snarl, how his blonde lick of hair had at last been tamed by the hammering storm, how beneath his tough exterior, back in the depths of his eyes, he was as afraid as the rest of us.

More afraid, I think.

I closed my eyes just as Champ hit the brakes again. I was thrown forward, and since I had been standing up, I went up and over the seat. My head hit Champ's head, and I landed in the aisle near the step well.

The bus came to a rough stop. "Jesus," I heard Champ saying. "Sweet Jesus."

He stepped over me out of the bus, into the rain. I pulled myself to my feet and followed.

"Get back in the bus," Champ said, but he didn't look at me, and there was no conviction in his voice.

I watched as he knelt to look under the bus. He collapsed to his knees and began to crawl underneath. I heard him sobbing. He stayed under the bus for a long time, so long that I gave up waiting for him to come back out. Since I was only a mile or so from my house, I began to walk. If I felt the rain on my shoulders that day, I do not remember it. Later, people talked about the storm and how hard it had rained that day. Some people even believed, for a short while, that the rain had played some part in Ty-Ty's death. Champ put an end to that. He never tried to hide what had happened, never tried to sugar coat it. I saw him interviewed once or twice on the local news after he got out of jail years later. He told it like it happened. He seemed, even then, to be baffled by Ty-Ty's behaviour and how he had ended up running the boy over with a school bus. Most of all he still seemed frightened.

I was frightened too.

I am still frightened, thirty years later, even though I

haven't touched a drop of alcohol in nearly ten years, nor have I lied to anyone about how tough I am for even longer.

My wife asked me the other day what I was afraid of. I thought for a while before remembering Ty-Ty—my mind always seems to turn back to that scrawny ninth grader with the defiant sneer, and the way he looked just before the bus hit him. I must have been silent, pondering this for a long while because my wife had to poke me in the ribs and say, "Hello, Trent. I asked you a question."

"I am afraid of people who are so scared they don't care anymore," I said. "I'm afraid of apathy, defiance, and . . ." I paused not even sure what I was trying to say. Ty-Ty, that's what I wanted to say. That look in his eyes. Whatever can make you look like that. That's the thing that scared me, still scares me. Only this was too difficult to explain, so I simply trailed off, leaving a sentence that I would likely never finish.

JAMES

(James at 12)

James had his hand up again. I almost called on him, but I hesitated. Calling on him could bring the lesson to a grinding halt, not to mention that I would have to deal with the derision of his classmates when he inevitably said something irrelevant, something that could only come from James.

On the other hand, James was still new in class. He had social issues, and if the classroom couldn't be a safe place for him to participate and feel included, then I suspected no place could.

"James," I said. "Go ahead. But make it quick."

But it was never quick with James. It was almost as if he had been silenced in social circles for so long, shunned by his peers so completely, that the classroom had become his outlet, his last place where someone would listen to him.

Moments later, after several ponderous and inappropriate comments, I found myself in the awkward position of having to stifle James, so we could move on with class.

"Okay, James. We need to get back on topic."

"One more thing. The dragon. That dragon is really cool."

Somebody snickered.

"What?" James said. "What? That dragon has two heads. I can just see it talking to itself. 'Hello head one. Hello head two.' And what if it got in a fight with itself?"

"And what if you shut up?" a voice from the back said softly. I chose to ignore it, but James couldn't.

"Who said that?"

"James," I warned. "Let's get back to reading."

"But..."

"I'm sorry." I went on, reading aloud from the novel; he kept talking too, trying to be heard, trying to stand up for himself. I raised my own voice to drown his out and eventually he fell silent.

I first met James a few weeks ago when he had been plucked from another teacher's room, because of behavioural issues. He came with a whispered warning from the counsellor: "Something's not right with him. The kids really pick on him. He just can't seem to fit in. We thought he might do better with a male role model."

As time went on, I saw what she meant. He was an easy mark, the kind of kid destined for conflict. He was a magnet for bullies and kids who needed someone to exclude. He made things harder on himself because he was always antagonistic. He never knew when to back off, when to recede to the background like so many kids who don't fit in. Try as they might, his peers couldn't force him to be an outsider because he would stay in their face, agitating them until he became public enemy number one of bullies and cool kids alike.

But James's interactions with his peers were only half the story. Like many teenagers that struggle with socialization, he was extremely smart, and he related better to adults than kids his own age. In fact, I found him affable and friendly between classes. He liked to talk to me about books and was enthusiastic about whatever subject we were covering at the time. He was a band kid, and I drove one of the band busses on Friday nights to the football games. So we had that too.

In our next seventh grade team meeting, I reported to my fellow teachers that the class change had been a success. Not an unqualified success, of course, but besides some minor issues, I thought James and I would get along fine.

But even as I spoke the words, I had my doubts. I knew James might be okay in the controlled environment of a classroom, but I wondered what his life would be like outside it. For some reason, I thought of my own son, Peyton, who is two and a half and sometimes very difficult. What if he became a James? What if one day, his teachers would listen to counsellors whisper words about him? The thought shook me up a little. I decided to be even kinder to James, to reach out to him, to try and help him fit in.

The next Friday, I sat behind the wheel of a school bus, waiting for the band to load up for an away football game. It was going to be a long trip. The kids were already in another gear, hopped up on adrenaline, sugar, and hormones. A bad mix for James.

As we started to pull away from the school, I saw him—hell, everybody saw him—sitting on a bench in front of the school, bawling his eyes out. In ten years of teaching middle school, I had seen just about everything there is to see, but I had never witnessed a face so contorted with pain, sadness, and utter frustration.

"Mr. Roswell must have had all he could handle," one of the chaperones seated behind me said. Roswell was the band director. A nice guy, but James could try even the most kind-hearted teacher's patience.

"Is he leaving him?" I said.

"Looks that way. He warned him the last time if he couldn't

behave, he would leave him. He probably called his mother to come pick him up."

I had to look away. His face—it hurt me just to see his face like that. But it wasn't only the pain that made it difficult; it was also a face I knew somehow. A face from a long time ago, a face I recognized because of the eyes. They were the distant, unfocused eyes of an outsider who would come inside if only he could find the key.

(James at 29)

I first encountered James at the swimming pool. This was back in college, and I was sharing an apartment with three other guys. We had pretty much taken over the pool one Saturday, playing a rough and loud game of football when James jumped into the water. We played around him for the most part, trying to ignore him, basically being assholes.

James was balding now, short, not muscular. He carried himself like a man waiting for the next blow. His body was tentative as he slid closer to the action, as if he were bracing himself, waiting for someone to splash water in his face, to shove him back, to tell him he was in the wrong place, yet again.

His face, however, was bright and eager, hopeful even, in a tragic way.

"Mind if I play?" he said to no one in particular.

We ignored him. Somebody missed a pass and the ball landed near James. He picked it up and tossed it back. It landed like a dead duck in the water.

"Mind if I play?" he said again.

We called him Sanctus because that's what the personalized tag on his Ferrari said. Next to the tag, he had a bumper sticker that read, "Pray the Rosary." He told us he inherited a bunch of money when his father died and decided it would be his only shot to own a fine sports car, so he blew it all on the Ferrari.

He lived upstairs from us, and after that day in the pool, he made it a habit of dropping by our apartment to chat. If he didn't come over, he would catch us outside in the parking lot, on our way to class. He always wanted to talk, to hang out, to be included.

We began checking the parking lot before we left the apartment, to ensure he wasn't around. Sometimes we'd fall silent when we heard footsteps on the stairs, so he would think we were gone or asleep and not stop by for one of his visits.

Once, in my haste to get inside and avoid him, I left my keys hanging in the outside of the door. I heard a knock, and a gentle voice: "Anybody home?" He pushed the door open. "Hey, man," he said. "Your keys."

I thanked him and when it was apparent he wasn't going to leave, I took a seat in the den. He sat across from me on the couch.

I have forever had a hard time with people who don't fit in. Part of me has always wanted to include them, to invite them in to the circle. But it was so much easier to let our group dynamic keep James at arm's length. But now, without my friends, I had nothing to protect me from James, nothing to keep me from doing the right thing.

We talked for a while, mostly about his father's death. A little about his Ferrari. He asked me some questions about my own life. I can't say why, but I felt uncomfortable. Yet, I couldn't seem to give him the cold shoulder. Inside me, a paradox developed. I wanted to befriend him, but I didn't want to leave the safe confines of my own circle in order to meet him out on the fringes of society.

So when he invited me to ride in his Ferrari, I didn't know how to answer. I knew I didn't want to ride. I knew I wanted him to go back upstairs and leave me alone. I wanted him to quit trying so damn hard to be my friend. But I didn't know how to tell him without sounding callous. And somewhere inside me, I knew what would happen to James if he never found a friend.

So I nodded slowly. "Sure. I've never ridden in a Ferrari."

The Ferrari's engine revved to life. James threw it into gear and we lurched out of the parking lot.

I tried to seem impressed as we made our way down Green Springs and out to Lakeshore, but in truth I was too uncomfortable to be impressed. I realized I had made a mistake. Here in the passenger's seat of his car, I was powerless. He could drive me anywhere, wreck the car on purpose, pull a gun from the glove compartment.

I noticed a change in James on the road. He seemed more at ease in his own skin, talking to me about the Ferrari and how he liked to come out here at night and really open her up. It was almost as if this was the moment he'd been waiting his whole life for: another human being, in the seat next to him, a captive audience. He talked and drove faster. I pretended to listen, while I tried to control the conflict blooming in my mind.

I wanted to be standoffish. I wanted him to know after this Ferrari ride he should never waste his time coming by again. I wanted him to stop speaking to us, to stop haunting the parking lot with those eager, unfocused eyes. I wanted him to drift away and leave us alone, so we could be assholes in peace, without having to worry about some social retard who didn't have any friends of his own.

On the other hand, I wanted to reach out to him, to listen to his stories, to engage with him on the level of a friend, an equal. I could see how badly he needed that.

So I settled for the middle ground, nodding along to what

he said, trying to appear interested, but also being sure not to give him any clear indication that I liked him, that I was willing to be a friend.

Finally I said, "I've got some studying to do. I'd better get back."

"A little further. I'll really open her up a little further down the road. She can really fly."

"That's okay, man."

He shrugged and found a place to turn around. We drove back mostly in silence. It was getting dark by the time we returned to the apartment complex. I thanked him for the ride and went inside, locking the door behind me.

A few weeks later, James stood at our door. I was the only one home again. It was the first time I'd seen him since the ride in the Ferrari.

"What's up, man?" he said. "Got a minute?"

I told him to come in.

"Listen, I was talking to one of your roommates the other day. He said you guys were breaking the apartment up, looking for a new place."

"Yeah. We're talking about it, but right now we're not sure who is going to go. Barry might get his own pad."

"I wanted to let you know that I've got some room at my apartment. I mean, if you need somewhere to stay until you find another one." He waited, obviously expecting me to say something, to offer some sign of what I thought about this idea.

"Isn't your apartment a one bedroom?" I said.

"Yeah, but that's no problem. I could sleep out in the den on the futon."

I looked at the door, really wishing one of my roommates would walk in. But the door mocked me, standing silent, waiting for my answer, too.

JOHN MANTOOTH

"I couldn't make you give up your bed."

"It wouldn't be a problem. I sleep out there most nights anyway. Hey, you've never seen my place before, anyway. Isn't that something? I've been here dozens of times, but none of you guys have been up to my apartment. You want to go up and check it out?"

"I don't know," I said. "I'm supposed to meet Barry in a few minutes at the library." There, I had lied. That should stop him.

"It'll only take a few minutes. You've got a few minutes, don't you?"

"Yeah . . . but, listen man. I don't think it would work out. We've pretty much already found a place." Another lie.

"You guys need another roommate?"

"Huh?"

"I just thought you might need a fourth if Barry is getting his own place."

"No, we've already got somebody lined up." This was true, at least.

"Oh."

I do not recall how I finally got rid of him that day. But what I do remember is he never convinced me to go up to his apartment. I also recall a sadness about him, almost as if—crazy as it sounds—we were his last shot at rejoining society, re-entering the world of friends, the inside.

Back then I hadn't seen James's face at twelve. Hadn't seen it crack like a dropped egg. At that time, I didn't know what it would be like to have a son, to know some people are born on the outside. Back then I didn't ask, what if. What if it were my son? What if it were me?

Barry and I were halfway out the door when he said, "Wait. Better check first."

"Right," I said.

We closed the door and went over to the sliding glass that opened up onto the porch of our little apartment. Pulling the blinds back slightly, we scanned the parking lot for signs of James.

"Looks like the coast is clear," Barry said.

I scanned once more to be sure. Since his offer to share his apartment, I had been diligent about avoiding him.

"Hold on," I said. "He's sitting in his car."

Barry's eyes jumped to the Ferrari, which was empty.

"His other car." I pointed. "There."

James sat in his Grand Prix, the one he owned before his father died. He seemed to be talking to someone because his lips were moving. We watched, fascinated.

He was the only one in the car. He had no phone.

"Who the hell is he talking to?" Barry said.

I shrugged. "Himself, I guess."

"Must be mad at himself," Barry said.

I saw what he meant. James wasn't just talking now; he looked like he was screaming. His neck was tight, his jaw jutting out, his lips curled back. And he was moving them fast, like he wasn't just yelling, but yelling rapid fire. He began to convulse, his body rocking back in forth.

"Is he having a seizure?" Barry said.

"I don't think so."

He might have been, of course. I was no doctor, and honestly had had little experience with people suffering seizures. But it didn't look like a seizure. It looked like a man in the midst of a rage, a tirade aimed at no one. Or maybe it was meant for everyone. Maybe it was meant for me.

I remember being scared at that moment. It was a deep kind of fear, the kind I have rarely experienced. It came from inside me and pulsed out to my skin, my fingers, my toes. What could make someone behave like this? Why wouldn't he stop?

I let go of the blinds, and they fell back into place.

"Hey," Barry said.

"I can't watch anymore," I said.

But when Barry pulled the blinds aside again, there I was, looming over his shoulder, trying to catch a glimpse of James. And despite the raging contortions and the silent vitriol coming from that Grand Prix, I recognized his face as another one I'd known. One I'd known as a boy, when I was no older than James had been when he was in my class. This other face, the one from my boyhood, was expressionless and void of any emotion other than the vague longing in his eyes.

(James at 47)

I lied earlier. I said I first met James in my seventh grade English class. That's not true. I first met James when he was an adult, a grown man in his forties, and I was a boy living in Montgomery, Alabama.

As you can imagine, life had not been kind to James. His hair had darkened and then grayed around the temples. In his forties, he'd taken to wearing dark slacks and long sleeve button downs. Even in the hot Montgomery summers, he never wore shorts. He ended up taller than I would have expected, nearly six feet, and somewhere along the way, he must have sold the Ferrari and downgraded to an old brown Buick. There was nothing unique about James as an adult. He wore his hair short as most men did in the eighties. He kept his shirt tucked in and his eyes to the ground. When I did see them, which was rare, I couldn't help but think they were his most memorable feature. He might have been a retired drill sergeant if not for the softness in his face and those vague uncertain eyes. They were the eyes of a man who has spent most of his life on the outside, straining to see what the rest of us were doing and wondering behind those sad pupils, how he too might join the fray.

By the time James was forty and lived across the street from me, he had given up his tactless advances, his desperate attempts to join the circle of life. He had settled in on the periphery, accepting in his status as outsider.

In our southern suburb, everyone waved; everyone greeted each other as a matter of course. These gestures were involuntary, like breathing or sneezing. Yet, the first time I saw him—the real first time—he refused to wave at me, even after I waved and shouted, "Hey," across the street. Instead, he continued on to his mailbox, eyes down, arms self-consciously stiff by his side.

I soon learned James treated all of his neighbours the same way, flatly ignoring them when they spoke, turning the other way when they waved, always, always focusing those eyes out instead of in.

I woke up in the middle of the night once when I was thirteen. I don't remember what woke me, but I do remember hearing the low hum of a car on the street outside my window. From the sound, I thought the car was stopped, the engine idling. Going over to my window, I saw a long dark car easing slowly down the road. Recognizing the car as James's Buick, I watched, expecting to see him pull into his driveway. But he kept going, his car creeping phantom-like along the road until the taillights disappeared like tiny cinders.

The night went silent again. I returned to bed and was almost asleep when I saw the headlights canvassing the walls of my room.

Out of bed again and over to the window, I watched James slide by, his brown Buick meandering down the silent neighbourhood streets. I felt like I was witnessing a secret ritual, one I could not explain or comprehend, a silent spectacle, a statement of sorts, a lonely man's prayer when there were no more words to offer up.

Mesmerized, I watched him—so unhurried, so without purpose—just driving, round and round the block.

I do not know how many times he circled the block. What I do know is other nights filled with this same lonesome ritual followed. Sometimes I only noticed them in the dregs of sleep and barely woke at all; other times, I went to my window and wondered at a man who had traded the prospect of human contact for the solitude of the night.

I think there was a time when I was young, that I forgot James, or maybe didn't understand him, his past, the way a person blooms like a tree and the wind and the sun and the ground feed it or starve it by turn, and it becomes rotten and it becomes strong, growing deep roots in the soil through no fault of it own.

Of course I was twelve and wouldn't understand such abstractions. And even at twenty-two, living in that little apartment, I had only a vague notion of what might become of a human neglected. It took me seeing James as a boy in my class, and then remembering his life to understand how James became an adult.

(James off the grid)
As the years passed, and I grew older and began to get caught up in the struggle of defining my own life, James became to me just another neighbourhood landmark—a mailbox, an old car that did not run, a fencepost in the back of the yard untouched by the feel of human skin—until I had no cause to notice him anymore.

I believe now, this is what he wanted. I believe this is why his eyes never focused on any of his neighbours, why they always drifted away to the horizon, that place outside of us; he had once raged against it, but was now only too glad to let it suck him away because trying to fight against the pull had hurt too much, and there comes a time to stop fighting and stop hurting and just let the world have its way.

Or perhaps, James did not go so passively. Perhaps he defined himself outside of us all? Perhaps he was a man apart, a man who found the opening in the fence, nudged his nose in the gap and found there was nothing holding him back from a place where the rest of us could never follow. I like this version better.

I did not learn the rest of James's story until I was in my thirties. After James with the Ferrari, but before James in my class.

Both my parents died in my mid twenties, so I hadn't been back to Montgomery for several years when I ran into a guy, Andy, who had grown up next door to me. I wasted little time asking about James.

"Whatever happened to that guy?"

Andy, who always reminded me a little of Robin Williams, smirked slightly and said, "Now that's funny."

"Funny?"

"Yeah, Mom and Dad were just talking about him the other day."

He went on to tell me a story I will never forget. After years of living in our neighbourhood in absolute solitude and silence, James walked across the street to Andy's parent's house and knocked on the door. Andy's parents were surprised to say the least, but they invited him in, eager to see what had brought about his visit. He got to the point quickly, telling them he would be going away for a while and asking them to pick up his mail while he was gone.

"Did he say where he was going?" I asked Andy.

"Wouldn't say. Just told them he had to go away for a while."

"And?"

"And, he did. He went away. Dad went over and got his mail every day. That was over a year ago. He's never come back. Never called. Nothing. Dad's filled up an entire plastic trashcan full of his mail. They haven't heard one peep from him."

I didn't know what to make of this. For the next few years, this mystery haunted me, held me as much as I held it. I wanted to know where he'd gone, when he was coming back, but lately, at least since meeting James in my class, I have realized the real question is not where, but why. Why did his roots slip the soil? Why did he resign himself to the horizon? Why did he drive away from the world in a big brown Buick?

But like all great mysteries, this one has no easy answers. I can piece together fragments from my own life, call them James. I create a chain of events that is not there. I can do this and make some sense out of James. I can add some causality to his life, force the pieces together, ignore the missing ones, and admire the half-formed creation.

James.

Perhaps I never knew you at all.

Maybe I only thought I did.

In my mind, I still see him. He's behind the wheel of that big Buick, or he's in his Ferrari, the top down, easing down a dark road. Or maybe he's on the bus now, a sole passenger, riding cross-country at a snail's pace, windows down, night breeze across his face, tangling his hair. I see him happy and free from whatever demons drove him to the periphery of life, beyond the circle of family and friends. He's out past the fence now, the one that holds us all. From here on, the road is clear. From here on, he can really open her up and fly.

LITANY

It was better in prison. Now that I'm free, I can't go an hour, a minute without thinking of them. And the dog. The damned little dog.

It's funny how life can get away from you. Thirty years of the good life, eight years in the joint. Now I'm forty and I don't have anything, just a body that won't sleep, a mind that won't rest.

I see their names when I close my eyes. They are the wild lights that cling to my eyelids, the flash of synapses in my brain.

Matthew Litton.

Kevin Funderburke.

Ann Lawson.

Demetria Thomas.

Over and over, I see the names. I hear them. I whisper them in secret to my godforsaken soul. I would rather still be in prison than here, this morass, this flooded valley of guilt.

Matthew Litton.

Kevin Funderburke.
Ann Lawson.
Demetria Thomas.

Picture a warm May day. Cinco de Mayo perhaps. You're a schoolteacher, happy, blissfully unaware of life and its catastrophes. You're like a child who picks up a snake in the back yard and is bitten. You pick it up because nothing else in the back yard bites; so why should the snake? But it does, and that changes everything.

You drive a bus. It's money that you need to supplement your salary, which isn't much, right? I'm not going to lie to you; it isn't anything. But you're happy. Did I mention that you have a wife and a daughter? Don't worry about their names. Names only make everything harder in the end.

Are you with me so far?

Good.

It's after school. You're sitting behind the wheel of the bus. The kids climb on, all ages. It's a small rural school, kindergartners and high school students all in the same building.

It's a good route. Thirty-five minutes in the morning. Thirty flat in the afternoon. For about an hour a day you're making an extra twelve, maybe thirteen grand a year. There is always something to spend it on: groceries, gas, furniture, bills, your daughter's college fund.

Money mattered then. It doesn't matter anymore. Nothing matters. No, that's not right. You have to understand this before anything else: All that matters is the litany.

Matthew Litton.
Kevin Funderburke.
Ann Lawson.
Demetria Thomas.

Those names. Maybe you think of the names so much

because you can't bear to think of the faces.

Lord, help me.

I'm sorry. I digress. You would understand if you were me. Maybe you can understand. God, I want you to understand.

Listen:

You hear the happy noises of children while the bus coughs and jumps onto the highway. A few years before, each stop had been a test of memory, but now, the drive is automatic.

Today you are thinking about your wife. It is her birthday. You are in a hurry because you have plans.

Hurry.

That's another word you will turn over and over in your mind one day. What does it mean? Why do we bother? A piece of advice: there are no answers.

Your wife? She is everything. Go ahead and imagine her, I won't care. She's spectacular. Fit and tan. A shine in her hair like the girls in shampoo commercials. Undress her, I don't care. You could fall in love with her for all I care. You'll never understand me, because when it's all said and done, you didn't kill anybody. I did.

But let's pretend. Let's pretend anyway that you did.

So, you can't wait to get home. There's a babysitter. Your daughter is out of the house. You'll go out, to a quaint little cafe, then back home for a tumble in the bed.

No, you won't.

But try to pretend anyway. Try to imagine.

You feel the steering wheel rumbling in your hands. It is never still. You make hard turns and don't slow down much. Your wife's at home. You've done this hundreds of times.

The first stop. Four kids get off. You can't remember their names. They've gone on with their lives. You've gone on too, only you had to leave your life behind.

At the next stop something happens that you will never forget. The dog, a little miniature schnauzer—hell, you think about that dog nearly every day—is under the bus.

One of the kids says, "Don't go anywhere. There's a dog underneath the bus." It's Demetria Thomas. You don't pull away, terrified that you might run over the dog. You have always loved animals, dogs in particular. Your family never had pets because your mom was allergic to them, but your grandmother always had them around.

You used to love going to your grandmother's. She always believed in you. Had high hopes. Sometimes, while you were in prison, you could think of the mint tea she used to make and your problems seemed to float away, smooth and soft like sunlight on a hazy summer day.

None of that stuff works anymore. You think of your grandmother's mint tea and you think of the names again.

Please, God. No.

But they have been written on your soul . . .

Matthew Litton.

. . . like verses of the Bible.

Kevin Funderburke.

They have their own cadence and rhythm.

Ann Lawson.

They do not heal . . .

Demetria Thomas.

They only bind.

I suppose I did it again. You're no doubt rolling your eyes at me now. Roll them. You won't bother me.

I must tell you about the dog. If I get distracted again, simply grab me by the shoulders and shake me as hard as you can. My brother did that to me the other day. He came in to visit me from—

You didn't shake me. Are you even listening? Hell, nobody's

ever listened to my side before. Oh, they heard it in court, but nobody really listened. Nobody wanted to know how it was only a mistake, an honest mistake.

It doesn't matter. I'm going to tell you anyway. Are you the kind that listens to killers? I've heard that you are. Then listen. Listen well.

The dog. The little dog. He's under the bus. You put the bus in park. The kids are all standing up, craning their necks hoping to catch a glimpse.

"He's clear!" someone shouts. You don't know who, but later you like to imagine it was Ann Lawson. She is a sweet girl. You can trust her. But you don't. You are too concerned for the animal. You are too concerned that you might roll over the little thing and kill it, leave it pasted to the road. You climb off the bus to verify that the dog is indeed clear. You see the little thing: shiny silver, a cute face. And your heart breaks. You would never have forgiven yourself if you had run over that.

Yes, you would.

In fact, you wish now that you had run over the damn dog twice. Three times.

But you don't. Instead, you climb back aboard the bus, buckle up, release the air brake, and put that death trap in drive, rumbling on down the road toward the seconds that will be the most important of your life.

Imagine a country road: clear, the sun shining bright. You've flipped the visor down because you forgot your sunglasses again. You remember hearing somewhere (bus school, maybe?) about a driver that wrecked a school bus because he didn't have sunglasses. He had been driving west at four in the afternoon; he didn't see the dump truck coming the other way. That could be me, you think. Except it won't be. Not now. Because there's a visor. They put them on all buses because bus drivers forget things like sunglasses. It's no big deal. People forget. They make mistakes, right?

Say yes. It's normal. The best of us make mistakes, all that garbage. Believe me, you'll need it later. You'll wear it as if it were a bulletproof vest. But nobody's shooting bullets and even the best armour can't stop glances, or murmurs, or a heaviness in your chest that sends your heart into your kneecaps and makes it difficult to walk.

But you don't know any of this yet. All you know is your wife at home, waiting for you, just waiting to love you. You know your daughter—God, she's beautiful. You know the damned little dog, the joy of saving its insignificant life. You know the beauty of the day, the next turn in the road, which is a doozy—hold on.

You swing the bus expertly around the turn. Three years of driving and you've never had a close call.

Through your windshield, you see the moon: a ghostly sliver in a clear blue sky. It's beautiful. The last beautiful thing you remember seeing. See it now. You will need its solemn wisdom later. Even in the daytime, the moon is a good listener.

And you, too, have been a good listener. I'm sorry for doubting you earlier. We're here now. We've come this far. You can't turn back.

You hear the blare of the train before you see it. The sound hardly registers. What's a snake to a child who's never seen one? Nothing, absolutely nothing . . . until it strikes.

One more bend and you see the tracks. A little blue house sits beside the road, and you think of how the trains must shake the walls, rattle the dishes, rouse the children. But also, how it must feel to lie in bed and listen to the trains speed past, like noisy flames, burning, burning, and then . . . gone, extinguished by the night.

You slow as you approach the tracks, thinking again of

your grandmother's mint tea. Hell, you can almost taste it, but that's not too unusual. It's a hot day, you're thirsty, and you're in the country. It's natural you would think of your grandmother. Her mint tea. You realize it's been a long time since you've seen her. You realize you won't ever see her again.

And then the train.

You follow procedure, opening the door as you approach the tracks, and you feel the first tinge of impatience creep into your veins. You really hope the train is not too close. Waiting takes so long. But there it is.

See it.

The smoke, coming out white and billowy like clouds. The wheels turning insistently. So many tons of steel. It is a long way off.

If there is a thought, you don't even remember it. You only remember a complete confidence. You have done this before. Other drivers have done this before. What are the chances? You close the door and drive over the tracks. Most of the bus clears the tracks before the engine coughs and grinds and sputters and then dies completely.

You waste far too much time, unmoving, thinking about what just happened. Is it possible, you wonder, really possible that the bus just stalled?

The first surge of fear grips your body like a hard freeze.

You force your hands to move, jam the gear shift into neutral, twist the key hard, give a hard stomp of gas.

Sputters, kicks, dies.

And so do you. You are stricken immobile.

Right then. Right there. You don't believe it could happen like that? I lived it. It happened like that.

It is the screaming that makes your blood move again, kick-starts your heart.

You stand. Look at the train. You would never say it was

far away now, not with a busload of kids on the tracks and panic coursing through you like adrenaline, but this is not adrenaline, it's not fight or flight. It's something more like dying.

That thought gets you moving again, gets you thinking. Suddenly, you are screaming at kids, directing them off the bus via the emergency exit in the back and through the main door. You plead with them to hurry. They seem to move so slowly. The engineer is blaring that horn like the world is ending, and somewhere behind the screaming kids and the impending steel, you know that it is.

By the time you think of saving yourself (oh, did you think you were going to be some kind of hero?), the train and the bus are only a dozen yards apart. The kids are still spilling out of the exits, running like water.

All at once, you know absolutely that everyone will not get off the bus. There is a logjam at the back door. No one in the front where you are. All you have to do is jump off and get clear. You take a long look down the aisle. You see

Matthew Litton
Kevin Funderburke
Ann Lawson
Demetria Thomas

at the very back. You shout: "Come to the front! There's time!"

But then you look at the train again. These kids are small. Kindergarten, maybe first grade. They've panicked. There's not time.

And as soon as you realize that they are going to die, no matter what you do, you run for the door.

Let me make sure you understand this. You should have stayed on. Even though it would have been five dead instead of four, you should have stayed on.

◻

A train makes a bus seem like a very small thing. The school bus barely slows the train. It tears through the bus, leaving remnants of glass and flesh on either side of the tracks. All you hear is the groaning of steel, the cries of anguish, the sickly sounds of souls escaping from healthy, eager bodies.

Don't you look away now. Don't you dare. See the carnage. See what you have wrought, the effects of a careless mistake. See their faces. Say their names . . .

Matthew Litton
Kevin Funderburke
Ann Lawson
Demetria Thomas.

Besides the names, I see the parents' faces. Their righteous anger still sends chills down my spine. How do you defend the indefensible? How do you tell a parent that their only child died because of your impatience? Does impatience sound better than carelessness? What about foolishness? Does it even matter? Shouldn't I have just stayed on the bus? At least then I would have never had to see the faces of the parents, heard the names of the children like an endless chant in my head.

Is there a heaven for people who make mistakes that can never be fixed? That's what I told the parents. I would fix it if I could. I would do anything. But they didn't listen. And I couldn't fix it.

Can you?

SUCKY

When Joe was three years old, he pointed at the claw-foot tub in the hall bathroom and said, "Sucky." His parents laughed. His father was proud, his mother vaguely worried that her three-year-old already used the word "sucky."

When he'd been four, he tried to tell them. They'd listened to him then. They listened and smiled and told him he had a great imagination and one day he would do something important like write a collection of poems or an article on tax reform that would win the Pulitzer Prize. As he got older, and was diagnosed with ADHD and dyslexia—"a damn fatal one-two punch," he'd overheard the doctor tell his parents when he didn't think Joe had been listening—his mom and dad said less stuff about poems and Pulitzers and more stuff like, "College is something you have to work for, Joe" and "The world is a cruel place to those who can't read." Joe could read. That wasn't the problem. But it was hard work sometimes because the words turned over on themselves and wouldn't ever quite straighten out for him and look like words were supposed to look, so much so he began to think of reading as something like walking through a minefield. Every word was a potential bomb. And when he took the tests, those stupid, computerized comprehension tests, he felt like his brain was floating in the middle of some far away ocean possibly getting pecked at by seagulls or sized up by sharks, while the rest of him was sitting in Ms. Fosett's second period, staring glass-eyed at a computer screen.

When he'd been seven, he'd tried to tell them again. He even got Dad up there to listen to the drain as he flipped the valve. The noise that usually sounded like a monster trying for all it was worth to suck the whole world through its tiny mouth hole, gurgled softly, nearly silent, like clear spring water sliding through a gap in the rocks.

Dad frowned. "It's time to stop being afraid of the bath tub, Joe."

Joe nodded, pretending he understood. But he didn't.

When he was ten and his mother mounted a showerhead over the tub and Joe took his first shower, he was reaching for the soap and slipped. His bangs had been longer then, and even though he managed to catch himself before he cracked his head open on the porcelain basin, some of his hair dangled dangerously close to the sucky. He heard it throttle down and inhale, a great, heaving, asthmatic groan. His bangs pulled against his scalp and he felt his head going down. He screamed and jerked himself up, cutting his head open on the tub's faucet. There was a lot of blood and more screaming. For the next several days, he was allowed to bathe in his parents' bathroom.

The sucky got worse. As he neared his thirteenth birthday, he heard it all the time. Sometimes he even found items in the bathroom missing. He lost a toothbrush, a roll of toilet paper, a sock, a page he'd torn out of his sixth grade yearbook showing Madeline Buckhorn's ass in a pair of tight blue jeans, half a deck of Magic: The Gathering trading cards, and a Victoria's Secret catalogue he'd swiped from the mail and hidden in the bathroom before his mother ever knew it came. He decided to talk to his parents again.

By this point, they had their own problems. Joe often wondered if they were going to get a divorce. Samantha, his mother, seemed to be forever rolling her eyes at Danny, his father. Danny never seemed happy about anything and frequently their disagreements spilled over into full-fledged fights.

Sometimes, after they thought Joe was asleep, they screamed at each other. He caught snippets, mostly, but he was smart enough to put them together. He might have had a "deadly combination" of ADHD and dyslexia, but he could think just fine. The snippets mostly went like this:

". . . just want a little space. Is that too much . . ."

". . . you'd be better off with somebody else . . ."

". . . ever since that woman started working there . . ."

". . . I do the dishes. I vacuum the floor, but that's not good enough . . ."

". . . go away for a while. I need space. Room . . ."

". . . are you going to drink another whole bottle tonight?"

". . . space. Just gimme some goddamn space . . ."

And worse. Much worse. When it got really bad, he covered his ears because he was sure he would hear his father slamming the door shut and leaving them. He'd been afraid of that almost as long as he'd been afraid of the sucky, ever since he woke up to a brutal fight one night when he was four. He'd cried and cried until his parents both came to check on him and reassure him they would never leave him.

"But, I heard daddy say he was leaving and never coming back," Joe said.

Dad sat on the edge of the bed then. He took Joe's hand in his. With his other hand, he brushed Joe's bangs out of his eyes. He said, "I promise I will never leave you, Joe."

Joe had nodded, forced his tears to stop, but he didn't

believe his father, not then, not nine years later.

But he did believe his father loved him. His mother too. That's why he decided he had to talk to them about the sucky.

Like many parents of thirteen-year-olds, Joe's mom and dad were incapable of listening to the actual words that came out of his mouth. When he spoke, they both heard a strange and vaguely pleasing sonic dissonance that neither recognized. His mother called the dissonance "a failure to communicate." His father—whom Joe had learned was once a punk rocker in the 1980s and should have known all about dissonance— just grunted at Joe when Joe tried to tell him anything.

But this time, his mother squinted at him strangely, and his father shook his head.

"Is this a joke?" he said.

"No, not a joke," Joe said.

"If this is a joke, it's not funny." The dissonance was making it difficult for Dad again.

Mom said, "I think he may need to see somebody, Danny."

"You mean like a shrink?"

"I mean like somebody who can help him. Do you think this is normal?"

"I think it's a joke."

Mom rolled her eyes. Always the first sign things were about to get ugly.

"I suppose his poor grades are a joke to you to? What about that I found a note in his book bag from a girl that was completely inappropriate? That a joke to you?"

Dad looked at Joe. "Can you believe this shit?"

Joe didn't respond.

"Can you believe how she acts?"

Joe might have shrugged.

"Holy Jesus. I'm going to work in the yard."

"You can't hide from your problems all your life," Joe's mother said.

"Then maybe I should just leave my problems," Joe's dad said as he was going out the door.

Joe was left with his mother who had started crying. Upstairs, the sucky began to purr.

He dreamed about it sometimes. In his dreams, he watched his old bath toys go down the drain one by one. In the dreams he could follow them. His eyes came out of his head and went down the drain too. There were mazes of pipes, then a great belly of water and waste that smelled like chemicals and shit, before the bath toys were diverted back into smaller pipes and rushed along in a current of mould and grime and old bath water to a spout that poked out of the ground in the middle of a vast desert. The desert was always empty, which is how Joe knew the sucky was always hungry and would always be hungry. It'd never fill that desert/belly, not in a million years of sucking. And somehow, this was the part that always jolted him out of sleep, this realization that some places are so empty, all the time in the world wouldn't be enough to fill them.

Joe's mom and dad went out of town on separate trips. Joe's dad went to the beach to "lay in the sun and read some paperbacks." Joe's mom went to her friend's house in Atlanta. They were going to have some "girls' nights" and do some "girl stuff." There were so many things wrong about this situation, Joe did not even try to count them.

At thirteen, he should have been jubilant to be by himself. Part of him was. But most of him couldn't concentrate on being jubilant because he kept listening to the upstairs bathroom, just waiting to hear a suck. But the first day, which was Friday, he didn't even hear a gurgle. When he had to pee, he went in his parents' bathroom. Their shower was pleasant and never gurgled.

On Saturday, his friend Roy came over with cigarettes, a six-pack of beer, and two sixth grade chicks, Rhonda and Melissa, both of whom had recently, as if by some arcane female magic, sprouted breasts.

For a while, amid the coughing and touching and giggling, Joe forgot (mostly) about the sucky.

"I've got to pee," Melissa said.

She was the prettier of the two, but less fun than Rhonda, who had already let Joe pop her bra strap and said she wanted a tongue ring for Christmas.

"Upstairs," Joe said. "First door on the—" But then he stopped, remembering. "You can use my parents'. It's in their room at the end of the hall."

Melissa ran up the steps. The party continued. Rhonda let Roy look down her shirt. They kissed. Joe was embarrassed and looked at the television where the Crimson Tide was leading Mississippi State by a touchdown.

A few minutes later, Melissa returned. "There's something seriously wrong with your bath tub," she said and plopped down on the couch between Roy and Rhonda.

"You used my parents', right?"

"No toilet paper. I used the hall one. Hey, do you get HBO?"

"What was it doing?" Joe asked. But he didn't wait for an answer. He heard it now, rumbling, sucking. Waiting.

Later, after the six-pack was gone and the cigarettes smoked, and they were all used to the rumbling coming from the upstairs bathroom, Rhonda said, "I hate my dad's new girlfriend. She's a total slut."

Roy said, "Sounds like a winner to me."

Melissa and Rhonda hit him at the same time.

"Ow. I was just kidding. Sort of. Anyway, that's kind of like saying the sky is blue, right? I mean, I hate everybody my parents have ever dated. They all seem so . . . I don't know . . . childish."

"You're calling somebody childish?" Melissa said. Her face was drawn and she looked a little pale.

"I know what he means," Rhonda said. "It's like my dad is a teenager. My mom, she's just, I don't know, a basket case. She'll never date again."

"So what about your parents, Joe?" Melissa said. "Are they on a romantic getaway?"

Joe shrugged. He could hear the sucky shifting gears, finding its torque. Its desert must be starving. "I don't think so."

"At least they're still together," Rhonda said.

"For now," Joe said.

"Mine are too," Melissa said. "But I get the feeling sometimes, it won't last."

"Me too," Joe said. He met Melissa's eyes. She smiled at him, a half wilted thing that made his stomach flip over.

"Dude," Roy said suddenly. "What in the hell is wrong with your bathtub?"

In Panama City, Florida, Joe's father, Danny, sat beside the hotel pool with Ralph, a high school buddy he'd started hanging with again since running into him at the Alabama game two weekends ago. Ralph had been the drummer in their punk band, The Bloody Dumplings. Then Ralph had been a skinny kid with rampant acne. Now Ralph was a hulk of a man, red-faced and huffing; his tits bigger than half the women lounging in various stages of undress around the pool.

But not bigger than the girl Danny and Ralph had been flirting with for the last half hour. Her name was Celebrity and when Danny asked her if that was her stage name or her real name, Celebrity hadn't even blinked.

"Both." She had a crooked smile and one of her teeth was going black.

Neither Ralph or Joe's dad asked for elaboration.

Later, when they were in the room and Celebrity excused herself to the pee, Danny thought about Samantha and shook his head. She deserved this. Hell, *he* deserved this. Then he thought about Joe, a photograph he used to have of his boy holding a drawing he'd done just for him. Joe's face beamed with joy, his squinty eyed smile a thing of innocence and beauty. Danny used to keep it folded neatly in his wallet, and when he was having a bad day at work, he'd pull it out and just like that he'd feel better. The photo had stayed with him until about three months ago when he and Joe's mom had taken a weekend trip to Atlanta. They'd had a huge fight that ended with all of his belongings, including the wallet with the photo of Joe landing in the pool. He dove in after the wallet, the photo, but he never found it. The only thing he could figure was that somehow it had been sucked down the drain at the bottom of the pool.

Ralph found a porno on the television. "You ever done this before?"

"Nope," Danny said, mentally letting the photograph fall back into the swimming pool. "But the way I figure it: there's a first time for everything."

Joe's mother, Samantha, was in a motel room too, but unlike her husband, she was alone. She couldn't bear to go to Jessica's house. Jessica and her husband, Rob, were so in love, it made Samantha sick. So she was alone, flipping through an endless litany of channels, wondering what Danny was doing. Twice, she almost called him, but each time she opened her cell phone, she saw the picture of Joe staring back at her and she asked herself the same question she had been asking herself for the last year: was it better to stick it out for Joe's sake or go ahead and split? After all, if she and Danny weren't happy, wouldn't that rub off on Joe? Hadn't it already?

She opened her cell phone a third time and looked at the picture of Joe taken last Christmas. He was such a frail boy. So nervous. Jumpy. When he didn't take his ADHD medicine, he could be almost intolerable, but then there were other moments, when he smiled at her so sweetly, she felt full, as if there could be nothing else she needed in the world besides her son's sweet smile.

Joe's parents talked on their cell phones. It went like this:

"Hello."

"You remember the night when Joe was three and we woke him up fighting?"

"Danny?"

"Do you remember?"

"Yes, where are you?"

"Doesn't matter."

Neither spoke. A small window of silence. In Panama City, Danny heard a car squeal off. Then the ocean, lapping against the continental shelf, and pulling pieces of it away, back to the dark, silent centre. In Atlanta, Samantha heard the distant throb of bass from the hotel bar. Earlier she'd seen a group of short-haired kids with dog collars setting up for a show. She'd thought of Dan then, the way she'd found him so cute that first night in Knoxville with his leather pants and faux-cockney accent. When he asked her to go for a walk after show, she felt like she was with Johnny Rotten or Joe Strummer. After a while, he took her hand and she looked at his profile and he pretended not to notice as she soaked him up, his almost elf like ears, his blunt, tough nose, the dark of his glassy eyes, the weight of his head, so right.

"Do you remember?"

"Yes. I stood at the door. I listened. You promised him you'd never leave."

"Yeah. He was so pitiful. My heart hurt that night."

"Because you knew it was a lie?"

"Yes. I knew it was a lie."

Danny carried the phone over to the sliding glass door and opened it. The salt air came in and he remembered a time when he'd been a kid, eighteen, and come with his buddies to this same beach. They'd gone out on a night like this one, when the spray of the ocean was in the air like fog and walked for what seemed like miles, passing girls their age in the deep dark, unable to discern their faces, so instead, they watched their forms: lithe bodies stuffed inside oversized sweatshirts that hung over blue jean cut-offs. In the dark, each girl was a girlfriend, a lover, a passionate wife they yearned for in the worst way. A yearning that did not know words and sat, like an ever-expanding balloon in the pits of their stomachs. They never said more than a couple of words to these perfect, invisible girls, and sometimes when Danny was lonely or sad he thought of them, their flip flops thwacking the hard sand, on their way to make some other boy happy.

He was too old to still yearn for such things, but he did. And this made him feel sick and alive at the same time. Beyond the pool, the ocean sucked the sand back out to sea.

"Danny?"

"Yeah?"

"Come home. I'm willing to try again."

"I don't think so."

"Why?"

"I need to go down to the beach, Samantha. I need to go for a swim."

"You're not coming home?"

"Samantha . . ."

"What about Joe?"

"I love Joe."

"What's going to happen to him? How's he going to make it without a dad?"

"Kids do it all the time. I barely had a dad."

"I can't believe I married you."

"Look, I didn't say I was never coming home. I just need some more time."

"You've always needed something, Danny. Always."

He didn't know what to say to this. It was true. He'd needed love or thought he did. Samantha had given him that. But it wasn't enough. Otherwise, he wouldn't have come here and fucked Celebrity. Otherwise, he wouldn't still think of that warm night and those faceless girls.

He hung up the phone. Not out of anger. He didn't think he could be angry at Samantha anymore. He hung up because he didn't have anything else to say.

"Danny? Oh, hell, Danny. You didn't just hang up. Shit."

Samantha tossed the phone across the motel room and went into the bathroom to take a shower. She always cried best in the shower. It was the only time she could ever really let herself go.

As she cried, she thought about her tears joining together with the hot water and sliding down her naked body into a pool at the bottom, near the drain. She tried to watch one as it fell off her face, but once it hit the water, it was impossible to know where her tears ended and the water began.

After his friends left, Joe watched movies. He read his comic books. He walked down to the 7-11 and tried to buy a *Hustler*. Dude wouldn't sell it to him. Naked girls always seemed to make Joe less afraid. He bought a slushy instead.

He drank it as he walked home, enjoying the sweet cherry flavour, until he neared the bottom and the straw made a gurgling, sucking sound. He thought of the sucky and tossed the cup in the road. An eighteen-wheeler crushed it under its front right tire a few seconds later.

There was a message on the machine when he got home. "This is your dad, Joe. Just checking in. I miss you . . ." He hesitated here, as if wanting to say more. In the background, Joe heard the ocean sucking, and he thought the ocean must be the original sucky. "I'll call you soon," his dad said at last.

There was something about his voice. Joe knew from the way he pronounced "soon" that his father wasn't coming home. And shortly after this realization, Joe had another: he could hear the sucky again. Gearing up for him, breathing out a huge blast of silence, making room in its iron lungs for a great pull.

Danny walked along the beach for a very long time. His bare feet got wet, and his ears got used to the rhythmic pull of the ocean. A very long time ago, he'd walked this same stretch of beach hoping to meet a faceless girl to hold him in her arms and tell him . . . What? That it would be okay? That she'd love him forever? No. The truth was, he didn't know or couldn't explain what made him want the faceless girl or any girl for that matter. Here he was nearly thirty-seven, and Danny had not gained one ounce of insight into what he wanted from women. This, despite being married to one for nearly fifteen years.

He passed two men smoking reefers, a stray dog, and three women whose hidden faces scrutinized him as he shuffled by.

He turned to the ocean now, another mystery. There was a moon high above him, and its shine lay on the waves, squirming with every deep pull of the undertow. He thought about Joe. The lie he'd told. Maybe, a voice inside him suggested, the easiest way would be to give up. He'd found the bottom of his life and from here, the only place that

looked inviting was the deep ocean. He wondered how far
he could swim, and when he finally stopped swimming, he
wondered how it would feel to let himself sink, the warm
seawater covering him and then soaking into him as he found
the undertow and rode it to wherever it was going.

Three steps in, he began to shed his clothes. Two more and
he was naked. Moments later he was swimming, the water
warm and salty on his lips.

Joe sat on the roof, outside his parents' bedroom, looking
at the moon. He wondered why they didn't come out here
on nights like this. Or maybe they did. His parents were a
mystery to him.

Tonight felt pleasant, warm and humid. Joe could feel the
air, and he liked that. The moon hung heavy and fat, a pale
pumpkin, streaked with wisps of smoky clouds. Somewhere
far away, the ocean pulsed. Beats just out of earshot, but
Joe knew they were there, just as he knew the desert/belly
waited for him and its infinite hunger would never be filled.

Inside the house, he heard the phone ringing. Grudgingly,
he pulled himself from his perch and climbed back inside.
The sucky roared. He felt no surprise at this. It would have
to happen tonight. All these years. It had been waiting for
tonight.

He picked up the phone, putting his free hand over his
other ear, to muffle the noise.

"Joe?" His mother's voice sounded very far away, and for
an instant he had an insane thought that she might be dead
and this was one of those ghost calls they always talked about
on the paranormal shows.

"Hey, Mom."

"I'm sorry we left you." Was she crying? It sounded like she
might be crying.

"It's okay. You'll be back tomorrow."

Mom made a weird sound. A murmur.

"What? You won't be back tomorrow?"

"Of course I will, Joe."

An awkward silence followed this statement, and in that silence, Joe read the language of intent, the unspoken dialogue he now saw was the province of adulthood.

"But Dad won't," he said.

"I can't speak for your father, but I will say he needs to talk to you himself. I'm very angry at him right now."

She didn't need to say this because Joe heard her voice shaking; he could even picture vividly the look on her face, her eyes locked on nothing, the corners of her mouth edging toward a grimace she could barely control. Or maybe she'd stopped trying now. Maybe it was so over, she didn't even care to control her disdain.

"Okay," Joe said even though it was not okay. It was far from okay. His parents were done, finished, sliced in two. He heard it in what his mother said and what she left unsaid. His mind went to the sucky and then through its great iron lungs until he found that awful gray desert, where not even light or darkness can exist, just the rotten, timeworn colours of no more laughing and despair.

"Are you okay, Joe?"

He nodded and then realized she couldn't hear him. "Yeah. I'm going to go take a bath."

He heard his mother smile. "I thought you'd be using our shower."

"I thought you didn't listen to me about the sucky," Joe said.

"No, we listened, but we decided it was better if we didn't make a big deal about things. It's funny because the sucky was one of the few things we agreed about. Anyway, I'm glad you're over it."

"Me too. Bye, Mom."

"Bye, Joe."

When he hung up the phone, he didn't let himself think about what he was doing, and he walked, zombie-like to the roar in the hall bathroom. The wallpaper was gone, and the walls looked threadbare underneath, as if the sucky was pulling layers of skin off it until there was nothing left but brittle bone. The toilet seat was up, straining against its bolts to come off; Joe actually heard the groaning of the screws. And as he stepped into the room, he felt himself stumbling forward, as if he'd entered a wind tunnel. He fought it long enough to strip off his clothes (they never hit the floor as he dropped them article by article; instead, they levitated over the rim of the tub before disappearing into the gaping black hole like diving birds); being naked made no rational sense. In the desert/belly he'd want clothes, but this was something he thought about later. At that moment, he acted instinctually, as he had thousands of times before. A bath meant being naked. That's all this was, Joe thought, a bath.

Now naked, he stopped fighting and let himself be pulled into the tub. An instant later the world was a slick darkness, and he fell.

Down, down, down into a darkness like no other, Joe fell. There was sludge and stink and something oppressive like the air just before a great storm. Joe didn't know where he was. He didn't know why he couldn't stop, or why his eyes were blanketed with a heavy, nearly total darkness.

When he stopped at last, it was only for an instant, a brief respite, before he heard the lungs kick into gear and he felt himself being jerked along a muddy path. Looking around, he saw the spillway from his dream, or something like it. In the dream there had been concrete and water and a certain manmade aspect to the setting that was missing here.

Here mud reigned and junk surrounded him. Old bicycles, clocks, clothing, trash, pieces of automobiles, and mangled paperback novels moved alongside him as if on a conveyor belt made of mud.

Above him, however, hung a dazzling blue-black sea. Looking up was like looking into an aquarium without the glass. The water itself formed a dome made of silky blue where schools of fish and other underwater things floated past. Despite the extreme unlikelihood of the sea being suspended above him, Joe did not doubt his eyes. It made sense. He'd gone underneath the world, to the very bottom, and when he was spit out at last into the dull, colourless desert that cannot be filled, he will have found hell.

Swimming with long strokes, Danny made his way out to sea. Occasionally, he stopped and floated on his back, staring at the moon. It looked bigger out here in the middle of all the water and space. He felt small, unimportant in the waves. Danny let himself sink into the water.

There was a pulse here. If you remained still, you could hear it thumping around you, transfiguring you until you become part of the current, part of the mystery. Danny was still. He waited, blanking his mind of Celebrity and Samantha and, most of all, Joe. He forgot about breathing for a while. He let the ocean push him like a marionette, here and there, there and here until he forgot even himself and there was no discernible difference between his body and a ripple in the current.

Like this, he made the decision to sink some more. He could be reborn after he was dead. This all came to him in a slow stream, like a current steadily pulling away the earth. He could not deny it. He was hypnotized by the rocking pulse. He didn't need his own anymore. So he let it go.

Last thought before darkness, not a good one: Joe, alone. Joe, facing the entire world and everything it squeezed you with. Joe, facing this by himself.

The desert with his eyes closed was a pleasant place. There was no heat. No cold. A dryness on his skin made him shiver and shake.

When he opened his eyes, he saw bruises everywhere. Bruises on the sky, bruises on his naked skin, bruises on the sand. In front of him there was nothing until the sky touched the ground, but even that disintegrated into ash and Joe couldn't tell sky from ground, up from down.

He turned and saw a body at his feet. For a long time, Joe looked at it without moving. For a long time, he was unsure who it was. In the desert/belly there weren't really fathers. Here there were only remnants, half-realized things, so hard to grasp they practically made themselves invisible. But part of him remembered Dad. Dad, who was supposed to come back home.

Joe dropped to the ground beside him and touched his heart. A slight pulse. A tiny, micro pulse, more of an echo than a reality.

Joe learned how to do CPR in health class two weeks ago. A fireman came in for a week and taught all the seventh graders how to save somebody's life. When he was done, the fireman handed out little badges that said, *I'm a Camden County Certified Lifesaver!*

He began to breathe into his father's mouth. At first softly, but then with more urgency. He tried to mimic what the fireman had done when he demonstrated on the dummy, but, most of all, he just tried to breathe hard. He did this for a very long time while the desert/belly waited.

☐

When his father woke up, the sky changed. The horizon came back, an inky dark slash in the distance. Dad sat up, salt water spilling from his mouth.

Joe stood behind his father and watched as he got up, shaking the sand off his naked body. The sun burned the ocean and bright streamers of light stretched almost to the beach. The sky dissolved into an intense blue.

Joe followed his father down the beach. They'd come out of the belly somehow, perhaps spit back up because something between them disagreed with it. Dad walked until he found a bundle of clothes half buried in the sand. He dug out a shirt and then a pair of pants. He did not put them on. Instead, he went through the pockets until he found his wallet. Then he emptied the wallet on the beach, shaking out bills, coins, photographs, credit cards. He went through them one by one, until he found what he wanted. Joe slipped up behind his father, so close, he smelled the seaweed in his hair. His father held a photograph in his hands. An old photo, Joe barely recognized the smiling little boy holding the scrawled illustration up to the camera. He'd been happy then.

He needed to be happy again. His father placed the photo up on dry sand and then took the rest of his belongs and tossed them as far as he could into the ocean. Just as Joe began to feel the fading (he couldn't tell if he was fading or the place was fading, but everything turned to grayscale, and the bright sun became a watermark in the sky, and then it was gone completely), he saw his father go pick up the photo, look at it once more and then evaporate like ocean spray.

After trashing his clothes and wallet in the ocean, Danny made a mad dash for his hotel room. He banged on the door until Ralph opened it.

"Jesus Christ, Dan. You're naked."

"And cold. Let me in."

Ralph moved aside. He had a beer open and porn on the television. "Why are you naked?" he asked.

"I need a shower," Danny said.

In the shower, Danny tried to remember what happened. He couldn't, and that was okay. He did remember the photo, finding it where it was supposed to be. Knowing he had to start over, get rid of everything that didn't matter, but at all costs hold on to his boy. He didn't feel so bad anymore. He knew he was going to let his boy down, but he also knew his boy would survive. Because that's what people did when they didn't die.

As he stepped out of the shower, one image flashed through his mind, fleeting, yet clear: Joe's face looming over his.

Danny held onto this one, tried to burn it into his synapses, thought a crazy thought: Joe had saved him so he could, in turn, save Joe. He did not know how, but it was true.

Danny smiled, liking the way it felt to believe something with his heart even when his mind said it wasn't possible.

Joe made it back home, eventually. The tub never so much as gurgled again. That doesn't mean everything was great for Joe from that point on. In fact, Joe's parents got divorced and stayed that way. Samantha met an ex-minor league baseball star who believed in drowning a day's problems in a fifth of Jack Daniels. Joe didn't like him at all, but even when he got drunk and threatened to kick Joe's ass, Joe never heard a peep from the sucky.

His father found a girl without a face and married her. Joe doesn't see him half as much as he'd like to. He never sees her.

There's part of Joe that is always coming back from the desert. During his trip down the sucky, he picked up a lot of dirt and grime and bathwater. In his mind, he is forever walking, shedding drop by drop all the nasty stuff. Bathing doesn't help. Only walking. And even that only helps a little. Some of the stuff, he knows, will stick to him forever.

THIRTEEN SCENES FROM YOUR TWENTY-FOURTH YEAR

Scene 9

A phone rings in the middle of the night waking you from dreams you will never remember.

"It's your brother," says William.

Alfred turns in his sleep. Outside the motel room, the city seems to do the same. You take the phone.

"John." A rough voice. Coarse. Your brother, Reg.

"Yeah?"

"Mom's in the hospital. She had a stroke."

William and Alfred are both up now, dark shapes across the room, breathing silently. They are your best friends in the world, yet in the darkness they recede like shadows.

"When?" You have never been able to say anything to your brother.

"Today."

"Is it bad?"

"I think so."

"Okay."

William and Alfred move as one, straightening up, readying themselves to speak words they do not know.

Scene 1

There is no soundtrack when you move home. It's late fall and the tree branches lay bare, cold-kissed by the wind until they are thin tendrils, icelike and brittle. The nights are cold and the air burns your lungs.

You leave friends, a job, school. And driving home, you feel like everything has been put on hold. When you turn into your old neighbourhood, you feel as if your heart might burst.

Mom is in her chair, wearing a sweat suit, still beautiful, still serene, long and tall and blonde—though her dark roots are finally showing past the hair dye. Her face is lined, her brow furrowed as if she has been concentrating fiercely.

You put a hand on her shoulder.

She says welcome home.

Scene 2

There are no friends here. Your father stays in his room, sitting in his chair, his half face glowing in the light from the television set. He emerges only for waffles and to empty his colostomy bag.

The house reeks.

Mom tries to be positive.

It's hard.

She's in the kitchen one day, running the faucet, knife in hand, peeling a peach. She's losing hair from the chemo. It never dawns on you how bad it is not only to have cancer, but to know you earned it from the stress of dealing with your husband who also has cancer and who hides in his room, never bothering to check on his wife who's caught cancer from him like the goddamned flu.

Anyway, she's in the kitchen, peeling that peach, and you want to talk, to share with her how you're feeling.

"If it's so bad, just go back to Birmingham. No one said you had to move home," she says, and her voice is cold and foreign. Not the Mom who kissed your tears away or held you close after your first dog got hit by a car.

There are words you want to say, aching words that fill you up like a helium balloon and make you come off the floor. You choke on them and something inside you snaps because she doesn't know how much you've given up for her.

You lose control. The balloon is airborne, no ceiling to hold it near the earth. It flies toward the hateful sun. And you close your eyes and let it take you.

What can make you hurt this much?

Mom and Dad.

You can't see anything except your anger.

When you come to your senses, you are on the floor in the hallway. Your hands and arms hurt from pounding on the carpet with your fists.

Your mother looks at you as if she doesn't recognize you anymore.

It gets worse before it gets better.

Scene 3

The moon is out tonight, full and bright and it sees you sitting in the car at the park, drinking your slushy.

You and William. Planning the trip.

"Memphis," William says. "That's the first stop."

"Beale Street," you say. "You ever been there?"

"No. Arkansas after that. Little Rock. You think Alfred's going to come?"

"He'd better."

"What if he backs out?"

"Then we'll go without his sorry ass. His loss, missing the trip of a lifetime."

William nods and tosses his half-consumed slushy out the window. You watch the moon, never wondering what will come after the trip. Perhaps you assume it will never end, or there will be other trips to equal it or maybe it is like a salve, and once rubbed, it will cool all of your scrapes and cuts and make them recede so not even the scars remain.

"Lubbock," William is saying. "We'll see the Hidey-Ho where Buddy Holly played his first show. Then we'll hit New Mexico . . ."

You decide to remember this night forever.

Scene 4

At work, there's a woman over by soundtracks who needs help. You help. She talks to you for a long time about Bette Midler. You don't bother to listen. Instead you think about the Grand Canyon, and the summer. You think about moving back to Birmingham. You think about your friends. You don't think about your mother.

The lady buys six CDs. Leartis, the shift manager, checks her out and tells you to vacuum. "We're closing early tonight," he says. "I got a gig."

You vacuum.

And think about the Grand Canyon. When Leartis goes to the back, you put on the Jayhawks. *Tomorrow the Green Grass*. It's kind of become like your theme song. Except it's the whole album. Listening to it makes you sad and happy at the same time. As long as there's happy, you think, as the opening chords of "Blue" ring out across the store, you can deal with sad.

Leartis comes back out and locks the door. It's fifteen minutes until ten. He doesn't care.

You don't either. You vacuum. And think about the Grand Canyon.

You've been home almost five months.

Scene 5

Mom is better. The cancer is gone. Radiation, chemo, surgery.

It all worked. Three months cancer free.

Mom is better.

After the trip, you'll move back to Birmingham for good.

Mom is better.

Tomorrow the green grass.

Scene 6

Memphis, The Ozarks in the rain, and now Red Rock Canyon State Park in Oklahoma. You grill hamburgers and hike. You go to sleep in a tent before eight o'clock, listening to the sounds of freedom and the rest of your life rolling out in front of you like a galaxy of stars, unending and bright with promise and mystery.

If you think of Mom, it is only a brief, half-formed thought, and it gets lost in the steady summer thrum of cicadas and bullfrogs.

And anyway, she's better now.

Scene 7

You buy a postcard at a gas station on the side of the road somewhere west of Monument Valley. The picture on front shows a stark view of Monument Valley at sunset. Plateaus are shrouded in shadow, as the sun burns like a photograph flash beneath heavy gray clouds. You write

> *Mom,*
> *Yes, the views here are really this beautiful. We are having a blast. So far the highlight was Red Rock Canyon in Oklahoma. Being here makes me so thankful you have your life back. One day, when you get stronger, I am going to bring you out here. I promise.*
> *Love,*
> *John*

Scene 8

You hike down three miles. Your legs are strong, your canteen full. Life may work out after all.

"Should we be thinking of heading back?" Alfred says. He's the smart one. Valedictorian. Med school.

"We'll be all right," William says. He's like you: tall, dark haired. More interested in sports than grades.

You agree. "Further," you say, though your legs are finally beginning to ache, and your back hurts beneath the weight of your pack.

Maybe you sense the half-way point looming near. The ninth day on a seventeen day trip. Middle of the day. Middle of the hike. When you turn around, you'll be moving away from the Grand Canyon, moving into the rest of your life. It scares the shit out of you.

You keep walking.

Finally, William gets winded and you turn around, start the journey back to the top, back to your life.

Now, it gets tough, and though you had been warned again and again, hiking down was the easy part and how it would be wise to turn back before you start feeling tired, you're still surprised when the uphill grind kicks in, and your legs go dead and you begin to doubt yourself.

Alfred sits down to rest, sweat pouring down the sides of his face. He grimaces and unstraps his pack.

"I can't carry it anymore," he says. "I got to rest."

William paces. He's always got such energy.

"I'll carry it," you say and pick up Alfred's pack.

Ten minutes later, when the sun tops out overhead and your legs have turned to jelly around your bones, you wonder why you are always trying to carry so much.

Scene 10

You are thankful for the dark when you hang up the phone.

William and Alfred do not see the tears that streak your face. Silently, you pull your shoes and shorts on. You leave the motel room without speaking.

The night greets you with a blast of warm air. Music and voices from the Riverwalk drift up to the third floor where you stand looking at the Space Needle as it towers over the city.

You walk, half hoping some happy person will approach you and demand to know why you have been crying, why your face is so broken and distraught, why your fists are clenched at the ends of you arms like tiny coiled hearts. You don't care about anything. You walk to the river.

Couples stroll by, laughing and smiling. Your life is over. "Over!" you want to scream. But you don't. You keep walking.

After a while you hope you are lost. After a while it is easier to get mugged or killed or abducted than to go back to that motel room and the rest of your sorry life.

Because your dad is dying of cancer and Mom had cancer and it went away but then she had a stroke because it came back in her brain, and oh shit. . . .

Just keep walking.

A long tunnel off the Riverwalk opens on your right. You turn into it without thinking. It's empty. Steps loom in front of you. You take them two at a time. On the other side you see a man wearing a trench coat, unshaven, with big, glazed eyes. They see you.

You keep walking. Maybe he'll have a gun. Or a knife. Or maybe he'll grab you and take you to his house and beat and torture you. Or . . .

But he staggers past, trying to focus on his own journey, trying not to fall. And you, you do the same.

When you return, at last, to the motel room, the one overlooking the Alamo, William and Alfred are sitting on the bed. They've waited up for you.

You tell them about the stroke. She can't speak. Probably from a tumour in the brain.

But they know all of this, already.

William's father has called. You're due at the airport at six. Your flight back to Dannelly Field in Montgomery leaves at seven.

Tomorrow you begin your new life.

Scene 11

She's frail. Like a baby. When she speaks, her voice sticks on the same word: "Just, just, just . . ." It is like the beginning of a plea: *Just help me please, just make it go away, just let me be healthy again, just, just, just...* Or perhaps it is justice she wants. Lord knows she deserves it. Living with Dad had been hell on her, but she never wavered, never complained, always put him and the children before herself. And where, exactly, had it gotten her?

You hold her hand. Tell her it will be okay. You tell her she beat cancer once, she will beat it again. It's a lie. She knows it, but maybe she thinks you believe it. That would be something.

"Just . . ." She wants to speak, but her brain will not send the words.

You tell her the doctors say this is normal right after a stroke. It takes months, they say, to regain verbal skills.

You neglect to tell her she's only got six left to live.

"I'm going to move back to be with you," you whisper. She strokes your hair.

This cancer will be efficient, the doctors say, speaking in solemn, almost reverent tones.

Chemo won't help.

Radiation?

No, no.

Surgery?

Out of the question. Best to let her ease into that good night with as little pain as possible. She'll need prescriptions of valium, ambien, Demerol, all the drugs that make you forget you have cancer.

You try to understand the words they say.

You'll want to bring a hospital bed in, of course, and contact hospice. Yes, you'll want to do that immediately.

You hear all of this, but all you comprehend is Mom is dying. Mom is dying.

Scene 12

You are somewhere in the middle of the fourth month, listening to your mother breathe and murmur over a baby monitor. You're in the den. Mom's in her room. She's had her meds. Maybe she'll sleep.

Dad's in his room, too. The television too loud. He's watching a war movie. Everybody's dying.

Mom's voice comes over the monitor, a whisper hidden among the static and buzz of voices from some house a block or so over, where enthusiastic voices cheer Junior as he rolls over or sits up or maybe experiences gas with a satisfied smile. But Mom's voice grips you. The static drops away until you hear her voice like a clear bell chiming out the secrets of the universe. You listen to a prayer.

She prays, not for herself, wasted to bone by cancer, but for her children. Three of them: Reg, John, and Anne. She calls them by name, prays for their lives when she is gone. She never asks God for her own.

There is a lesson here.

Scene 13

All day long, you know. The hospice nurse, Lou, arrives at nine that morning and tells you to be ready because today will be the day.

"She's not eating," you say.

"That's because she's not hungry," the nurse says.

"I just want her to be comfortable."

"Don't worry."

But you worry because that's all you have now.

Around four that afternoon, somebody suggests it would be good for all of the children to go in one at a time and say goodbye. Reg first, followed by Anne. You watch as they both come out red faced and swollen-eyed.

It is your turn. The room is dark, the shades drawn. Mom can't speak anymore. You sit beside her bed, hold her hand and talk.

At first the words won't come, but then they flow more easily and you are telling her everything you always wanted to tell her. You tell her no one else ever mattered in your life like her. You tell her you believe in heaven and God because of her. You tell her you will do everything you can to live a life that honours her.

Finally you break and lay your head on her emaciated belly. Her hands find your hair and caress it in a way you will always remember, and through the long days and nights that follow without her love, you will miss this caress more than anything else. There is communication in her fingers. They speak to you in a way that makes words irrelevant.

When you leave her, she is still. You go to your father's room and tell him it's his turn.

He looks at you for a moment, perplexed, before he rises and slowly makes his way down the hall.

ACKNOWLEDGEMENTS

These stories represent about five years of my life. Best I can recall, the first of them was "Chicken," which I finished in 2006, and the last of them was "The Best Part" (finished in October of 2011). Along the way, I had a lot of help and met a lot of nice people who were willing to accept me and my ragged batch of stories unconditionally. The most important of these are the people in my writing group—Sam W. Anderson, Kim Despins, Kurt Dinan, Petra Miller, and Erik Williams. These five read most of these stories numerous times and were instrumental in helping me get from first draft to something ready to send out into the world. I owe you guys a huge debt.

And now, a list of others who helped out in one way or another: Laird Barron, Jason Bickell, Doug Clegg, Ron Currie, Ellen Datlow, Boyd Harris, John Hornor Jacobs, Joey Kennedy, John Langan, Nick Mamatas, Alfred Newman, John Rector, Mary Rees, William "Hank" Richardson, Ian Rogers, Erik Smetana, Ben Stokes, Paul Tremblay (thanks for answering all the emails!), Kevin Wallis, and Lawrence Wharton (Larry, I hope this book reaches you).

I'd also like to thank Brett Savory, Sandra Kasturi, and my editor, Helen Marshall. Brett and Sandra—thanks for taking a chance on me and for all the love you put into the process. Helen—wow, you're amazing. You made these stories so much better.

Thanks to Danny Evarts and Erik Mohr for the gorgeous art. You guys "got" the stories, and it shows.

Also, I'd be remiss not to mention my fabulous agent, Beth Fleisher. Thanks for all of your hard work, Beth.

And last, a resounding note of appreciation to Becky, my wife. You've been so incredibly generous to allow me the space and time to write. It takes a special person to be married to an aspiring writer, especially one as single-minded and stubborn as I can often be. Thanks for being that person again and again.

PUBLICATION HISTORY

"Halloween Comes to County Rd. Seven" originally appeared in *Thuglit* (May/June, 2009).

"The Water Tower" originally appeared in *Fantasy Magazine* (July, 2009); reprinted in *The Year's Best Dark Fantasy and Horror* (2010, Prime).

"Long Fall into Nothing" originally appeared in *Crime Factory*, Issue 6 (May, 2011)

"Shoebox Train Wreck" originally appeared in *Haunted Legends* (2010, Tor).

"Walk the Wheat" originally appeared in *On Spec*, Issue 80 (Spring, 2010).

"On the Mountain" originally appeared in *Shroud*, Issue 4 (Fall, 2008).

"Chicken" originally appeared in *Greatest Uncommon Denominator*, Issue 0 (Spring, 2007).

"Litany" originally appeared in *Shimmer*, Issue 3 (Spring, 2006).

"This is Where the Road Ends" originally appeared in *Tales from the Yellow Rose Diner and Fill Station* (2011, Sideshow Press).

ABOUT THE AUTHOR

John Mantooth is an award-winning author whose short stories have been recognized in numerous year's best anthologies. His short fiction has been published in *Fantasy Magazine*, *Crime Factory*, *Thuglit*, and the Bram Stoker Award-winning anthology, *Haunted Legends* (Tor, 2010), among others.

ABOUT THE ILLUSTRATOR

Danny Evarts is an illustrator, editor and graphic designer, and currently holds down the role of Art Director and Technical Editor for Shroud Publishing. He has been attempting to perfect his obsession with layout and design since the mid-1980s. Danny abandoned a career in journalistic and fiction writing in the early '90s as he came to realize that his visions were better suited to illustration, first for underground magazines and mini-comics. He soon fell in love with relief printmaking, and after a brief stint as a designer in the music industry, his works—most often original prints made through carving into wood or linoleum—now pepper the pages of books and magazines. He is also the illustrator of the Unchildren's Book *It's Okay to be a Zombie*, and is fomenting further adventures in this series alongside many other projects. Danny lives with his partner in the Maine woods, where they spend most of their time working on their property and fleeing from irate wildlife.

EMB
RACE
THE
ODD

COMING IN SPRING FROM
WORLD FANTASY AWARD-
NOMINATED PRESS

ChiZine Publications

THE STEEL SERAGLIO
MIKE CAREY, LINDA CAREY & LOUISE CAREY

AVAILABLE MARCH 15, 2012
FROM CHIZINE PUBLICATIONS

978-1-926851-53-2

ALSO AVAILABLE FROM CHIZINE PUBLICATIONS

WESTLAKE SOUL
RIO YOUERS

AVAILABLE APRIL 15, 2012
FROM CHIZINE PUBLICATIONS

978-1-926851-55-6

CHIZINEPUB.COM CZP

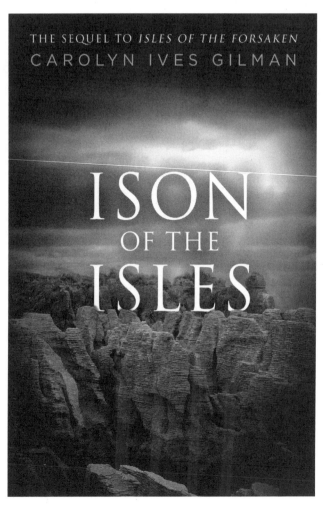

ISON OF THE ISLES
CAROLYN IVES GILMAN

AVAILABLE APRIL 15, 2012
FROM CHIZINE PUBLICATIONS

978-1-926851-56-3

ALSO AVAILABLE FROM CHIZINE PUBLICATIONS

A TREE OF BONES

VOLUME THREE OF THE HEXSLINGER SERIES

GEMMA FILES

AVAILABLE MAY 15, 2012
FROM CHIZINE PUBLICATIONS

978-1-926851-57-0

NINJA VERSUS PIRATE FEATURING ZOMBIES
JAMES MARSHALL

AVAILABLE MAY 15, 2011
FROM CHIZINE PUBLICATIONS

978-1-926851-58-7

RASPUTIN'S BASTARDS
DAVID NICKLE

AVAILABLE JUNE 15, 2011
FROM CHIZINE PUBLICATIONS

978-1-926851-59-4

ALSO AVAILABLE FROM CHIZINE PUBLICATIONS

978-1-926851-35-8

TONE MILAZZO

PICKING UP THE GHOST

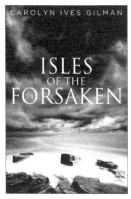

978-1-926851-43-3

CAROLYN IVES GILMAN

ISLES OF THE FORSAKEN

978-1-926851-44-0

TIM PRATT

BRIARPATCH

978-1-926851-43-3

CAITLIN SWEET

THE PATTERN SCARS

978-1-926851-46-4

TERESA MILBRODT

BEARDED WOMEN

978-1-926851-45-7

MICHAEL ROWE

ENTER, NIGHT

"THE BEST WORK IN DARK FANTASY AND HORROR FICTION THESE DAYS IS BEING PUBLISHED BY SMALL PRESSES, HAUNTED LITERARY BOUTIQUES ESTABLISHED (MOSTLY) IN OUT-OF-THE-WAY PLACES, [INCLUDING] CHIZINE IN TORONTO. THEY'RE ALL DEVOTED TO THE WEIRD, TO THE STRANGE AND—MOST IMPORTANT—TO GOOD WRITING."

—DANA JENNINGS, THE NEW YORK TIMES

978-1-926851-10-5

TOM PICCIRILLI

EVERY SHALLOW CUT

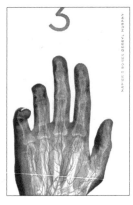

978-1-926851-09-9

DERRYL MURPHY

NAPIER'S BONES

978-1-926851-11-2

DAVID NICKLE

EUTOPIA

978-1-926851-12-9

CLAUDE LALUMIÈRE

**THE DOOR TO
LOST PAGES**

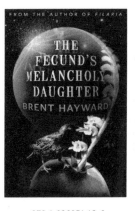

978-1-926851-13-6

BRENT HAYWARD

**THE FECUND'S
MELANCHOLY
DAUGHTER**

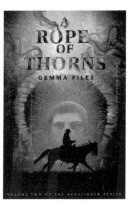

978-1-926851-14-3

GEMMA FILES

A ROPE OF THORNS

"I'VE REVIEWED ALMOST A DOZEN OF THEIR RELEASES OVER THE LAST FEW YEARS . . . AND HAVE NOT BEEN DISAPPOINTED ONCE. IN FACT, EVERY SINGLE RELEASE HAS BEEN NOTHING SHORT OF SPECTACULAR. READERS IN SEARCH OF A VIRTUAL CACHE OF DARK LITERARY SPECULATIVE FICTION NEED LOOK NO FARTHER THAN THIS OUTSTANDING SMALL PUBLISHER."
—PAUL GOAT ALLEN, BARNES & NOBLE COMMUNITY BLOG

ALSO AVAILABLE FROM CHIZINE PUBLICATIONS

978-0-9813746-6-6

GORD ZAJAC

MAJOR KARNAGE

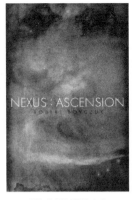

978-0-9813746-8-0

ROBERT BOYCZUK

NEXUS: ASCENSION

978-1-926851-00-6

CRAIG DAVIDSON

SARAH COURT

978-1-926851-06-8

PAUL TREMBLAY

*IN THE
MEAN TIME*

978-1-926851-02-0

HALLI VILLEGAS

*THE HAIR WREATH
AND OTHER STORIES*

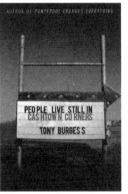

978-1-926851-04-4

TONY BURGESS

*PEOPLE LIVE STILL
IN CASHTOWN
CORNERS*

"IF I COULD SUBSCRIBE TO A PUBLISHER LIKE A MAGAZINE OR A BOOK CLUB—ONE FLAT ANNUAL FEE TO GET EVERYTHING THEY PUBLISH—I WOULD SUBSCRIBE TO CHIZINE PUBLICATIONS."

—ROSE FOX, *PUBLISHERS WEEKLY*

CHIZINEPUB.COM CZP

978-0-9812978-9-7

TIM LEBBON

**THE THIEF OF
BROKEN TOYS**

978-0-9812978-8-0

PHILIP NUTMAN

CITIES OF NIGHT

978-0-9812978-7-3

SIMON LOGAN

**KATJA FROM THE
PUNK BAND**

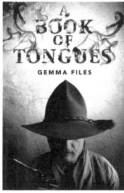

978-0-9812978-6-6

GEMMA FILES

**A BOOK OF
TONGUES**

978-0-9812978-5-9

DOUGLAS SMITH

CHIMERASCOPE

978-0-9812978-4-2

NICHOLAS KAUFMANN

**CHASING THE
DRAGON**

"IF YOUR TASTE IN FICTION RUNS TO THE DISTURBING, DARK, AND AT LEAST PARTIALLY WEIRD, CHANCES ARE YOU'VE HEARD OF CHIZINE PUBLICATIONS— CZP—A YOUNG IMPRINT THAT IS NONETHELESS PRODUCING STARTLINGLY BEAUTIFUL BOOKS OF STARKLY, DARKLY LITERARY QUALITY."
—DAVID MIDDLETON, *JANUARY MAGAZINE*

ALSO AVAILABLE FROM CHIZINE PUBLICATIONS

978-0-9809410-9-8

ROBERT J. WIERSEMA

**THE WORLD MORE
FULL OF WEEPING**

978-0-9812978-2-8

CLAUDE LALUMIÈRE

**OBJECTS OF
WORSHIP**

978-0-9809410-7-4

DANIEL A. RABUZZI

THE CHOIR BOATS

978-0-9809410-5-0

LAVIE TIDHAR AND NIR YANIV

**THE TEL AVIV
DOSSIER**

978-0-9809410-3-6

ROBERT BOYCZUK

**HORROR STORY
AND OTHER
HORROR STORIES**

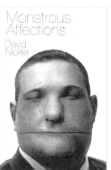

978-0-9812978-3-5

DAVID NICKLE

**MONSTROUS
AFFECTIONS**

978-0-9809410-1-2

BRENT HAYWARD

FILARIA

"CHIZINE PUBLICATIONS REPRESENTS SOMETHING WHICH IS COMMON IN
THE MUSIC INDUSTRY BUT SADLY RARER WITHIN THE PUBLISHING INDUSTRY:
THAT A CLEVER INDEPENDENT CAN RUN RINGS ROUND THE MAJORS IN
TERMS OF STYLE AND CONTENT."

—MARTIN LEWIS, *SF SITE*